Sunray Alice

Sunray Alice

by
Jeremy Hepler

www.silvershamrockpublishing.com

CONTENT WARNINGS
This book may contain content that triggers undesired reactions.
NAZIS, CHILD ASSAULT, GUNS, GUN VIOLENCE, ALCOHOLISM, RACISM

Copyright © 2022 Jeremy Hepler

Front Cover Design by Kealan Patrick Burke
Interior art by Bob Veon
Formatted by Kenneth W. Cain
Edited by Kenneth W. Cain

All rights reserved.

This is a work of fiction. Names, characters, businesses, places, events and incidents are either the products of the authors' imagination or used in a fictitious manner. Any resemblance to actual persons, living or dead, or actual events is purely coincidental.

No part of this publication may be reproduced, stored in a retrieval system, or transmitted in any form or by any means, without the prior permission in writing of the publisher, nor be otherwise circulated in any form of binding or cover than that in which it is published and without a similar condition including this condition being imposed on the subsequent purchaser.

For Tricia, the true Queen Green Thumb

" The kiss of the sun for pardon,
The song of the birds for mirth,
One is nearer God's heart in a garden
Than anywhere else on earth."

— Dorothy Frances Gurney

PRESENT

1

Alice Mayes couldn't remember the last time butterflies spawned in her stomach. She'd found sensations like that came less and less with age and experience, and with less intensity when they did. But as she approached Emily, who was waiting by the hurricane fence staring out at the garden, a kaleidoscope kicked up a storm in her belly. She'd always dreamed of finding someone like Emily. Someone worthy. She rested the shovel she'd plucked from the barn against the fence and gave Emily a motherly hug.

"Did you sleep well?" Alice asked.

Emily flashed a smile, nodded, and turned her attention back to the garden, where the first light of dawn was awakening the foliage.

Keeping her eyes on Emily, Alice placed her hand on her fluttering abdomen. Emily had been helping tend the garden since she was six years old, nearly fifteen years now, and she'd lived in the apartment above Alice's garage for the last two. She had cautious, grass-green eyes and a quietly beautiful face that suggested vulnerability. And she was as slender as a rake, her slight figure suggesting weakness or frailty. But she was far from either.

She was the most resilient person Alice had ever known.

Abandoned outside an Amarillo fire station as an infant, Emily spent five years bouncing around the Texas Panhandle—three different towns and four foster homes in all—before landing a permanent home in Sunray with the Newel family on McGee Street, two houses down from Alice. From the first time they had met—the day Alice had caught the skinny, freckle-faced little girl stealing tomatoes and pears from the garden and chased her down and wrenched them from her hands—Alice had felt an uncanny bond with Emily. The little girl with a pixie chin and eyes hardened beyond her years was a replica of her younger self: headstrong, determined, thick-skinned, independent. Someone who did what she wanted to do, what she felt she had to do, and people could either accept it or move on.

Alice eventually followed Emily's gaze and looked toward the roughly two hundred acres of abundance that locals called the Garden of Sunray. The butterflies in her stomach settled some as her eyes slid back and forth over the thick vegetation, pausing to momentarily admire a fuzzy leaf, a bee on a rose petal, an orange-breasted robin on an oak branch, sunshine winking on a drop of morning dew. She'd experienced thousands of calming sunrises in the garden, hundreds with Emily, but knew she had few to spare. She hadn't received any dire prognosis from a doctor, and she hadn't been blessed with prophetic visions or messages like Pastor Fred Lewis's wife, Hazel, supposedly had been, either. She simply knew from a lifetime of listening to her body. The message was clear. For weeks her heart had been telling her it had a limited number of beats left, her lungs something similar. But that was okay. She wasn't scared or upset or worried. And she didn't want pity or prayers. After ninety-three years of love and pain, joy and loss, she was ready to move on. She just needed to tie up this one last loose end first.

The loose end.

She tousled the back of Emily's short hair. "Did you bring everything?" She'd texted Emily the night before, asking her to please gather a couple of bottles of water and dry snacks from the pantry, a hand trowel and rag from the barn, and bring them with her in the morning. Alice had everything else she needed in her cargo pant pocket.

Emily patted the backpack pulled snug against her spine. "Right here." She met eyes with Alice. "What do we need to do out there, anyway? Did I screw something up?"

Alice had allowed Emily to maintain the garden on her own for the first time this spring. Over the last two months, often helped by friends Becca, Juan, Charles, and a few others, she'd turned soil and re-seeded, transplanted the greenhouse-grown sprouts, pruned the fruit trees, removed weeds, and cleaned winter debris out of the canals that brought overflow water in from Regreso Creek. All the while, Alice had sat in her rocker on the back porch, or in front of her bedroom window upstairs, and pretended not to watch, hiding the binoculars or aiming them in an obscure direction when necessary, only taking walks through the garden to inspect the work when Emily wasn't around. She didn't want Emily to think she didn't trust her. Trust with Emily was hard earned.

Alice shook her head. "No. You've done fine. There's just something I need to show you near the creek."

Emily cocked a suspicious eyebrow, the pierced one. "What is it? I thought I knew every inch of this place."

What is it? Alice mused as the butterflies in her belly picked up steam again. She looked out at the garden. Such a simple question. *What is it?* Three little words. But in this case, they carried so much weight. She'd stayed up all night wondering exactly where to begin, *how* exactly to begin. She remembered everything from those five horrific days in the summer of '44 as clearly as she remembered what she'd eaten for breakfast—half a piece of toast with jelly—and although she still thought of them often, daily on one level or another, she hadn't spoken about them aloud in over seventy years. And she'd never told anyone the full truth. All she'd seen, what she'd done.

When she met eyes with Emily, Emily smirked. "What? Do you have a chest of gold buried out there or something?" Emily chuckled softly then playfully flared her eyes. "A body you need me to bury? A werewolf you shot with a silver bullet?" She put the tip of her pinky to the corner of her mouth like a devious villain. "A vampire you staked through the heart?"

Alice forced a smile she hoped didn't look forced and lightly shook her head as if amused. "Come on." She tilted the shovel handle toward Emily. "Take this and follow me."

Emily took the shovel. "You sure you feel up for the walk?" She thumbed over her shoulder at the barn next to the garage. "Both of the four wheelers are gassed up and ready to go."

Alice appreciated the gesture, but it was important for her to walk the garden with Emily this one last time. That was how she'd always imagined it. "I'll be fine," she said. "I want to walk."

Emily adjusted the weight of her backpack and followed Alice through the wooden gate and into the garden. They negotiated a narrow path with clusters of tomato plants, herbs, and sunflowers on their left, vines that would grow fat with watermelons in the coming month on their right. Wild flowers and Spanish lavender abound. An apple tree here, an oak tree there. Where the path forked, they curved left, and as they looped around a patch of mulberry trees, an engine sounded overhead.

Alice looked skyward, shielding the sunshine from her eyes. A small prop plane flew into view, curving low around the garden's outer rim. Fly-bys were a common occurrence, planes often carrying the pilot's visiting relatives or friends they wanted to impress. Sometimes they showed up at Alice's front door afterward, like countless others who'd heard of the garden or simply driven by, requesting to walk the grounds and take pictures, sometimes asking to return for an engagement proposal or a family portrait. A few had even requested to have an actual wedding on the site. A few others to scatter a loved one's ashes.

Alice had gotten a bird's eye view of the land from local crop duster Frank Kilgore's plane in the summer of '92, after nearly all two hundred acres were flourishing. He'd been telling her for years how amazing it looked from up there, and that she *had* to fly over with him. "I've never seen anything like it around here," he'd said. "It looks like it doesn't belong." And he was right. From overhead, the riot of flowers, vines, and vegetables, clusters of berry bushes, plentiful fruit and ornamental trees, all of it, a hoarder's garden, in one huge gulp, looked both amazing and miraculously out of place, as though the heart of some lush South American rainforest had been ripped out and transplanted into the chest of the arid Texas plains.

Alice waited until the plane was out of earshot, then looked back over her shoulder and locked eyes with Emily. The butterflies were relentless. It was time. Now or never. She took a deep breath, straightened her bifocals. "Remember when you first heard rumors about me and all that Nazi prisoner mess, and I told you the rumors were just that, and I didn't know much more about it than anyone else?"

"Yeah," Emily said, drawing out the word, seemingly dumbstruck by the out-of-the-blue question.

Alice held Emily's gaze for a long moment, until she believed Emily had registered the sincerity in her eyes, the gravity of her coming words. "Well, I lied. I know everything. More than everything, in fact. More than anyone." She pressed her hand against her abdomen again. "And you need to know it, too."

PAST

1

I was sixteen that summer—full of vinegar and piss, as Mom used to say—and couldn't stand living in Sunray. Like most small panhandle boom towns, it was a good ten or fifteen years behind the rest of western civilization. Yes, the entire town was wired for electricity and most homes had phones, but only about half had indoor plumbing, and only one building in town—the Morley—had modern air conditioning. The population had dropped from a peak of thirty-five hundred in the mid-thirties down to around a thousand, and of those, most were Bible-thumping locals or unsavory, labor-seeking transients. Standing in the center of town square, you couldn't throw a rock north or south without hitting a liquor store or bar on Main Street, and you couldn't throw one east or west without hitting a church on Ozmer. Where those two roads intersected— the only two paved roads in town—two worlds collided. One world filled with indulgence and ignorance, the other filled with salvation and sanctimony.

I was with Mom in the heart of the salvation and sanctimony—the Trinity Lutheran Church—when word hit town about the escape. Back then, the church sat on a spacious lot half a mile east of town square, across the street from where the newer church sits now. Mom and I had been there for nearly two hours, scrubbing, sweeping, and polishing. She cleaned four of Sunray's fourteen churches once a week, a few oil-rich assholes' houses twice a month, and I'd been forced to spend my summers and weekends helping her clean since I turned five years old. We were on opposite ends of the sanctuary that August afternoon, polishing pews with a homemade mixture of lemon juice and olive oil, when Pastor Lewis stepped into the open front doorway and called us over.

"Martha, Alice, could I have a word with you, please?"

He ordinarily spoke with a soft, disarming drawl—when he wasn't fevered on scripture and bellowing from the pulpit, that was—but his request came across firm and urgent.

Mom shot me a stern look and discretely tugged at her shirt as she sidled between pews with her back to him. The heat had been relentless that week, well over a hundred degrees for days. We'd turned on the ceiling fans, raised the windows, and propped open the front and back doors for better air circulation. I'd also tied the front of my sweat-soaked t-shirt into a knot, baring my midriff, which was an unacceptable appearance for a young lady in Mom's eyes. Especially unacceptable in the presence of Fred Lewis. Not only was he the revered head of Sunray's largest and wealthiest church, he was also one of Mom's best-paying employers, a family friend, and our nearest neighbor.

Not in the mood to listen to another one of Mom's lectures about respect after Pastor Lewis left (I'd already heard one on the ride to the church after an early morning argument about walking around the house in my underwear), I unknotted my shirt and followed her up the center aisle.

We greeted him just inside the entrance where the sun gave way to shadow. As usual, he wore black slacks and a short-sleeved black button up adorned with a clerical collar. He was eighty percent arms and legs, and at six-foot five, towered over me and Mom. His thinning hair clung to his scalp. He pulled a handkerchief out of his pocket and dabbed the sweat off his forehead and upper lip.

"Have you heard?" he asked.

Over the next few days, as the mess thickened, that vague question would become the common greeting in Sunray. When you crossed paths with someone or answered the phone, there was no more "How are you?" or "How's work going?" or "What do you think of this weather?" Only, "Have you heard?"

Mom and I shook our heads.

His eyes bounced from her to me then back to her. "A handful of Nazis escaped from Camp Hutchinson this morning, and a few of them jumped on a train that came through Sunray Depot a few hours ago."

The news stung.

Two years earlier, in the summer of '42, as the war raged on in Europe and the Pacific, the government had secured a large chunk of farmland twenty miles southwest of Sunray and built the first of many POW camps in Texas. Camp Hutchinson was the second largest internment facility in the United States at the time. It consisted of four compounds surrounded by chain-link fences and rows of barbed-wire, each housing a thousand prisoners. Italians filled three of the sheet-iron structures crammed end to end with cots and footlockers, German Nazis the other. They'd been housed together initially but brawls had broken out, resulting in a few deaths, forcing the separation. Provisions for the inmates and the soldiers who managed the prison were delivered by train. The same tracks that passed within a mile of the camp also passed through the depot in eastern Sunray.

Mom's eyebrows shot up. "Have they been caught?"

Pastor Lewis shook his head. "Sheriff Bennington told me the train was searched and found empty shortly after reaching Mercy, and the only place it had stopped before that was here. The entire track has been temporarily shut down, and the Army is checking cars on the two roads going in and out of town, and supposedly setting up checkpoints on some other roads in the county, too. I'm going to talk to Mayor Wilson right now to see if he knows anything else. I just wanted to stop in real quick and make sure you knew what was going on and ask you to help spread the word." His eyes tightened with warning. "Those men are desperate, Martha. Some as evil as they come. The Devil's Disciples, as I've said before. They beat four of the guards with fence posts during the escape and tied them up. We all need to stay alert and look out for one another until we know they've been caught."

Mom nodded with conviction. She'd heard. We all had. News about the Third Reich's brutality had been trickling out of Europe for years, and the first concentration camps had recently been discovered in Poland, confirming the worst of it. Pastor Lewis and other church leaders had been using rumors of Nazi atrocities to fuel their sermons for the better part of a year, naming Hitler as the anti-Christ, claiming his rise to power was a sign of the end of times, a warning for everyone on Earth to take a side, choose a path of righteous or wicked, and that rhetoric had drastically increased after the prisoners began arriving in the autumn of '43.

"Is this your only job today?" Pastor Lewis asked.

Mom nodded. "We have to clean United Methodist tomorrow, but yeah, this is it for today."

"Good, good. I think it'd be better if we're all inside before nightfall, just in case." He patted at the moisture on his forehead and upper lip again. "And if you need anything, anything at all, or if you just don't want to be home alone until we know more, Hazel and the boys are at the house. They know what's going on, and I'm sure they'd love to have you over."

Mom thanked him for his generosity, and we followed him out onto the porch where I raised my hand to shield my eyes from the bright sunshine and surveyed Ozmer Street. My thoughts moved with my eyes. Was one of the prisoners hiding in the First Baptist Church of Sunray next door? The pentecostal church next to that? The backseat of the Ford parked across the street? The abandoned house on the corner? The shoddy storage shed behind Miss Carla's Luncheonette?

Then my thoughts moved deeper, inward, and I felt my shoulders tense. I wondered if one of the men could be the one who'd killed my dad; the one who'd kick-started the waves of ache and anger that had ebbed and flowed inside my chest for eight long months. I bit my bottom lip to keep the possibility from spilling out of my mouth. Mom didn't like talking about Dad much, rarely brought him up herself, and she'd already rejected the possibility of his killer living in Camp Hutchinson when I'd posed it months earlier, saying she refused to entertain such foolish thoughts.

Foolish or not, I couldn't help entertaining them. My imagination was too rampant, my eagerness to find a specific person to finger for Dad's death too great. I wanted someone—a face, a name, a monster—to be held accountable.

Foolish or not, I had fantasies of revenge.

When Pastor Lewis reached the roadside, Mom waved to him and marched back inside. "Come on," she said, making a beeline toward the pews, her legs whipping against the inside of her full-length skirt. "Let's hurry and finish so we can get out of here."

2

At home, I helped Mom unload the cleaning supplies from our beat-up '35 Chevy Pickup and store them in the downstairs bedroom, then I went upstairs to my room. I grabbed Dad's old fishing jeans off the top of my dresser and held them close to my nose for a moment—long enough to catch the scent of creek water and Red Man tobacco clinging to the fabric—before changing into them. That smell—*his* smell—made me feel close to him, like he was right behind me, about to laugh or say my name, maybe goose my side to make me squeal, or throw his arms around me and lift me off the ground in a bear hug and say it was time to squeeze the nonsense out of me again. It had the power to bring tears to my eyes, a smile to my face, inspiration to my desire, grit to my resolve, so many things. Right then, it gave me comfort.

I'd chopped the lower legs off and wore them rolled up just above my knees. They were baggy and had to be held afloat with a leather belt. Dried fish blood streaked one thigh, and a green patch covered the crotch where the hem had split. Much to Mom's dismay, I'd worn them nearly every day that summer. The only times I didn't was when we attended church on Sunday mornings and when I helped Mom clean. I was afraid the overwhelming scent of perfume and cologne the sanctuary reeked of on Sunday mornings, or the strong odor of the cleaning products that inevitably got all over my clothes when we cleaned, would override Dad's smell. He'd always refused to let Mom wash them, saying doing so would ruin his familiarity with the fish, drive them twenty miles downstream, and he'd never catch anything ever again. I refused to wash them, too. I didn't want to drive what little remained of him farther away from me, either.

He'd quit his supervisor job at the Alloy carbon black plant and joined the Army shortly after the attack on Pearl Harbor. The last time I saw him, he came into my room to tell me goodbye because I refused to go downstairs and see him off. I threw my arms around him and cried and begged him not to go. "Why, Daddy? Why are you doing this? What if something horrible happens? What if you don't come back?" He smiled an easy smile that said, don't worry, I'll be fine. "It's okay to be scared," he'd said. "There are many times in life when you're going to be scared of what's ahead of you, but that doesn't mean you should turn and run. Especially if the cause is worth the risk." He caressed my back. "I'd love to stay here with you and Mom, but sometimes sacrifices have to be made. This is one of those times for me, Ali." He was the only person who called me Ali, and no one has ever called me that since. A few tried, but I nipped that in the bud immediately.

That was the last word he ever said to me: Ali.

He was killed during the Fifth Army Bernhardt Line offensive in the winter of '43. A bullet to the chest, they'd said. Died instantly and without suffering, they'd said. I bet they told everyone that. We received his dog tags with the news of his death, but like many soldiers, his body remained overseas, buried with five others in an unmarked grave. He did have a tombstone in Sunray Cemetery, and Mom and I occasionally placed flowers in front of the small slab with DOUGLAS ALLEN MAYES 1905-1943 etched across it, but it was a resting place in name only.

I made my way to my window as Mom started talking (*Have you heard?*) on the phone downstairs. Our house was one of only three houses on McGee Street, the center dot on the southernmost road in Sunray. The Lewis's house was about half a mile east, the Dalton's, half a mile west. My window faced south, looking out over the land that stretched south as far as the eye could see—land that would later become the Garden of Sunray. At the time, we only used an acre or so directly behind the house for personal produce and our small chicken coop. The rest was flat and featureless save a crippled windmill, patches of mesquite thicket here and there, and the area on the eastern edge of the land where Regreso Creek sliced through the prairie on its way to merge with the Brazos River, allowing plump bushes and several elm and oak trees to thrive along its bank.

The land had belonged to Dad's family since the early 1900s, a good quarter century before Sunray sprouted up and became an official town, and they'd leased it to cattle farmers until the dust bowl years erased that option. As an only child, Dad had inherited the acreage, along with the two-story farmhouse his ancestors had built by hand, after his parents passed.

He and Mom were leasing a tiny two-bedroom home in north Sunray when I was born, but we moved into the farmhouse with Nana Mayes after Grandpa died from a heart attack when I was seven. Years before his death, a stroke had left Nana's left side paralyzed, making it impossible for her to manage on her own. She was a bitter woman who fought death as hard as she fought expressing gratitude and relenting control, but she eventually passed in her sleep in the downstairs bedroom a few months before Dad left for boot camp.

Dad had dreams for the land. He'd told me that when he returned from the war, he'd like to build a house close enough to the creek that he could fish off the back porch. "And maybe a barn next to that so we can have some horses" he'd also said. He'd always loved horses and was obsessed with the Pony Express. He'd worked on the Chase Ranch, tending their horses and swine, from the age of eight until he married Mom and took a better paying job at the carbon black plant. He'd taken me out there many times to ride. Of course, he never returned from the war, and starting a few months after his death, I'd overheard Mom discuss selling the land multiple times, saying she didn't have any desire to be responsible for that much land and needed a fresh start in a "modern house that isn't drafty and had proper indoor plumbing."

I stared out the window, scanning the horizon, thinking about the train tracks that ran just east of our property line, about Dad and

Camp Hutchinson and the escape prisoners, wondering about possible, impossible connections, until Mom hung up the phone and hollered my name.

When I entered the kitchen, she eyed my shorts with prim disapproval before looking me in the face. At the beginning of the summer, her expression would've been accompanied by a disapproving comment, a reminder of how unladylike I appeared, but she'd given up on that front. "Hazel wants us to come over for dinner so we can talk about all this prisoner mess," she said. "She has a feeling it's not going to end well."

Hazel Lewis, Pastor Lewis's wife, was always having "feelings." She claimed to have been regularly blessed with prophetic insights, visions, and messages since the age of five when she'd nearly died from tuberculosis and "touched heaven's doorstep." Mom and many other Bible-thumpers, members of the Trinity Lutheran Church congregation in particular, glommed on to her every word, heeded her every warning. Pastor Lewis sometimes even incorporated her dreams and visions into his sermons. Dad, on the other hand, had been one of many who found Hazel flaky and delusional. He never believed she was purposefully putting on a ruse, and he treated her with respect and kindness to her face, but behind closed doors, especially around like-minded friends after he had a few drinks in him, he occasionally mocked her and laughed at her, claiming she was "off her rocker," another "Bible-enthused fortune teller." Hazel always treated me kindly, and I believed that *she* believed in her ability, but I had too much Mayes skepticism running through my veins to buy it. I sided with Dad.

I snickered to myself and whispered, "Of course she does," thinking if Dad had been there, he would've shot me a wink behind Mom's back.

Mom ignored my flippancy and gestured at the pantry. "Grab a half dozen eggs and the butter. I'm going to go wrap up what's left of the salt pork."

We loaded the supplies in a cloth sack, locked the front and back doors, which we rarely did, and walked to the Lewis's.

Unlike our paint-faded, patch-work shiplap home, their two-story brick house was as architecturally ornate inside and out as the finest church. In fact, it had been built by the same ritzy construction company out of Mercy that had built the Trinity Lutheran Church. Both structures had wide, spade-shaped archways, intricately engraved doors, shiny brass hardware throughout, indoor plumbing, and even matching round stained-glass windows. A cross surrounded by a rainbow of colors dotted the wall above the church pulpit, and a slightly smaller identical one served as the sole window in the house's attic, facing McGee Street for all to see.

Hazel flung the door open before Mom could lower her hand after knocking. Hazel was a big-boned woman with gentle eyes and hair the color of root beer. Rumor had it she came from a family of moderate wealth—pre-Civil War plantation wealth, most believed—and her appearance seemed to validate that speculation. She was a few years older than Mom but appeared significantly younger. Her milky skin showed little if any signs of weathering, and her hands were as velvety soft as a lamb's ear leaf.

"Martha, Alice. Hi. Come in, come in."

We followed her to the kitchen, and after I set the sack of groceries on the counter, her eyes caught mine. "The boys are upstairs playing cards if you'd like to go up."

"Thanks," I said, and made my way upstairs as Hazel and Mom began an energetic back-and-forth about the Nazi mess.

I slowed as I reached the doorway to Robert's and Thomas's bedroom, careful to dodge the squeaky spots on the floor, and peeked inside. They were sitting on Thomas's bed on the left side of the room, their attention on the cards in their hands. Robert's back was to me, blocking Thomas's view of the doorway. I raised my hands into the air, fingers curled like hungry werewolf claws, and roared as I jumped through the doorway, landing flat-footed on the wooden floor with a thunderous smack.

Thomas, the younger of the two, squealed, dropped his cards, and jumped to his feet on the bed. Robert quickly twisted my direction. He had turned sixteen two months earlier but was taller and more thoughtful than most grown men. Surprise held his mouth open and eyebrows high as we locked eyes. When I laughed and half-heartedly roared and clawed at the air again, his eyes softened and the corners of his mouth rose. He flicked his handful of cards my way.

"You're not funny," he said, though his growing smile said otherwise.

"Yeah," Thomas added. "That's not funny. Why do you always do stuff like that?" His tone was harsh, brow pinched. For an eleven-year-old, he had little play in him, and I had made it my mission to change that.

I winked at him. "Because it's so easy."

I collected the cards off the floor while Robert gathered the others. Thomas hopped down, and we sat in our customary triangle on the round rug between their two beds—Robert directly across from me, Thomas to my right.

Thomas snatched the cards out of Robert's hand and then reached for the ones I had. I playfully jerked them back, and he whined, "You picked the game last time, Alice. It's my turn."

I held steady for a moment before shooting him an exaggerated, eye-squinting smile and passed the cards to him. As he began shuffling, I looked at Robert. His attention hung on my shorts for a moment before shifting to my face.

"So, what do you think about the prisoner thing?" he asked. "Are you worried at all?"

"No," I said. "Not really. I'm more... I don't know..."

"Intrigued?" he filled in.

I confirmed his assumption with a quick nod and coy smile. We'd had countless *what if* conversations about Camp Hutchinson and the Nazis, including one a few weeks earlier about whether or not my dad's killer could've somehow, someway, wound up so close to Sunray. He knew how bad I wanted it to be a possibility, so it was hard to tell if he was indulging me out of pity by saying the idea wasn't foolish like Mom had insisted, or if he truly thought it wasn't. I wanted to believe the latter, but I never pressed him on it.

"Do you think the prisoners are really *here*...in Sunray?" I asked.

He lightly shook his head. "I doubt it. Those guys could've jumped off anywhere, and I figure they'd want to get as far away from the camp as possible. And just because they searched the train in Mercy and didn't find them doesn't mean they're here."

"Yeah," I agreed. "They could've hopped off when the train slowed in one of the small towns between here and there and stolen a car, or hopped onto another train in Mercy before the one they rode in on was checked."

"They could be anywhere."

"Memory is the game," Thomas interjected without looking up, and started placing cards face-down in long rows. Memory was his go-to. He wasn't the best at reading people, but he could memorize the freckle pattern on a person's face with one good glance. When he finished, he flipped over two cards, the six of hearts and eight of spades, and turned them back over. Then he looked at his brother. "Mom thinks they're definitely here. I heard her tell Mrs. Hanna on the phone earlier that there are enough abandoned buildings in town to hide an entire Nazi army. She said they could be anywhere."

There was no arguing about the buildings. If prisoners were in town, they had plenty of places to hide. One-room shacks had been brought in on skids during the oil boom in the early '30s and dropped wherever they'd fit, and when those filled up, more ramshackle housing units were thrown together using oil rig scraps or whatever else could be salvaged from the town dump. Meaning, after the oil wells ran dry and the workers moved on, Sunray was left with as many abandoned houses as used ones. Other than the prostitutes, drunkards, and transients who occasionally took advantage of the free spaces, and kids who dared one another to venture inside the spookier ones, most hadn't been touched in years.

Thomas's ominous remark lingered in the air, and we played in silence for the next five minutes or so, Robert and I stealing occasional glances at each other, Thomas concentrating on the cards as though his life depended on it, the ceiling fan whirring overhead, the relentless hush of Mom's and Hazel's conversation drifting up the stairs. Thomas was retrieving the final pair to claim victory when a loud knock on the front door brought us to our feet.

Standing shoulder to shoulder behind the upstairs banister, we watched Hazel peek out the window next to the front door. "It's Sheriff Bennington." She straightened her blouse and spine before unlocking and opening the door to greet him.

Ace Bennington was round without being particularly overweight, sturdy but far from muscle-bound. Born and raised in Mercy, he'd moved to Sunray during the oil boom when the need for more lawmen arose and worked his way from deputy to sheriff rather quickly. He'd been one of Dad's best friends for as long as I could remember. They were fishing buddies, drinking buddies, home repair buddies. St. Louis Cardinal-fan buddies. *Watch-over-my-wife-and-daughter-while-I'm-gone* buddies.

He removed his sheriff-star-pinned cattleman's hat as he stepped inside, exposing his pale bald head, a stark contrast to his dark mop of a mustache and sun-reddened face. When he noticed us, he called out, "Hi, gang," and we trickled downstairs.

"What brings you by?" Hazel asked. "If you're looking for Fred,

I think he's over at Mayor Wilson's office."

"Thank you, but that's not why I'm here." He gestured at Mom with his hat. "I stopped by because I tried to call Martha to make sure she'd heard what had happened. When she didn't answer, I went by her house. And when she wasn't there, I figured I'd try my luck here." He met eyes with Mom and a scrape of a smile crept to life on his face. Hers too. "Third time's a charm, I guess."

"Did you catch the prisoners yet, Sheriff?" Thomas blurted out. "Dad said the Army stopped the train and set up roadblocks and everything."

"Thomas," Hazel scolded, taking him by the shoulders and easing him back. "Don't interrupt."

"It's okay," Ace said, eyeing Thomas. "No, son. We haven't found any signs of them here in town either, which is good. Two were captured in the fields before they reached the train, though. Apparently, one caught his foot in a groundhog hole and snapped his ankle, and the other had a bum hip due to a grenade injury or something and never made it to the tracks."

"Do you know how many are still missing?" I asked.

"We've been told four, but we're still waiting on an official count from the Army."

I nodded as Ace started fanning his sweat-slicked face with his hat.

"Where are my manners?" Hazel reprimanded herself. "You must be burning up in that uniform. Would you like a cool glass of tea?"

"I'd love one," Ace said.

"Dry or sweet?"

"The sweeter the better."

In the kitchen, Ace sat at the table in the center of the room, drinking his tea. Thomas sat across from him, peppering him with hypothetical questions about the prisoners and escape, ninety-nine percent of which Ace could only answer with "I couldn't say," "I have no idea," and "I don't know." The phone rang during Thomas's barrage, summoning Hazel to the living room (*Have you heard?*) where her excited tone suggested she'd stay for some time, so Mom asked Robert and me to help prep for dinner. She tasked Robert with chopping potatoes, me with mixing dough. I went to the pantry to grab the flour and found the jar nearly empty.

"There's not enough flour," I said, angling the open jar at Mom.

Mom stared at it for a moment, her mental gears grinding. "We don't have any at our house either. I was going to stop by Fulton's after we finished cleaning the church, but it must've slipped my mind."

Ace downed what remained of his tea and stood. "I'll go get some for you."

"You don't have to do that," Mom said. "I know you're busy with all that's happening. We can manage without it."

He shuffled around the table and handed Mom his empty glass. "It's no problem. Nobody's expecting me back at the station for a while."

They held eye contact for a long second. I could tell by the way Mom's lips subtly worked that she was fighting the urge to reject the offer again. I could also tell by the firm expression on Ace's face he wouldn't take no for an answer.

"I can go with him to speed things up," I offered. "He can wait in the car while I run in so he doesn't have to risk being cornered and questioned by anybody."

Ace slipped on his hat and cocked a finger-gun at me. "Sounds like a plan."

"I should probably ride along, too," Robert said. He sounded drab, as though he didn't have a choice. "You know," he looked my way, an ornery twinkle in his eyes, "in case the flour sack is too heavy for her."

I punched him in the upper arm, eliciting a burst of laughter from him and smiles from everyone else except Mom. She put her free hand on her hip and shot me her standard *Why Alice, why?* look. *That's not ladylike.*

Thomas jumped up, shoving his chair with the backs of his knees, and angled his eyes up at Ace like a needy puppy. "I want to go, too. Can I, can I?"

"Sorry, son, there's not enough room. Deputy Weber has the department car right now, so I'm in my truck. The cab can only hold three, and the bed's full of junk."

Thomas crossed his arms over his chest and plopped back down in his seat, pouting.

Mom met eyes with Ace. "You're sure it's not a bother?"

"Of course not," he assured her. "We'll go straight there and back. It won't take ten minutes. Fifteen tops if Fulton's is still bustling like it was when I passed by on my way here."

He spoke with the utmost confidence, as if his prediction of events and timeline were ironclad, already written in the history books.

We'd soon find out they weren't.

3

Fulton's Grocery Store was located just north of town square on Main Street, wedged between Jimmy's Liquors and the Sunoco filling station—where the Kroger was today.

Ace slowed the truck and rolled down his window as we approached the intersection of Main and Ozmer.

Back then, the patch of land the roads looped around in the center of the intersection was called the Heart of Town Square by some, simply the roundabout by others, and it was grassland, not the cement-covered, curbed-in, fenced-off eyesore it is today. A young

Texas red oak stood in the center, tall and proud behind the Texas-shaped slab of limestone marked with the name Sunray and the year of the town's official birth. They were both placed there during a small ceremony in the spring of 1930, four years after the boom began. Though now, of course, only the slab remains.

Garrett Show, the aptly named owner of the Morley, stood by the oak tree, smoking in the shade. His suit was crisply pressed, hair bedraggled as usual. His black mutt, Spade, sat at his feet. The green scarf wrapped around Spade's neck matched the color of Garrett's bowtie. He'd moved to town six years earlier to oversee the construction of and manage the movie theater for his father who owned a similar one in Mercy. He quickly became a favorite patron at local bars (and supposedly with many of the ladies of the night who frequented such places) due to his generous spending and magnetic personality. He waved to us as we passed, and Ace held up an acknowledging hand.

Fulton's was still bustling, as much as any place in Sunray could bustle, anyway. Five or six parked cars lined Main Street in front of the store. A small cluster of well-dressed women huddled on the walkway, gossiping.

Ace eased to a stop behind the parked cars. "I'm probably going to be using this truck all night, so I'm going to go next door and top off with gas while you go get the flour," he said as Robert and I hopped out. "I'll wait for you there."

The well-dressed women, two of whom were the Gideon sisters, looked our way as we passed by. Greta and Anne Gideon, forty-four-year-old twins who dressed the same, walked with the same hitch in their hips, and had matching neck moles, had always lived together and would die within hours of each other twenty years later. Their father, one of the richest oil tycoons in the Texas Panhandle, had died two years earlier. He'd left his estate, including the five-thousand-square-foot house on the western edge of Sunray that Mom had cleaned twice a month for ten years, to them. They continued to employ her but didn't treat her as well as Mr. Gideon had. They were never outright hateful or mean, just cold and dismissive. They considered "dirt gatherers and toilet scrubbers" like Mom, although necessary, less than, the bottom of the social pyramid, and treated her as such. I held my chin high and pretended not to notice when their gazes slid to my fish-gut shorts. I welcomed their silent judgment. I welcomed their disgust. They're the ones who felt it, not me.

Mary Fulton ran the cash register and greeted us by name when we entered the store. She and her husband, Greg, had opened Sunray's one and only grocery store a few years before the oil boom and lived in a small house directly behind it. They both worked sunup to sundown, six days a week, come rain, hail, sleet, or snow, but were somehow always energetic and lively, overeager to help and please. Mom said that was because they didn't have any kids or extended family of their own in town.

"What can I get for you kids?" Mary asked, her generous smile exposing the large gap between her front teeth.

"We just need a bag of flour," Robert said, returning a smile. "We can get it."

"Well, holler if you need help. Greg's back there somewhere."

Robert made a beeline for the flour and I followed. Ten or fifteen other shoppers lingered in the aisles, most talking to one another rather than searching for items on the shelves. I heard the words "Nazi" and "camp" mentioned more than once as we navigated the aisles, greeting people with smiles as we excused ourselves past them. A couple I recognized from church, a few others from school. One guy had a crewcut and the rigid stance of an off-duty soldier—a common sight around Sunray ever since Camp Hutchinson's completion. Sunray was the nearest town to the camp, therefore the closest place for soldiers to find cheap booze and cheaper women, or an invigorating Sunday morning sermon, or a greasy homemade hamburger and fries, whatever floated their boat.

At the back of the store, Greg was restocking the two-pound, five-pound, and twelve-pound sacks of Pike's Peak Flour. He was squat and a good hundred pounds overweight, which he carried around his waist like a tire. Sweat drenched his shirt, and he huffed and puffed as he worked. But he still had a pleasant expression on his face.

He greeted us, shaking Robert's hand, then mine, cupping each one of ours in both of his. "You need flour?"

I pointed at the five-pound sacks. "One of those, please."

He grabbed one, dusted the white off the top, and shook it a little. "Just making sure there aren't any leaks." He handed it to me. "Is that it?"

I nodded, thanked him, and carrying the sack in the crook of my arm like a football, headed back toward the front of the store with Robert by my side. We hadn't taken three steps before he gingerly placed his hand on my shoulder and lowered his face down close to mine.

"You need some help, little lady," he asked in an over-the-top, awe-shucks sarcastic tone. "You seem to be struggling a bit. Perhaps you should've gotten the two-pounder."

I jerked my shoulder away and cut my eyes at him, giving him an equally over-the-top, back-off glare. His mouth dropped open in mock dismay, and he put his hands over his heart. "Ouch."

I shook my head without breaking stride, fighting back a smile, and lightly rolled my eyes. "You're dumber than a bucket full of hair," I said, a saying I'd borrowed from Dad, one I regularly used around Robert and Thomas. So much so that Thomas had gotten in trouble for saying it to a kid at church who failed to recite all sixty-six books of the Bible in correct order.

Robert stepped in front of me as we approached the register and told Mrs. Fulton to put the flour on his mom's tab, as well as a box of

Chuckles. After he signed the ledger, we agreed we'd tell our mothers she'd said hello, and walked back outside. I surveyed Main Street when Robert paused to open the box of sugar-coated jelly candies.

Two older men had joined the group of well-dressed ladies huddled together on the wooden walkway, and a man and woman with sourpuss expressions on their faces were standing outside of Jimmy's Liquors next door with beer bottles in hand, their attention aimed toward the paved road. Across the street, a few cars were parked at an angle in front of the bar called The Mug, another two in front of the Go Club next door to that. Doris Klepper, a feisty twenty-four-year-old who worked as a waitress at Miss Carla's Luncheonette and was known to enjoy a drink or ten, had her long hair tossed to the side and her arms propped on the driver-side door of one car, flirting with the bearded man inside.

Ace was standing next to his truck at the Sunoco, facing our way. Ronald Faraday, a scrawny twig of a man with bad breath who pumped gas for a living, had his foot up on the stool that sat between the pumps and was bending Ace's ear.

Robert popped a couple of candies into his mouth, poured some in my hand so I could do the same, and as we headed for the Sunoco lot, I noticed his dad standing under the oak tree in the center of the roundabout, squatting in front of Garrett Show, petting Spade.

"Look, there's your dad," I said, pointing as I chewed, the sticky sweets gumming to my teeth. "I wonder if—"

"Stop him!" a deep voice behind me bellowed.

The command demanded attention. Robert and I spun around. Doris shot upright and looked over the top of the bearded man's car. The group huddled on the walkway in front of Fulton's jerked their heads toward Main Street.

A man in ragged jeans and a dirty long-sleeved shirt was running down the walkway in front of the Go Club, stumbling, struggling to maintain his balance. He glanced behind him as he veered around the two cars in front of The Mug and continued down the Main Street, moving toward the roundabout, picking up speed. His hair was short, the same length as his flimsy beard. One foot was in a shoe, the other bare. Blood smeared the left side of his face and neck.

"Don't let him get away!" Billy Smarten yelled as he darted out from in between The Mug and Go Club, giving a face to the booming commands. He was a pigeon-toed local who worked at the variety store a block over on Union Street. He ran onto the paved road, chasing the man, swinging a baseball bat in his hand like a baton. "He's one of the Nazis!"

My eyes widened, breath caught in my throat.

They *were* here. At least one, anyway. A Nazi. In Sunray.

Time slowed to a crawl as I searched the man's face. A naive part of me expected to see telltale signs of a demon hiding in human skin: pitch black irises, a menacing grin, horns or pointed teeth even… But I saw nothing of the sort. I didn't see the giant, blonde-haired, blue-eyed, tanned, muscular man with bloodthirsty eyes we'd all been told German soldiers were, either. The man was light-haired and stout, but he was far from tanned or giant. And his eyes were filled with desperation, not hate. I'd be lying if I said I wasn't a little disappointed.

The two men standing on the walkway with the group of well-dressed women rushed out onto the road, yelling for the man to stop. So did the young man who'd been standing in front of the liquor store, holding his beer bottle head-high, ready to strike. By the time the Nazi reached the north edge of the roundabout, two men who'd emerged from The Mug and the military man who'd been inside Fulton's had joined the chase. Doris trotted down the middle of the road behind the gang. I dropped the flour, a small cloud of white dust powdering my feet as I bolted out onto the road. Robert hurried after me and grabbed my arm, pulling me to a stop.

"Let go!" I snapped at him, fighting his grip.

He held steady. "No."

I jerked away from him and ran, the flour forgotten.

"Alice!" he hollered after me.

Pastor Lewis and Garrett Show stepped out from under the oak tree and stood side by side as the man approached, arms outstretched in a human fence.

Spade darted at the Nazi, barking furiously, and he kicked at the mutt with his shoed foot but missed. Spade latched onto his shin, and he shook and thrust his leg, screaming.

When Garrett moved to grab Spade's scarf, the Nazi lunged at him, tackling him to the ground, punching at his face. Garrett, a timid man by nature, struggled to protect himself. Pastor Lewis grabbed the back of the Nazi's shirt and pulled him off of Garrett, and the Nazi wheeled around and decked Pastor Lewis in the face. Pastor Lewis stumbled backward, and the Nazi thrust his fingers in Spade's mouth and pried the mutt off of his leg as Ace and Ronald Faraday sprinted toward the roundabout.

Ace had his arm outstretched, gun drawn. His hat flew off as he crossed the road, yelling, ordering the man to put his hands up.

The Nazi tried to run for it instead, but it was too late. The gang of chasers (around a dozen men by now, mostly young and middle-aged, at least two with guns in their hands) had caught up. A beer bottle flew from the gang, hitting the Nazi in the back. He staggered forward, and when he glanced back over his shoulder, Billy Smarten reared back and hit him in the knee with the wooden baseball bat.

I stopped at the edge of the grass next to Doris as the man crumpled to all fours and was surrounded. Robert flanked me. Pastor Lewis wedged himself into the group. Ace forced his way to the front. The Nazi remained motionless. So many people were yelling I couldn't make out who was saying what. The choir of angry, contemptuous voices hurled curses, insults, and commands. All accentuated by Spade's relentless barking.

When the Nazi tried to crawl forward, legs and arms flew at him and the yelling intensified. He tried to stand, to fight, but the blows were too many. So many legs and arms were moving I couldn't tell whose was whose. Fists and feet pounded the Nazi's face and torso until he crumpled back onto the ground, then they pounded more.

When two quick gunshots rang out, everything stopped. A pall of silence dropped over the crowd. The mob slowly backed up, all attention on the Nazi curled up in a ball at Ace's feet.

"Who fired those shots?" Robert asked. "Was it Bennington?"

"I don't know," I said, glancing back at him. Greta, Anne, and a small horde of others stood behind Robert. Mary and Greg Fulton were on the walkway in front of their store, watching, and other pockets of people watched from the roadside up to a block away, a couple of kids straddling bikes included.

"Was he shot?" someone asked.

"I hope so," Either Anne or Greta said.

"Would someone please go find Deputy Weber and Dr. Mobley and bring them here," Ace announced, scanning the onlookers. "And the rest of you need to move out. Everything's over. Everything's fine. I've got it from here."

The Nazi remained motionless, curled in a fetal position, as the mob encircling him reluctantly dispersed, sneaking glances back over their shoulders as they went. Pastor Lewis exchanged words with Ace and then headed our way after Ace pointed us out.

"Is he dead?" I asked, stepping toward Pastor Lewis as he drew close. He had a small cut on his left cheekbone where the Nazi's knuckles had landed. The tender skin around the eye above it was pink and puffy.

"No," Pastor Lewis answered. "He's not."

"Did the sheriff shoot him?" someone behind me asked.

"Where was he hiding?" someone else hollered.

Pastor Lewis held his hands up, fingers-splayed like he did when he wanted to silence his congregation, as other questions followed. "Listen, I know everyone has a bunch of questions. I do, too. But now is not the time for answers. You all need to get off the roads and go home like Sheriff Bennington said. We'll get answers in due time. Now...go. Go home."

The people obeyed, murmuring their way back to their cars, or workplace, or homeward bound, and Pastor Lewis's attention turned to Robert and me. "I told Sheriff Bennington I'd walk you two home since he's going to have his hands full for a while."

Robert stared at his dad's swollen cheek. I'd never seen Pastor Lewis physically injured and doubted he had either. "Are you okay, Dad?"

"I'm fine," Pastor Lewis said curtly, pulling a handkerchief out of his pocket and patting at the cut as he marched away. "Let's go."

Pastor Lewis had a car, a newer Ford Tudor sedan, but he rarely drove. He walked everywhere, said it helped him "keep a good read on the town's pulse," but I think he did it in an attempt to control the pulse. He reveled in staying at the forefront of town gossip almost as much as he did preaching from the pulpit.

I kept glancing back over my shoulder as he guided us across the street and east down Ozmer. His long, purposeful stride combined with my wandering thoughts made it hard for me to keep up. Just before Ace and the Nazi were out of sight, Deputy Weber pulled up in the sheriff's cruiser and hustled over to his boss, leaving the driver's door open. The last thing I saw was them lifting the Nazi to his feet and partially leading, partially dragging him toward the cruiser.

We walked in silence, the setting sun hot on our backs, until we reached the Trinity Lutheran Church. Pastor Lewis told Robert and me to "stay put" while he circled the building and double-checked that the doors were locked, windows secure. Then we continued east, passing the First Baptist and Methodist churches, a couple of abandoned homes, and the small shack called The Pathway where some of the non-denominationals met, before stopping at Miss Carla's Luncheonette on the corner of Ozmer and Knoll Street. Again, Pastor Lewis told us to "stay put" while he went inside to briefly talk to Miss Carla.

The early dinner crowd in the luncheonette was sparse, only two cars parked outside. War rations had limited Miss Carla to serving meat only three times a week: hamburgers on Wednesdays and Saturdays, bacon on Sundays. Though Pastor Lewis occasionally asked his congregation, of which Carla Reed was a member, to donate ration stamps so she could host an Easter feast, or a Fourth of July meal, things like that.

Robert and I stood in front of the store, a few feet from the propped open door, our backs against the glass with MISS CARLA'S LUNCHEONETTE painted in a rainbow arc on it.

"That was crazy," Robert said. "I guess we were wrong about them being here, huh?"

I nodded and pinched my lips together to prevent the thoughts and questions racing through my mind from flying out of my mouth. *Was that him? Was that the monster who killed my dad? I want to go back and see him. Talk to him. Or was he dead? Where are the others?* I would've loved to discuss and speculate with Robert, and I know he would've indulged me, but it wasn't the time. I needed to allow what had just happened to settle, align my thoughts and feelings first. Besides, I didn't want to get into a *what if* conversation in front of Pastor Lewis. He had a tendency to spin everything into a dreadfully long sermon-style lesson.

Robert slid his beanpole leg my way and tapped the tip of his shoe on top of mine. My aged Keds appeared whiter than navy blue. "Looks like you've been trampling through snow."

Sticking out my tongue and panting like a winded dog, I wiped at the sweat on my forehead and slung my hand at the ground as if it were so thick with liquid, I couldn't hold it all. "What makes you think I haven't?"

We had a good laugh and turned our attention back toward the road. He pulled the box of Chuckles out of his pocket and offered to dump some in my hand. I accepted, and we chewed in watchful silence for a while.

"Do you think your mom will be mad we didn't get the flour?" he eventually asked.

"Not once she hears what happened," I said.

He nodded. "And the way this town's gossip vine runs, they'll probably know before we get back."

"They definitely will," I agreed.

We finished the box of candies and followed Pastor Lewis south on Knoll after he emerged from Miss Carla's. He led us in a meandering path toward our street, conveniently passing many of the Trinity Lutheran Church's wealthiest members' houses, two of which Mom cleaned. Robert and I quietly stood by and watched while he told the ones who answered his knock what had happened and to spread the word.

It was after seven o'clock, the sun two hours from vanishing, when we reached McGee Street. A walk we could've made in ten or fifteen minutes (I know because I'd made the walk to Fulton's and back home hundreds of times, not to mention walking to and from school for years) had taken nearly an hour.

4

Hazel fawned over Pastor Lewis's minor injury the second we walked through the door, acting like he'd been in a full-on boxing brawl. She'd already received a call from someone who'd been downtown. He shrugged off her efforts to clean the wound and led everyone into the living room where she, Mom, and Thomas listened to a description of what had happened with rapt attention. Pastor Lewis stood in the center of the room and did a majority of the talking, using his hands as an animation tool, like he did in church. Mom and Hazel sat on the couch on the edge of their seats, shaking their heads and covering their mouths at the appropriate moments. Thomas sat on the floor in front of his dad, wide-eyed, soaking it all in. Robert and I chimed in with a few details from our perspective, including my apology for losing the flour along the way.

Everyone except Pastor Lewis moved to the kitchen when Hazel insisted we still eat dinner. He stayed in the living room, pacing back and forth as far as the phone cord allowed, calling person after person, spreading the news.

Robert, Thomas, and I sat around the table in the middle of the kitchen and ate small helpings of fried eggs and seared salt pork, listening to our mothers rehash what they'd learned.

When Hazel enthusiastically reminded Mom how she'd "had a bad feeling about this," how she'd known "something bad was going to happen," Robert shot me a gloating, *I told you so* look. He and I had had many conversations about Hazel's "feelings" over the years—healthy debates, he called them, the same term his dad used to describe arguments about scripture with nonbelievers. And although, like Dad, I never outright disrespected her or called her a fake, he knew where I stood. We had an unspoken truce. He didn't hold my skepticism against me any more than I held his belief against him. But I wasn't above giving him the occasional *really?* eye-roll when warranted, nor he me the occasional *I told you so* look. Cracking a subtle smile, I gave him a single nod of surrender. What else could I do? Technically, Hazel had been right.

About half an hour later, Pastor Lewis entered the kitchen, suggested Mom and I head home before the sun fully set, and offered to walk us. Mom agreed that leaving was for the best but politely refused his offer to accompany us, promising to call Hazel once we arrived home to let them know we were safe.

Mom kept a calm face and pace as we marched down McGee Street, strolling as though her world were right as rain, but as we entered our house, her actions betrayed her nervousness. She moved through the entire house, flicking on lights as she went, making sure windows were locked, rooms and closets were undisturbed. Then she made her way to the detached garage. Dad and some of his buddies had built the two-story structure that Mom called the Hideous Catch-All shortly after we'd moved in with Nana Mayes, and it was packed with tools, fishing and hunting equipment, Papa and Nana Mayes's old furniture and clothes, and everything else Dad had noticed in the landfill north of town and saw potential in. The large barn-style front door had been nailed shut years earlier after a thunderstorm damaged it; the only way in was through the door in the back—a flimsy door with no lock.

When Mom returned from the garage, she said she'd taken two strips of Dad's cellulose tape and stuck them to the top of the door and the frame so we'd know if anyone had gone inside, then forced me to accompany her to the outhouse. She insisted I "go now" and "get it all out" because she didn't want me outside alone after dark.

At the time, the house hadn't been updated with proper indoor plumbing, an issue Mom had reminded Dad of regularly. His go-to response: "We don't have enough in savings for that yet, and I'm not taking out a loan. Besides, we're doing just fine with the way things are." This was the same sentiment Nana Mayes had delivered to Mom for years, and she hated it. Along with the outhouse, our plumbing system consisted of a water pump out back that pulled from a well, a second smaller pump in the kitchen over the sink (installed by Dad and Ace at Mom's insistence), a large portable basin for bathing inside or out, and chamber pots under each bed for emergencies.

In the kitchen, Mom called Hazel, and after I washed up, I went upstairs, and changed into the large t-shirt I used as a nightgown, then got my diary out of the chest at the foot of my bed and wrote about what I'd witnessed downtown. When I finished, I made my way to my window and opened it, allowing the breeze to kiss my face. After surveying the land, I glanced up at the first-born star in the sky. "Was that him, Dad? He didn't look like I thought he would."

"What?" Mom said, startling me.

I whipped around and saw her standing in my doorway. "You scared me."

"I didn't mean to." She stepped into the room. The stress of the day weighed on her eyes. She was ready for her nightly drink. "Who were you talking to?"

I looked back at the open window as if someone might be there. "No one. I was just…" I shrugged and headed to my bed. "Talking to myself, I guess."

"Oh," she remarked as she walked toward my open window. "I want to keep all the windows closed tonight." She closed and locked it, then drew the curtains together.

"No one's going to get in that unless they can fly," I argued. "You know how hot it gets up here. I'll sweat like a pig with it closed all night."

"I don't care." She flicked on the overhead fan. "There. That'll do."

I groaned.

"You need to say—"

She cut off and snapped her head at the doorway when the phone trilled downstairs. She looked back at me. "Say your prayers and get some rest. We have to get up early and go clean the Methodist church tomorrow."

She pulled my door mostly closed, and as she hurried downstairs and answered the phone, I turned off my bedside lamp, crept over to the window, unlocked and opened it. Kneeling, I rested my arms on the sill, my chin on my arms, and welcomed the night air on my face again. I sat there a good ten or fifteen minutes before tiptoeing to the top of the stairs to eavesdrop on Mom.

Crouching on the second to top step, I could see a little less than half of the kitchen. Mom sat in a chair with her back to me, the phone to her right ear, her left hand curled around a tumbler filled with a mixture of tea and Southern Comfort. She didn't think I knew she hid a bottle of Southern Comfort in the dresser in Nana Mayes's old room downstairs and added a little to her bedtime tea every night. Or, if she did know, she wanted to pretend I didn't.

She'd been a social drinker my whole life, sipping wine at Christmas and birthday parties with other adults, even having a beer or two here and there in good fun, but as far as I knew, the liquor drinking, the alone drinking, secret stress drinking, didn't start until after Dad left for boot camp. And it didn't become a nightly ritual (and occasional afternoon thing) until after he died. I didn't hold it against her. She was knee deep in grief, and she'd come from a long line of alcoholics who'd turned to the bottle for a lot less, if anything at all.

Mom had grown up in Button, Oklahoma, dirt-poor. Her father and mother were both uneducated day laborers who drank twice as much as they worked and were free with their fists. She was the youngest of five siblings who all shared one mattress in one room. She had one sister (Henrietta) who was ten years older than her, and three brothers (Bill, Frank, and Louis) who were closer to her in age. Louis was the second youngest, a year and a half older than her, and the one she'd had the closest bond with. She called him her shield because he always stepped in and redirected their parents' aggression at himself when it was aimed at her.

So, shortly after her sixteenth birthday in the summer of '26, when he told her he was moving to the Texas Panhandle to work in the oil fields and wanted her to go with him, she couldn't say yes fast enough. Their other three siblings had already scattered. Henrietta lived in Arkansas with a pig farmer and had three kids of her own. Frank lived in southern Texas, working on fishing boats in the gulf. And Bill, a carbon copy of their drunk, angry father, lived on the other side of Button with his girlfriend.

Mom had always dreaded the day Louis would move away, too, and she'd be left in the house alone with their parents. Fortunately, that didn't happen. But six months after they arrived in Sunray, a derrick collapsed and crushed Louis and three others, leaving Mom two choices: take the live-in maid job she'd been offered by Mrs. Killeen, a rich lady at the church she'd been attending, and stay in Sunray, or return to Oklahoma. Of course, she took the job, and that's how she met Dad. One day he saw her walking down the street, struggling to carry groceries back to Mrs. Killeen's house, and offered her a hand. They were married two months later, and I was born within a year.

I couldn't make out exactly what was said as I listened to Mom talk to her best friend, Ruth Henry, the lady who cleaned churches with her when I couldn't during the school year, but I heard enough to know it was about Camp Hutchinson and Nazis.

When they finished talking, Mom hung up the phone, downed what remained of her drink, and moved to the other side of the kitchen, out of sight. A minute or two later, I heard the radio on the kitchen counter click on, and she came back and sat down, her tumbler refilled. She reached across the table and slid her Bible into view as Mercy's KGNT radio host, Opal Felton, delivered the Panhandle Daily News, headlining the Camp Hutchinson prisoner escape. The six-shooter she normally left in its holster in her bedside table upstairs—the six-shooter that had belonged to bitter Nana

Mayes—was on top of her leather Bible. She picked up the gun and set it next to her tumbler, her eyes pausing on it for a moment before she opened the Good Book. She found a suitable passage, wrapped her fingers around the tumbler, and began reading.

Remembering her sitting there now, the image in my mind like a Monet watercolor, it strikes me how predictable humans are. No matter the time period, race, religion, or location, or the exact cause for the fear, pain, anxiety, stress, or grief, a majority of us in the know tend to lean on at least one of three crutches for comfort: gods, weapons, or liquors.

That night, Mom leaned on all three.

5

Kassie Chisolm, Sunray's daytime phone operator, probably played connect the dots on her switchboard more before sunrise the following morning than she had the entire previous month. Our phone rang five separate times alone, and from my bedroom, I heard Mom make a few calls of her own between those. A special town meeting had been scheduled for 9:00 a.m., and word spread fast, reaching every ear in Sunray within an hour or two.

A bowl of cold oatmeal and a spoon were sitting on the table where the Bible, six-shooter, and tumbler had been the night before. Mom was wearing one of her nicer dresses, her hair up in a tight bun, eyes and lips touched with makeup. She looked exhausted, like a woman in the grip of a heavy migraine. She covered the talk-end of the phone with her hand and told me about the meeting and to hurry and eat, all without glancing at my fish-gut shorts. I scooped up the bowl and walked out onto the back porch as she continued her conversation. I sat in Nana Mayes's wooden rocker and listened to the blue jays serenade the morning sun while I quickly ate, then I fed the chickens—one of my daily chores—and hurried back inside.

"Lock that door," Mom said as she hung up the phone, "and go put on your shoes."

"Are we still going to clean the Methodist church today?"

"We'll do it this afternoon," she said. "I'm sure Pastor Hughes will be at the meeting, and I'll tell him that we'll be sure to get it done. Now, hurry. Get your shoes. I want to stop by Fulton's first and grab some flour and a few other things, and I don't want to be late. I'll get the truck keys and meet you outside. Lock the front door on your way out."

At Fulton's, Mom had me run in and grab everything on her list so she wouldn't "get stuck in conversation" with anyone. Then we rode the rest of the way in silence, the windows down, my hand swimming through the warm, dry air.

The Morley Theater had been built in '38 on the western edge of town, across the street from the three-room brick building that served as the Sunray Public School as well as the Sunray Public Library. As the only building in Sunray with modern air conditioning, the Morley was used not only for movies, but also for graduations, plays, elections, weddings, dances, group baptisms, memorial services, town meetings, weekly drawings to give away groceries, dishes, and household items, you name it.

Typically, I'd say around one fifth of the locals attended Mayor Wilson's monthly town meetings, but as we turned onto Warwick Lane, I knew this meeting would be at least twice as big. More cars and trucks lined the dirt road than I'd ever seen in any one place in Sunray. The only other time I remembered seeing that many parked cars was at the Tri-State Fair in Mercy the previous summer.

We parked two blocks away in front of the only hotel in town, the Desoto Hotel, a two-story brick establishment with about fifty beds to offer, and joined the smattering of people walking toward the Morley.

Goose bumps sprouted on my arms and legs the moment we entered the building and the artificially cool air hit my skin. Some people milled about in the lobby, waiting for relatives or friends, but Mom and I headed straight into the theater. The cavernous room could seat around three hundred souls and was two-thirds full, the air alive with a steady, tense murmur. Another thirty or forty people, mostly older men, stood silently against the back and side walls, eyeing the crowd. Ace's two top deputies, Weber and Putnam, loomed just inside the entrance like sentries, dressed in full uniform, thumbs hooked into belts. Mayor Wilson, Sheriff Bennington, Pastor Lewis, Garrett Show, Pastor Hughes, two men in military garb, and a couple of rich oil tycoons were on the elevated stage, bunched around the podium, chatting. The thick red curtain was closed behind them, concealing a bulk of the stage and the movie screen.

"Alice!"

I spun left when I heard my name. Rising from his seat, Robert waved and motioned me over. Our friend Benny Garrison, his twin sister, Nancy, and Thomas sat in the three seats to his left, but the seat to his right was empty. Tessa Sanders and a couple of other girly girls from school sat in front of him, heads angled my way.

"Go ahead," Mom said. "I'm going to go sit with Ruth and Hazel and the others up at the front."

Tessa and her friends flashed flimsy, etiquette-mandatory smiles as I approached but gave little effort in disguising the revulsion in their eyes as they took me in. Times may have been way different, but teens and cliques were the same. To most, including Mom, Tessa and her friends were considered elegant, wholesome, refined... ladylike. A real catch. What a young woman should be. And I was rough around the edges, a tomboy who kept her plain brown hair pulled back and never used makeup, wore big t-shirts and fish-gut shorts. An outcast. The opposite of them. The divide between us was wide, and I couldn't care any less. God may not have blessed me with much, but he blessed me with that. I've always had a natural immunity to judgement when it comes to the way I look or carry myself.

I ignored the girls, greeted Benny, Nancy, and Thomas with a "hey guys," and sat next to Robert.

"Glad you made it," he said. "You guys drive?"

I nodded, briefly catching his eyes before surveying the room. "I didn't know this many people still lived in Sunray," I joked.

Robert flashed an approving smile, scanning the room himself. "Right. I've never seen it this full."

Over the next ten minutes, we made sporadic small talk and watched the room fill up, acknowledging people with smiles and head nods. Eventually every seat was taken, the standing room sparse. Smaller kids sat on adults' laps, some in the aisles leading up to the stage.

My thoughts ran wild as my eyes searched the room, landing on worried faces, serious faces, bored faces, expectant faces. Eyes I knew and eyes I didn't. Eyes that revealed everything and eyes that held secrets. How many others had lost loved ones to the war? I knew some. Mrs. Keats, Mrs. Bakersfield, Mrs. Herbert, Mrs. Jones, and Mrs. Cole had all lost husbands, brothers, or sons. I'd attended their loved one's funerals, as they had Dad's. Had any of them contemplated the idea that their loved one's killer lived in Camp Hutchinson, or was I an outcast in that realm, too? Did they fantasize about revenge, think the Nazi beaten in the street could've been "the one," like I did? There were so many people in the room, so many possibilities. How many more men would die in the coming months or years? How many people sitting in there had loved ones they thought were still alive, fighting over there, in a tank, in a plane; loved ones they hoped would come home and throw their arms around them and kiss them again someday?

Hope.

The thought of the word brought a swell of emotion to my throat, and I suddenly felt pain gnawing at my bones, as fresh and hungry as it had been the day the military knocked on the front door with Dad's tags. I closed my eyes and tried to pretend I hadn't learned of his death. No news is good news, right? What you don't know can't hurt you? In that moment, I wanted my hope back more than I wanted anything in the world. But I knew better. It was too late for that. I inhaled deeply though my nose, opened my eyes, and swallowed the lump down when Mayor Wilson tapped on the microphone, silencing the room.

Wearing a brown tie and brown slacks held up by suspenders, he appeared crooked behind the podium. He'd had polio as a child and one of his legs was two inches shorter than the other, making it appear as though he were perpetually tilting to his right. He presented his usual, carefree smile, but it was tinged with angst. Sweat moistened his upper lip and thick hairline. The older of the two men in military garb stood ramrod straight behind him, as though waiting his turn in line at the bank.

"Hello, hello, hello," Wilson tested for volume. He cleared his throat. "I'd like to thank everyone for showing up on such short notice, and I'm sure you all know why we're here. I know everyone wants answers about the prisoners, so I'll get right to it."

He told the story about the Nazi being chased down in the Heart of Town Square the day before, confirming the man was indeed an escaped prisoner, and adding only one detail I was unaware of: Billy Smarten, the pigeon-toed variety store worker with the booming voice, had caught the man trying to steal supplies from the back storage room. Billy figured he was one of the prisoners because he had numbers written on the front of his shirt and screeched in a foreign tongue when Billy scooped up the baseball bat that was used to prop the back door open and chased after him.

"Is he dead?" a man hollered from the back of the room.

Mayor Wilson hesitated, glancing sideways at no one in particular. "Yes. He is dead."

The crowd hummed with quiet remarks, and I felt Robert's gaze briefly fall on me.

"Serves him right!" a female at the front near Mom and Hazel called out, eliciting a few nods and words of agreement.

"Did you shoot him, Sheriff?" someone yelled.

All eyes, including Mayor Wilson's, moved to Ace who stood against the wall to the right of the stage. Ace's head shook as he took a single step forward. He held a hand in the air and announced, "No, I didn't shoot him. No one did."

Greg Fulton, a few seats in front of me, said, "How'd he die, then?"

"I sure as hell would've shot him if I'd caught him stealing from me," Mr. Turner, owner of the department store called T's Fittings, yelled, cheeks red as beets.

"He's dead," Mayor Wilson said, "and that's all we can say for now."

"I don't care how he died," feisty waitress Doris Klepper said. She was sitting directly across the aisle to my right. "Good riddance."

A couple of claps.

"They shouldn't be anywhere near here, anyway," Miss Carla hollered, one of the many well-dressed church women near Mom wearing a fancy hat.

"Yeah!" Many people echoed, then the disgruntled comments rained.

"That camp should've never been built!"

"We don't want their kind here!"

"It's bad enough they're killing our men over there! We shouldn't have to worry about them killing us here, too!"

"I told you something horrible like this was going to happen!"

"Those men are like animals!"

"They don't belong here!"

"It's causing nothing but grief!"

Mayor Wilson moved his hands up and down as if he could tamp down the escalating noise and hostility permeating the room. "Calm down, everyone. Calm down."

"Yes, calm down," Rod Rogers yelled from the back of the room, turning all heads his way. He wore overalls and a frayed straw hat, had sun-hardened skin and deep-set eyes. On the street, he could've passed as a homeless drunk, but he was one of the wealthiest cotton farmers in the panhandle. He jerked the toothpick out of his mouth, eyes strong with knowhow. "Their kind is keeping most of us on the right side of a ghost town, folks. Without them, who'd work my fields?" He pointed at wheat farmer Gil Hedges. "Or his?" At sorghum farmer Jesse Tatum. "Or his?" A few others. "His, his, or his? Not to mention the dairy farmers and factories they help out." He shoved the toothpick back in his mouth, moved it around. "I've gotten to know some of the men who work my fields, and a lot of them didn't want to be a part of this war any more than we did. They have families back home. Wives and kids they're worried about like you. They're not all bad guys, and like it or not, we need them right now."

Sally Cole jumped up and shot daggers at Rod with her eyes. In her dark purple dress, she looked like an angry eggplant. "No, we don't, Rod." On the verge of tears, she swung her fat arm through the air. "Look how few men are here today. That's because of *them* and the madness *they've* brought to our world. They're liars and thieves and murderers." She swallowed hard, forcing an emotional lump down her throat. "My boy's not here today because of them…and he never will be."

Rod put his hands up as if to block her anger and grief from assaulting him. "I understand your pain, Sally. I do. And I'm sorry about Riley. He was a good kid. But—"

"No!" Mae Keats interjected, standing up next to Sally. "No buts." Her husband's funeral had been two months earlier, the official beginning to her life as a single mother of three. "You don't have a wife or kids to lose. You can't understand. All you care about, all you'll ever *understand,* is your bottom line. You should be ashamed of yourself. There are more important things at stake here than money."

"That's not fair, Mrs. Keats," Gil Hedges said, defending his fellow farmer. "Family or not, Rod is a law-abiding Christian and has always given generously to families in need, especially due to the war."

Ignoring Hedges, Mrs. Keats whipped toward Mayor Wilson. "Exactly how many more of these escaped prisoners are running loose around here, anyway, Mayor?"

Mayor Wilson looked back over his shoulder, and the elder military man sidled up next to him. Wilson met eyes with Mrs. Keats, "Mrs. Keats," he scanned the crowd, "everyone, I understand we're all a little on edge after what happened yesterday, but if you'd please be seated, Corporal Tanis would like to speak. As many of you already know, he's in charge of Camp Hutchinson, and I believe he will be able to address your concerns about the prisoners better than I can at this point."

Mayor Wilson eagerly moved aside, allowing Tanis to step up to the podium. He didn't smile or appear angry or nervous. He looked in control. The way he held his shoulders and chin, his razor-sharp silver crewcut and firm jawline, all radiated meticulousness, self-importance. He surveyed the crowd for a long moment, the unspoken message in his eyes speaking volumes. He wanted unfettered attention and respect, and he was used to getting it.

"Before I address your question, Mrs. Keats…it is Mrs. Keats, right, dear?" He glanced at her and she gave a curt nod. "I'd like to first apologize to everyone for this troubling and inconvenient situation and assure you that we are doing everything we can to remedy it and make sure it never happens again. I would also like to thank each and every one who helped locate and subdue that prisoner yesterday. You should be proud. Your vigilance was a prime example of the American spirit that I'm honored to be a part of. It's easy to see that even though you're not overseas with our brave men, you're willing to do your part and fight right along with them."

He was good. His voice was smooth, delivery effortless. He didn't take sides or place blame. He asked forgiveness, praised and bonded, gave assurances. Public speaking 101. Or sheep corralling, as Dad liked to call it.

"I'm also very pleased to let you know another prisoner was caught late last night just outside of Mercy," he continued. "I'm going there directly from here to question him and escort him back to the camp. We're hoping he'll have some information that can help our search efforts." He glanced at Mrs. Keats again. "Which brings me to your question, Mrs. Keats. There are now two prisoners still unaccounted for, but we are taking every possible measure to find them. We have shut down traffic on all railroads in the area and have checkpoints set up on all major roadways across the panhandle. Teams are being assembled to keep watch in every town, large and small, within twenty miles of the Rock Island Railroad tracks from here to Kansas."

His gaze traveled over the assemblage. "We don't know too much about them, only that they were captured together and were close friends by all accounts, so we believe they're probably moving together as well. If you see anyone or anything suspicious, please immediately notify Specialist Henning." He gestured at the second man in military clothes who'd been on the stage earlier. The bony man with a slash of a mouth, beak of a nose, and slits for eyes raised his hand for visual identification. "He'll be in charge of our Sunray search team and can be reached through the mayor's office. Of course, you can also always notify Sheriff Bennington, Deputy Weber or Putnam, or any other soldier you come across. I believe if we all stay calm and work together, this issue will be resolved in no time."

"Corporal, when will—"

Tanis held up a finger, indicating he wasn't finished. "There's one more thing you all need to be aware of. I have been notified by state officials down in Austin that since the man who died from his injuries yesterday was a federal prisoner, the Hutchinson County district attorney has been assigned to come investigate the death. He will be arriving here later today to start an inquiry. I'm told he will start at Camp Hutchinson and then make his way up here, so we're all in the same boat. I'll give you the same advice I gave my staff: don't do or say anything that'll make this more of a mess than it already is. Our country doesn't need that right now. God bless."

With that, Corporal Tanis turned and marched off stage, refusing to acknowledge the questions hurled his way as Mayor Wilson manned the podium.

"Folks, folks," Wilson said, quieting the crowd. "That's all the information we have about the prisoners for now. This is a fluid situation, and when we learn more, so will you. You know y'all are like family to me, and I want everyone to feel safe and protected. With that in mind, I'd like to remind everyone to please lock your doors, and to let you know we're going to setup some watch groups around town to patrol the streets and keep an eye out. Pastor Lewis has volunteered to head one for the south side of town, Neil Shore the north, and Mr. and Mrs. Fulton the central downtown area. If you live or work in those areas and want to be in the loop, reach out to one of those folks. To echo what Corporal Tanis said, I believe if we all stay calm and work together—and trust in our Lord, of course—everything will be just fine. Remember, I'm always here if you need anything. Thank you. Good day."

The crowd erupted in a buzz of conversation. A few people, mostly ranchers and farmers, headed straight for the door. Others hurried toward Mayor Wilson and the watch group leaders. But most lingered, socializing, enjoying the air conditioning for as long as possible. Robert, Benny, Nancy, Thomas, and I sliced our way through the lingerers, and after Benny and Thomas used the restroom, we gathered in the lobby near the ticket booth where we exchanged opinions about the dead Nazi, Tanis, Rod, and Mrs. Keats.

Thomas, the youngest among us by five years, spoke the most. The combination of terror and fascination roiling inside him uncontainable, he spat out run-on after run-on, question after question. Robert and I replied to some of his brother's questions with short answers or head nods, but little else. Benny and Nancy said nothing. For twins, they didn't look too similar—Benny was thinner, had bushier hair and a rounder face—but they both had their mother's canted eyes, and both of their eyes carried a large dose of trepidation. They'd been carrying it whenever they were around large groups of people since Pearl Harbor, and I hated seeing it, feeling it.

Outside of Robert (and Thomas, I guess), they were my closest friends. My only other true friends. Before the Japanese attacked, they'd been fun-loving jokesters, mostly carefree about their "outcast" appearance and the muted dislike that came along with it. But immediately after Pearl Harbor, they were singled out by many locals and transients with outright hatred. Insults (*Go home, gooks!*) chased them down roads, into the schools, hit their ears on answered phone calls. Bottles and trash were hurled more than once, their home vandalized. Few gave them the chance to explain that Jasmine (Gokongwei) Garrison's family had immigrated from the Philippines, not Japan. Nor did they care that her husband, Benny and Nancy's dad, Pete Garrison, one of Sunray's best plumbers, was as American-white as their own reflections.

To his credit, Pete never faltered defending her or the twins, taking the loss in business because of his "slant-eyed wife and kids" in stride, even getting into a few fist fights on their behalf. The Garrisons attended Trinity Lutheran Church, tithed every month, and eventually turned to Pastor Lewis for help. Only after he explained the Garrison's situation to the congregation, confirmed they weren't "the enemy," weren't Japanese sympathizers or spies or anything else, and asked them to help spread the word, did the open meanness lessen. Of course, the discrimination never fully ended. Disdainful whispers and scrutinizing eyes still followed the Garrisons around town, hence the ready trepidation Benny and Nancy carried in their eyes.

That trepidation heightened when Tessa and her friends ambled by, whispering and giggling with hand-covered mouths. When Tessa glanced at me, I gave her a sarcastic, face-scrunched curtsy. She rolled her eyes and then smiled at Robert who smiled back. They held eye contact for a moment before Tessa batted her eyes, turned, and left with her friends, giggling.

I nudged Robert's arm as he watched them go. "Why don't you go tell her how much you *love* her?"

The joke brought a joyful expression to Benny's and Nancy's faces, elicited a chuckle from Thomas.

Robert's brow lifted. "What? I'm just trying to be nice."

"Yeah," Nancy said. "*Nice* is the word written all over your face. Not love."

I high-fived her.

Robert's cheeks blushed as bright as pomegranates. His eyes flitted from Benny to Nancy to me. "You know I don't like her like that."

"But you liked the way she sashayed away, right?" Benny asked, winking, tossing his own hips back and forth.

Laughing, I patted Robert's shoulder. "It's okay. I like the way she—"

"Benny. Nancy. Come. We need to go now," their mom said. She stood by the exit, all four-foot nine of her. Her husband Pete was behind her, six-foot two and holding the door open, smiling at us over her head. When he waved, we waved back.

"See you at church tomorrow," Benny said.

We watched them leave, and I turned to the Lewis brothers. "And then there were three."

We meandered around the lobby for about twenty more minutes, eyeing and ranking the candy on the shelves next to the popcorn machine behind the register, chatting with people as they exited the theater, making fun of others. Few people remained by the time we grew impatient and opened the theater door to check on our parents. Mom, Pastor Lewis and Hazel, Ace, Deputies Putnam and Weber, Mayor Wilson, and a handful of other locals were grouped in front of the stage.

They glanced our way as we entered the room, and before the door had shut behind us, Lily Thomas bolted into the lobby from outside hollering, "Sheriff, Sheriff." She pushed passed us into the theater and hurried to Ace. She was wearing a knee-length robe, her long red hair dripping wet. "I just saw one of them!" Her hysterical, flute-like voice echoed in the spacious room. "A Nazi!"

"How do you know it was one of them?" Ace asked.

"He had swastikas tattooed on his forearms." She held up her arms as though hers were marked, too. "He was in the kitchen when I got out of the shower. He tried to grab me. I think he wanted to…" Her eyes welled with tears as she shook her head and cinched her robe snug. "But I hit him over the head with a pan and ran to my car and drove straight to the station, but no one was there, so I came here because I remembered the meeting was happening."

Silence dominated as Lily collapsed forward, burying her head in Ace's chest. He wrapped his arms around her. It was a paralyzing silence, an unsettling silence. In retrospect, a meaningful silence.

Sunray had been tilted on its axis by the escape, knocked farther askew by the discovery of the first Nazi, and her accusation had completely flipped it upside down, leaving nothing but that powerful silence in its wake.

6

Ace broke the silence by ordering Deputy Weber to go find Specialist Henning, notify him of the incident, and then meet him at Lily's house to help conduct a search of the surrounding area. After he passed Lily off to Deputy Putnam and asked Pastor Lewis and Mayor Wilson to quickly spread the word, have everyone, especially on that side of town, keep their eyes peeled but stay inside, he rushed out of the theater.

As Putnam shepherded Lily into the lobby with Mayor Wilson and the other locals in tow, Pastor Lewis ordered Hazel and his sons to follow him to their car so he could drive them home. He suggested Mom and I head home as well, follow them in our truck, which Mom consented to with a nod.

Pastor Lewis slowed his Tudor to a stop on the dirt road in front of our house and waited for Mom to park in front of the detached garage. Hazel hollered out the passenger window after Mom and I had gotten out of the truck, inviting us over to their house for the afternoon. Mom politely declined, saying we needed to do some chores around the house, promising we'd stay cautious and in touch.

Inside, while I put away the groceries we'd purchased before the meeting, Mom called Pastor Hughes and asked if we could please delay cleaning the Methodist church until the following afternoon, until we knew a little more about the latest prisoner. She promised we'd have it done before Mr. Hodges's—another soldier who'd died overseas like Dad—memorial service on Tuesday. Having just hung up with Mayor Wilson who'd told him about Lily's encounter, Hughes agreed postponing the job a day or two was fine.

I helped Mom with our weekly Saturday downstairs chores, which included scrubbing the stove, sink, and tub, retrieving the laundry from the clothesline out back and putting it away, and sweeping the wooden floors. Afterward, we ate egg salad and crackers, and then she sent me upstairs to tidy up my room. When I finished, I got my diary from the chest at the foot of my bed, tossed my pillow on the floor in front of my window, and sat down. I had detailed about half of the morning's events when the phone rang. I snuck to the landing and crouched on the second step, bringing half of the kitchen into view as always.

Mom stood next to the table with her back to me, the phone to her right ear. About a minute or two passed before she hung up the phone, retrieved a tumbler from a cabinet, the jar of tea from the fridge, and filled the tumbler half full. Knowing what was coming and not wanting to hear another lecture about eavesdropping, I scurried into my room.

Waiting just inside my doorway with my back to the wall, I heard her pad through the living room with more care than usual, surely stealing a glance up the stairs to make sure I wasn't watching. She entered the spare bedroom where she hid her bottle of Southern Comfort, and then padded back to the kitchen. I returned to the second step after soft swing music began drifting up the stairs from the kitchen radio. Mom filled the remaining half of the tumbler with whiskey, moved out of sight to hide the bottle somewhere in the kitchen in case I walked in, returned to her seat, picked up the glass, and began to remedy her rattled nerves.

I sat on the stairs for the next hour or so, watching and listening as she sipped her drink and fielded *Have you heard?* phone call after *Have you heard?* phone call. With each conversation, I gleaned more information about the Lily Thomas incident and its aftermath.

Lily Thomas and her husband, Tony, lived on Maple Street on the eastside, about a block south of the train depot. Their house and the surrounding area were searched by Ace, Weber, Henning, and a mix of other soldiers and locals to no avail. Other than the frying pan on the kitchen floor and the wide-open back door, there were no leads. No neighbors had seen or heard anything suspicious. The newly formed watch groups began patrolling the streets as the search played out, many brandishing rifles and pistols for all to see, discovering nothing as well. Tony, twenty-two years old and as meek as men come, worked at the Alloy carbon black plant and had been summoned to the sheriff station by Deputy Putnam to escort Lily home once the search had ended. She had been checked by Dr. Mobley at the station and had no external injuries. He gave her a sedative of some sort to calm her frazzled nerves, and she'd passed out on the couch at home.

I stayed as still and quiet as a field mouse as long as I could, fighting the urge to visit the outhouse until I started to cramp. When I finally headed downstairs, I slapped my bare feet on the wooden steps loud enough for Mom to hear me coming, giving her time to hurry to the sink and rinse the whiskey smell out of the tumbler. She watched me walk past her, and as I approached the back door, I noticed her Bible and gun on the kitchen counter near the radio.

"Where are you going?" she asked.

"To Timbuktu. Might come back with a camel or two."

She rolled her eyes the same way she had every time Dad had said the same phrase. She'd often called him stupid when he spouted his "rhyming nonsense," but she spared me the comment.

"The bathroom," I said, and placed my hand over my lower abdomen. "My bladder's about to—"

She waved me off. "Just hurry."

The phone rang, and she answered it and sat back down as I headed outside.

The outhouse was about fifteen yards off the back porch at the time, to the right. Dad had relocated it every three or four years, usually around Halloween, and had moved it there just before leaving. I slipped my feet into the "summer outhouse shoes" we left outside and hopped off the porch. We used the shoes—Dad's tattered pair of fabric Oxfords—to protect our feet from the goatheads and spiky weeds that invaded the yard each spring. We had a similarly large pair of his old galoshes we used for "winter bathroom shoes" to protect our feet and legs from the frigid northern air and snow in the winter.

The Oxfords flopped around my feet as I hurried toward the outhouse in the hot afternoon sun. I did what I needed and was closing the door behind me, when I noticed him to my left, facing me—a young man, maybe twenty-five years old, squatting in the garden between the pumpkin vines and squash plants, motionless, dressed in tattered jeans and a shirt with numbers written on the left breast. The shade from the chicken coop to his right cut him in half, a sunlit half and a dark half. His left arm dangled in the lit half, a half dollar-sized black swastika obvious on the top of his pale forearm. The hand attached to the arm held one of our yellow squashes.

Something visceral erupted inside me at the sight. A swarm of angry butterflies spawned in my chest. My face flushed. I could hear the tick of my pulse in my ears, feel it thudding against my tonsils. My mind exploded with accusation.

There he is, it screamed. *A monster masquerading as a man. The one who attacked Lily and slaughtered Dad and God knows how many others. The one who's been living a good life twenty miles away in Camp Hutchinson with his buddies, eating and enjoying meals made with our local crops, working in our local fields or factories, receiving services from our local dentists and doctors, feeling our warm Texas Panhandle sunshine on his face, all while Dad was buried alone in a cold dark grave somewhere in Europe—eating nothing, enjoying nothing, feeling nothing.*

Foolish or not, I never considered the man's strength or size, or yelling for Mom, or finding a weapon, or whether the other escaped prisoner was nearby.

Adrenaline and rage ruled me, and I reacted.

I rushed at him, the Oxfords flying off as I ran. He rose and backpedaled, as if he hadn't expected me to attack. His foot caught on the edge of the coop and he stumbled, catching himself from hitting the ground with one of his hands just before I reached him.

"That's my dad's squash," I said through gritted teeth as I attacked him, arms churning like pistons, fists pounding whatever they could.

Backing away, he dropped the squash and used his forearms as shields. When he turned to run, I launched myself onto his back, tackling him to the ground. We grappled for position. I grunted and struggled to stay on top of him, swinging, scratching, biting his wrist when it grazed my mouth. He fought to evade and block, and at twice my size and weight, gained the upper hand quickly. He grabbed both of my wrists, forced me onto my back, and pinned my shoulders into place with his knees. His face was sheeted with sweat, blue eyes like saucers.

"Calm down," he said, thick with a German accent. The words came out weak, as though he didn't feel confident using them.

I thrust my hips repeatedly, attempting to buck him off. "Get off me, monster!"

He sat back on my torso to stop me, his weight making it hard for me to breathe. Then he glanced toward the house. "Shhhh," he said. "I won't hurt you. I promise."

"Is that what you told Lily before you tried to rape her and she took a pan to your head?" I managed, eyeing the red knot on his forehead.

A look of fear passed over his face like a shadow. "I didn't... I just wanted food. I thought no one was home."

I wanted to rebel, to scream *"Liar! Thief! Rapist! Murderer!"* But I couldn't take in enough air. "Monster" was all I eked out.

A tense moment spooled out, my short breaths a quick rhythm behind his deep ones. Birds chirped. The chickens shuffled around in the coop, pecking at the ground. I searched his eyes for murderous intent, justification for my rage, but registered eyes brimming with trepidation much like Benny's and Nancy's. Tired eyes, wounded eyes. The longer we locked eyes, the less my rage and adrenaline controlled my mind.

"Please believe me," he said. "I've never hurt anyone."

The sincerity in his voice complimented the emotion in his eyes so well I was taken aback. I stared at him, unsure, teetering on the fine line between expectation and reality.

Is he lying? Monsters lie. But...

"I'm going to rise so you can breathe," he said, and glanced at my house. "Please don't scream."

He slowly lifted his backend off my diaphragm, and we held eye contact as I took in a series of deep breaths.

I thought about screaming, about my mom on the phone inside, of her gun on the kitchen counter, and I know it sounds corny, or stupid, or far-fetched, or like a cop out, but something inside of me, an innate command as instinctual as my initial rage had been, compelled me to stay quiet.

We breathed, our air colliding in the space between our faces. I followed his gaze when his eyes slid to his hand pinning my left wrist to the ground. The sight of the six-inch gash on my forearm released the surge of pain I should've already felt had my adrenaline not blinded me to it. Blood flowed from the wound, coloring the man's thumb shiny red. He eased his knees off my shoulders, shifted off of me, and pulled me into a sitting position.

"I can prove it," he said with an air of desperation.

"Prove what?"

"That I would never hurt you."

He let go of my right wrist but not the left one. I pulled my knees to my chest but didn't resist his grip. The gash stung and gaped wider as he twisted sideways to grab one of the squash plants with his free hand.

Then he closed his eyes and revealed himself to me.

Tiny explosions of tingly, prickly pleasure assaulted my arm beneath his hand, trickled down to the gash and intensified. I gasped and reflexively tried to jerk my hand away, but he held firm. Every hair I had stood on end as a rush of energy, an electricity of sorts, funneled down my arm and surged through my entire body. The world seemed to swell, magnify, slow, heightening my senses, clarifying colors and shapes, sharpening my thoughts. I could see every pore on his face, the multiple shades of discoloration of the swollen knot on his forehead, the speckled details in his blue irises. The sweetness of nearby honeysuckle saturated my taste buds. I could smell the difference between his sweat and mine, between the scent of nearby fresh and decaying vegetation. Hear the buzz of unseen insects as though they were swarming around my face.

I can't say for certain, but I'd bet my mouth fell open as the gash on my arm healed, the wound diminishing as though an unseen hand had run an invisible zipper along it. Simultaneously, the squash plant withered, wilted, turned to ash and crumbled in his hand.

Having been raised on Jesus and the Bible and knowing little else of religion, I called myself a Christian. And I truly did believe in forgiveness and the goodness of the gospels' parables. But either due to my inherit Mayes skepticism, the same skepticism that wouldn't allow me to believe in Hazel's "feelings," or the influence of Dad's regular mocking of stories like Noah's ark and the burning bush, a habit that had caused more than one fight between him and Mom, I'd always struggled to embrace the idea of real-life, divine intervention, unexplainable miracles—the raised from the dead, part the Red Sea, heal the blind, cure the leper stuff. But right then and there in the garden, reality had cracked right in front of my eyes, literally on my arm, exposing a layer of magic just below the surface few have been privy to.

The physical sensation of elation faded when he opened his eyes and let go of my arm, leaving me dumbstruck with awe. I rubbed my hand back and forth over my forearm where the cut had been, smearing fresh blood around. There was no wound. No scab. No scar. No pain. The skin looked unharmed. My eyes bounced from the man to the plant ashes and back to him as he stood and surveyed me.

I staggered to my feet, bracing my healed arm as though it needed support, and we locked eyes. A long time seemed to pass before I recovered the ability to speak.

"What... Who are you?" I asked.

He smiled faintly but proudly. "Karl. Karl Wag—"

He broke off and looked toward McGee Street when a car engine sounded in the distance. The smile disappeared, and a hunted-animal look rose in his face. He watched Pastor Lewis's Tudor slow as it glided past my house, a cloud of dust in its wake. Our eyes connected for a second, then he turned and ran. He weaved through a small copse of mesquite trees in the field adjacent to our yard, heading in the opposite direction of Lewis's car, toward the Dalton's house.

"Wait," I called after him, but the word came out as a whisper.

PRESENT

2

Recalling the memory of meeting Karl made Alice simper. She looked at her forearm where the short-lived wound had been and ran her fingers over the skin. So much time had passed. So much of her had worn down. She now needed bifocals to see her arm clearly, medication to keep her arthritic fingers free from pain when she used them. Her skin was paper thin, decorated with liver spots and trivial scars from gardening accidents. But the awe she felt inside, roiling beneath the ugly symptoms of her physical decline, felt as fresh as it had that hot August afternoon. As proof, the hairs on her arm stood at attention.

"Are you serious right now?" Emily asked, though her grass-green eyes showed no signs of disbelief.

They'd paused on the shade-side of a clump of eight-foot-high honeysuckles, the white and yellow blossoms' sweet scent engulfing them. Alice had found it difficult to recite certain parts of the story while also navigating the garden's terrain. Her equilibrium wasn't what it used to be, her ankles and knees feeble at best—an unseen rock or stubborn vine away from a fall. Reciting the memories, speaking them aloud for the first time in close to eighty years, had proven more overwhelming than she'd expected. Not the speaking part itself, but the mental jump. She paused each time she caught herself drifting back in time and was unable to focus on the present. She couldn't afford an injury. Not this close to the finish line.

A slew of sunflowers poked up behind the field of eggplant sprouts to their right, eager to flower and fruit later in the summer. To their left stood four acres of healthy corn stalks that would triple in height in the next few months and eventually yield hundreds of ears for locals. Pear trees, some nearby, some farther away, most at least fifty years old, randomly dotted this area of the garden, too. So did sporadic bursts of colorful perennials.

Emily leaned forward and took a closer look at Alice's forearm as though she had the ability to see what couldn't be seen. She met eyes with Alice. "So he actually healed you with a plant? Like Jesus-healed you? Like a miracle?" She cocked her head. "You haven't been binge watching Stranger Things again, have you?" The twinkle in her eyes spoke to the awe she was experiencing from hearing the story, too. "And you're okay, right? You're not having a stroke or seizure or some kind of delusional, elderly mental lapse I need to be worried about?"

Alice didn't respond. Emily's questions were a reflex, not real questions—her mind's attempt to rationalize the irrational. Denial was the most predictable initial human response to the unexplainable. Alice had spent the entire afternoon asking herself similar questions the day she'd met Karl.

"Can I have some water please?" Alice asked.

Emily removed her backpack, pulled out a bottle, and handed it to Alice. "And you're sure it wasn't a trick of the…" Emily held up a finger, halting herself before the entire question had tumbled out of her mouth. "Wait, that doesn't make sense because you felt it, too, right? But…" She caught Alice's eye. "Did I ever tell you about the time Darla and I went to that psychic in Dallas?"

She had, of course, but Alice didn't see the point in saying so. Emily's thoughts were barreling downhill, and Alice knew she'd regurgitate the story either way. It was part of the process to reach acceptance. Alice shook her head, giving Emily the okay to go on, took a swig from the water bottle and passed it back. Emily slipped it into her backpack and re-slung the anime-patch-covered tote over her shoulders. To Alice, Emily seemed as stimulated and eager for adventure as she had when she'd left for Dallas a week after her high school graduation.

Like most Sunray teens, Emily had planned to bail on the "piss-ant-sized, boring-as-fuck" town the first chance she got. She wanted to move to a big city where a better life awaited. An exciting life. A fulfilling life. Life fraught with progression and beneficial experiences, untapped knowledge and possibility. She sought Nirvana, Atlantis, the idealistic dreamland, and hoped the University of North Texas in Denton, just north of Dallas, would serve as her springboard to such a place.

The selfish part of Alice hadn't wanted Emily to leave Sunray. They worked in the garden together nearly every day, rocked on the back porch and chatted about life as the sun rose or set, ate TV dinners in Alice's living room a couple of times a week, watching HGTV or the Cooking Channel. They were more than friends. They were family. But Alice had encouraged the move anyway. The mature, motherly part of her knew it was for the best. The change would prove if Alice's instincts about the girl were right. Emily needed to go, and Alice couldn't stand in the way.

Neither Alice nor Betty and Burt Newel—the kind couple who'd adopted Emily and lived down the street from Alice—heard from Emily much the first few months after she'd left for Denton. She didn't return home once. Her new environment had seized her attention.

When she called or texted, the messages were short snippets about how awesome the Dallas Aquarium and Six Flags were, how magnificent it was to walk beneath lit skyscrapers downtown in the middle of the night listening to Pink Floyd. That summer she went to a "real" Texas Rangers baseball game, ate "real" sushi, met a "real" musician from Jamaica and a "real" artist from Italy.

But as the summer changed into fall, the newness slowly wore off and reality set in. Her calls and texts became more frequent, the back and forth longer, the topics less about the offerings of the big city and more about what was happening in Sunray. She wanted to know what the weather was like, if Gina Ferry had finally had her baby, who was mowing Miss Sutter's lawn now. She wanted to know every detail about the garden, hear the rundown of exactly what Alice had done that day and would do the next. Her roommate on campus, Darla Whitfield, was a good friend, but she wasn't Juan or Becca, Emily's two closest lifelong Sunray friends who'd she'd left behind. After graduation, Juan had taken a job at the Alloy carbon black plant alongside his father, and Becca continued working on her parents' ranch (Cattle Crossing), tending horses and helping with hippotherapy sessions.

As fall swept into winter, Emily drove her used Taurus home more and more. She spent Thanksgiving, the entire Christmas break, and several weekends in Sunray hanging out with Juan and Becca, visiting with her parents and Alice.

As winter changed to spring, Emily's impressions of the big city had done a one-eighty, and Alice could tell Emily would return to Sunray full time soon. Emily was driving home every single weekend, complaining nonstop about Darla, traffic in Dallas, her professors and classmates, her part-time job at Dunkin' Donuts, the abundance of concrete, the lack of open spaces and anything green.

After the spring semester had ended at North Texas University, Emily had returned to Sunray with everything she owned and asked

Alice if she could move into the apartment above the garage for the summer and help in the garden. Alice agreed, no questions asked. And when autumn rolled around and Emily started working part-time at Cattle Crossing Ranch with Becca rather than returning to college and asked if she could remain in the apartment a little longer, until she "figured out what to do next," Alice again agreed with no questions asked.

It was obvious to her that Emily had missed Sunray more than she'd hated Dallas. Sunray was the only stable home she'd ever known, the Newels and Alice the first adults she'd ever allowed herself to trust and love. Her two truest friends, Juan and Becca, two people who would take a bat to anyone who threatened her, lived there. Her passion for open pastures, gardening, and riding horses were all there. Her peace of mind was there. Her heart was there. But Alice kept all that to herself. She knew that in her own time, Emily would realize the truth. Trying to force it on her would do no good. Alice was just glad to have Emily home and know her instincts about the girl had been right. Emily had chosen Sunray. Just like Alice had so many decades earlier.

Alice patiently listened to Emily's story about the psychic Nora the Knowing. Nora had read Emily's and Darla's palms the first time they'd ventured downtown together and insisted the two girls had a special connection. To prove it, she'd told them to stand and face each other, focus on each other, and for Darla to close her eyes. A few seconds later, she quietly tapped Emily's shoulder. When Darla opened her eyes, Nora asked if she'd felt anything anywhere on her body. Darla replied with a soft yes and lightly touched her own shoulder. Their minds were blown. But a month later, while spooning mint chocolate ice cream into her mouth at one in the morning, Emily had seen a show on the Discovery Science channel that showed the truth behind magic tricks. One of the tricks was the shoulder touch one she'd later see David Blaine perform on TV as well.

"So, see, even though you felt it," Emily said, "do you think it could've been a trick?"

"It was real," Alice said calmly. "He healed me. No ifs, ands, or buts about it."

"How can you be so sure? I mean...did you ever see him do it again?"

One side of Alice's mouth crept upward into a knowing smirk.

Emily's eyes swelled more than seemed possible, and she lightly slapped Alice's upper arm. "Real—" She glanced at the spot she'd slapped. "I'm so sorry. I didn't mean... It was a reflex." She gingerly rubbed the spot as if to erase any pain.

Alice's smirk expanded to a full-fledged smile. She loved Emily's unbridled enthusiasm. She'd been the same once upon a time. "It's okay. I'm fine."

Emily apologized again and then eagerly wrung her hands in front of her chest. "So...when did you see him again? Did he come back?"

Alice nodded. "That night."

PAST

7

After Karl ran off, I stood motionless in the garden for a moment, looking back and forth from my forearm to the pile of plant ash before collecting the summer outhouse shoes and dashing back inside.

Mom was still sitting at the table with the phone glued to her ear. She obviously hadn't seen or heard what had happened outside. She didn't say a word to me and barely looked my way as I locked the back door and headed upstairs, keeping my bloody, not-injured arm pinned to my side and out of sight.

Behind my closed bedroom door, I stripped off my shorts, turned them inside out, and with the help of a little spit, wiped the sticky blood off my arm. With no water of any kind upstairs at the time and Mom usually washing all my clothes and our towels, I didn't want to have to explain a blood stain to her. And forget about explaining what had happened out in the garden. She would never believe me. She would think I was mocking her fears, testing her patience, "pushing again." I needed time alone. Time to collect my thoughts and wrap my head around what I'd seen, what I'd felt.

I paced for hours, the fan whirring overhead, talking out loud, replaying, relentlessly asking and answering my own questions, stealing glances at the garden out the window, pausing to examine my forearm each time a surge of awe flooded through me and my hairs stood on end. I was amped. The afternoon passed in a flash. And although I never left my room, I felt like I'd traveled a thousand miles.

Around six o'clock, Mom called me down for dinner—peanut butter sandwiches and salted cucumbers—and I immediately knew she'd downed another tumbler or two while I'd been upstairs. She had an obvious glaze of alcohol in her eyes. We gazed at our own plates as we ate. I had no desire to question her about any rumors she'd heard on the phone, or to give her a reason to spread more by telling her about Karl. And I think she realized she'd drunk too much and consequently focused her energy on trying too hard to sound and act normal. So we ate without conversation, a re-airing of President Roosevelt's June 12th Fireside Chat quietly playing on the radio in the background.

Upstairs, as Mom jumped back on the Sunray gossip train downstairs, I closed my door, grabbed my diary, and sat on the floor in front of my open window. I detailed my experience with Karl, then propped my arms on the sill, my chin on my arms, and watched the garden and land beyond until the sun abandoned the sky. I no longer tried to rationalize what had happened. I'd questioned my denial to death. I accepted. I believed. I knew. But knowing only brought more questions. Questions about Karl: *Nazi* Karl? *Magic* Karl? *Generous* Karl? Where had he gone? Was he alone? With the other prisoner? How had he done what he'd done to my arm? Why? What were his motives, desires, morals, background? And on and on.

I was still sitting there thinking about him when he came back.

Not long after the night critters had awoken, I noticed movement in the garden to the right of the chicken coop. A person, hunched over, looping around the pumpkin vines, continually glancing at the back porch. I couldn't see him clearly, but I knew it was Karl. Butterflies jumped to life in my stomach, quickening my pulse. I ducked low enough to barely peek over the sill. He crept around the back of the coop and was out of sight for a long moment. I rose an inch or two, waited with bated breath. When his upper body finally emerged from behind the coop, the bright moonlight revealed his face. It was definitely Karl. His focus was on the kitchen window, and I wondered if he could see Mom. I could hear the radio faintly, but I hadn't heard her voice in quite a while. Was she off the phone? Sitting at the table? Reading her Bible? Was her pistol nearby? If she saw…would he…? Would she…?

I rose, slightly leaned out the window, and cleared my throat. Karl immediately looked up at me, and after a brief pause, raised his hand and spread his fingers wide in a peaceful gesture. My eyes stayed trained on his hand as I took in a deep, shaky breath and slowly raised my own hand, fingers spread like his. A wisp of a smile touched his mouth. He gave a single nod, lowered his hand, and slipped back behind the coop.

I snuck to my usual eaves-dropping perch at the top of the stairs. The kitchen light was on, but Mom wasn't in her chair. Her Bible and pistol weren't on the table either. I glanced down the hall at her bedroom. The door stood wide open, her bedside lamp off. I cocked my head, aiming my ear downstairs, and listened for a minute. The only sound was the radio in the kitchen—Mercy's Opal Felton giving the nightly KGNT war update.

I stealthily made my way downstairs, and as I approached the living room, heard the rhythmic purr of Mom's snore. The heavy dose of afternoon whiskey had knocked her out early. She lay on her back on the small couch she and Dad had brought with them when we'd moved into the house with Nana. Her feet were propped on one armrest, head on the other. She'd unpinned her hair, and it hung down the side of the couch. She still had her shoes and dress on. Her open Bible rested face-down on her chest, the pistol on the floor between the couch and coffee table.

Wanting a warning if Mom awoke, I turned off the living room lamp and kitchen light. If she did get up, she'd have to turn on a light or two to navigate the house, which would alert me. And just in case things went bad outside, I grabbed a steak knife from the kitchen and slid it into the back pocket of my shorts before unlocking and easing open the back door. The door popped and creaked a bit, so I paused to confirm Mom's snoring had continued, then stepped outside, slid on the summer outhouse shoes, and headed for the garden.

I stopped about ten feet from the coop and softly cleared my throat. Karl peeked out at me and stepped into the moonlight. He seemed as hesitant to move any closer to me as I was to step toward him. I lifted my left arm as though to remind him of our previous encounter, of how he'd healed me.

"How'd you do it?" I asked.

He gave a barely noticeable shrug. "I just do." He sounded tired, like he'd already answered the question a thousand times.

"Are you some kind of super Nazi soldier or something?"

He shook his head. "I'm not a Nazi. I'm Karl Wagner."

"What you mean, *not* a Nazi? You have a Camp Hutchinson prisoner number on your shirt." I waggled my finger at him. "And you have swastikas tattooed on your arms for God's sake."

He glanced at his arms as if to verify my claim, and the corners of his mouth turned down as he ran his finger over one of the marks. "If I had a knife, I'd cut them off right now." His eyes pled with mine. "You must believe me."

"Believe what? That you don't know how you healed my arm? That you're not a Nazi? That you'd get rid of your tattoos if you could?" I took a single step forward. "If you want me to believe you, then you have to be honest with me."

"I am," he said.

Holding his gaze, I lifted my arm again. "How'd you do it?"

He eyed my unblemished skin for a long spell. "The only way I... I'm a bridge."

"*A bridge?*"

"Yes." The confirmation came out brighter than anything I'd ever heard him say. His hands rose head-high as if he was under arrest, and he wiggled his fingers. "A bridge between God's hands is what Mama always says."

I stared at him, at a loss for words, uncertain how to proceed.

He seemed to understand my confusion, lowered his hands and squatted. "Watch." He took a dandelion in each hand. When he closed his eyes, one weed withered to ash as the other nearly doubled in size. He opened his eyes as he stood. "See."

I did see. "But how…"

"I don't know how it works. Or why. I just can do it."

I believed him. How could I not? I gestured at the ash and foliage at his feet. "Is that all you can do? Magically, I mean. Bridge…things?"

He nodded.

"Who else knows you can do it?"

"Only one person from the camp."

"The other missing prisoner? The one you were captured with?"

He nodded again. "Hans."

Placing my hand on the knife handle protruding from my back pocket, I scanned the area with quick glances, right, left, back over my shoulder. "Where is he? Is he here?"

"No. I don't know where he is."

I took in a deep breath, scanned the area again. "Why did you come back here? What do you want from me?"

We held eye contact for a long moment. Silence stretched to the point I thought he might not answer, and when I was about to repeat the question, he finally said, "I need help. I need a friend."

My eyes swam from his to the numbers on his shirt to his tattoos. Conflicting emotions sparred inside me. I didn't know what to do. He was special, no doubt. And everything about him screamed harmless and vulnerable and sincere. Maybe farmer Rod Rogers was right. Maybe some of the prisoners weren't bad guys. But…Karl was a Nazi, right? One of *them*. The enemy. One of the Devil's Disciples. Just look at his tattoos. *Right?*

He crossed his arms in front of his chest and attempted to cover the swastikas with his hands. Shame crushed his eyes, and his chin dropped. "I don't know how to—"

"Alice?" someone whispered with force. "Is that you?"

Karl's head shot up, and I spun around. Footsteps crunched the brittle prairie grass somewhere to our left, maybe thirty yards away. When I looked back at Karl, he'd already turned to run.

"Wait," I whispered, making a decision in the white panic of exposure that would change the course of my life forever.

I rushed to his side, grabbed his shirt, and led him behind the chicken coop where we ducked down. I pointed southeast, the direction of Regreso Creek. "There's a bend in the creek beyond the prairie that way with a big elm tree on the west bank. You can't miss it. It stands ten feet above all the others. It has a cavity in a crook about head-high, and there's a canteen and some crackers wrapped in a blanket in there. It was my dad's emergency stash. I can meet you out there tomorrow morning."

The footsteps stopped. "Alice?" Another forceful whisper. Closer. A male's voice.

"It's safe?" Karl whispered.

"Yes. It's my family's land. No one goes out there but me."

I peeked out from behind the coop when the footfalls continued our way and saw Robert taking slow measured steps, scanning the darkness. "Alice?"

"Sunup, tomorrow morning," I whispered to Karl, and then I jumped out from behind the structure, startling Robert.

He gasped and hopped back a step. When he registered who I was, he touched his chest and said, "What the heck are you doing? Trying to give me a heart attack?"

I hurried to him. I wanted to keep him as far away from the coop as possible. "I'm sorry. I didn't mean to scare you, I swear."

He peered over the top of my head at the coop. "What were you doing over there?"

I glanced back over my shoulder at the coop, too. "Hiding. I panicked when I heard you coming. I didn't know who you were."

He looked down at me. "Sorry. I didn't mean to scare you, either." He gestured at the coop with his eyes. "Is someone else over there?"

"No," I lied. "Why?"

"I thought I heard two voices."

"Nope. It was just me. Walking around talking to myself like a crazy person as usual."

He put his hands on his hips and surveyed our surroundings. "Why are you out here, anyway? It's dangerous to be out here alone with those prisoners still on the loose."

"But *you're* out here," I countered. "Alone. Why is it any less dangerous for you?"

A light smile formed on his face. He knew where I was headed. Our boy-versus-girl debates had been ongoing since grade school.

I pulled the knife out of my back pocket and held it tip-high between us. "Besides, I brought this for protection, just in case. What about you?"

His smile grew wide enough to take up half of his long face. He patted down his front and back short pockets as though he might find a forgotten weapon. "Nope. Nothing. You win."

Beaming with exaggerated cockiness, I slid the knife back into my pocket. "Now that that's settled, to what do I owe the pleasure, Mr. Lewis?"

"I don't know." He nervously kicked at the dirt for a moment. "I don't want you to take this the wrong way, but I remembered how right after your dad died you said you hated the nights and had a lot of trouble sleeping. I thought you might be having trouble again with all that's going on, so, since I was having trouble sleeping myself, I thought I'd come check on you."

His words brought a genuine smile to my face. "Thank you," I said, touching his shoulder. "And you're right. I couldn't sleep either, which was why I came out here and was rambling to myself like a fool."

He chuckled.

"How'd you get out, anyway?" I asked. "Your front and back doors have a hundred locks each."

"My window." He made movements as if climbing a ladder.

My mouth dropped open in amplified dismay. "You climbed down the trellis? The trellis with your mom's coveted cross vine growing on it? Did you destroy any of it?"

A proud gleam touched his eyes. "Not a leaf."

I nudged his upper arm with my palm. "What a rebel. Are your parents still awake?"

"I think Dad was. He was downstairs in his office with the door closed, probably on the phone or working on tomorrow's sermon. He's fallen asleep in there the past two nights. Mom was already asleep, though. Snoring louder than a freight train when I left."

"What is it with moms and snoring? My mom's doing the same. I'll need earplugs if I want to get any sleep tonight."

We had a good laugh and held eye contact when the humor faded. I could tell he wanted to kiss me. Really kiss me. He'd been looking at me like that more and more lately. My heart sped up. We'd kissed once before, just a peck about a month earlier after a bout of water splashing on the bank of Regreso Creek, but we hadn't spoken about it since.

"Alice," he said. "I've been wanting to—"

His attention jerked toward the coop when a crunching noise, a sound like a twig snapping, came from that direction. "What was that?"

"Just the chickens fighting," I said, and quickly stepped into his personal space. I put my hand on the back of his head and pulled his face down to mine. Our lips touched, and I slid my tongue into his mouth. He wrapped his arm around my waist, and we kissed long and hard. He was a passionate kisser. An emotional kisser, if that makes sense. He had soft lips and a warm, sweet tongue that moved in unison with mine like two tango dancers.

He wasn't the first boy I'd made-out with—I'd gone to second base with Billy something-or-other behind a tent at the Tri-State Fair in Mercy a year earlier—and he definitely wouldn't be the last. But, thanks to Karl hiding behind the coop, he was the first one I initiated the act on. In more ways than one, it was one of the best decisions of my life.

After we separated, I told him I should head inside, "because it's so dangerous outside," I joked, and he should get home, too, before he got into trouble. He agreed and walked me to the back porch. We stole quick glances and shot quick smiles at each other as we went, but didn't speak. I slipped off the summer outhouse Oxfords, told him I'd talk to him tomorrow, and crept inside as quietly as possible as he trotted off in the moonlight.

Mom's position on the couch and snoring rhythm hadn't changed a lick. I quietly put away the steak knife, turned the kitchen light and living room lamp back on, then went upstairs to my bedroom. I sat on the floor in front of my window and watched the garden for a long time, whispering to Dad, hoping I'd made the right decision about Karl, before fatigue finally won me over and I made my way to bed.

8

Mom had her back to me when I entered the kitchen just before sunrise the next morning. She stood in front of the sink, wiping down a plate. She'd changed out of the dress she'd fallen asleep in and into one of her other nice dresses. Her hair was wound in a perfect bun on the top of her head. The room smelled of fresh baked biscuits. Two sat on a plate on the table along with a small glass of milk.

"Morning," I said.

She glanced back at me. Her face carried a ready smile that quickly faded as she took in my attire. She set the plate down and faced me. "We've talked about this. That's not acceptable for church."

I examined myself as though unaware I was wearing the same t-shirt and fish-gut shorts I'd fallen asleep in. Or that I'd slipped on my flour-dusted Keds.

"You need to go change. And hurry. We're giving Ruth a ride to church today, so we're leaving early."

"I'm not going."

Mom's right hand found her hip. She eyed me, her lips pressed into a tight slash, seemingly daring me to repeat myself.

"I'm going fishing like I used to with Dad on some Sundays," I said.

"That's foolish and ridiculous and… No, you're not."

"Yes I am."

Her nostrils flared as she drew in a blade of air.

"You can't stop me," I added. "I need this. I'm going whether you like it or not."

I expected her to yell at me, insist I go change right now, but instead she spoke in a low, measured tone. "Why, Alice? Why? Why do you have to constantly push like this? Do you enjoy making my life difficult? Is it your goal to make me miserable?"

"This has nothing to do with *you*. I'm going for me." I tapped my chest. "For *me*."

"How can you say it has nothing to do with me? With all that's happening around here right now. Two prisoners still out there. It's dangerous." She pointed a firm finger at me, and her volume ticked up a notch. "You're my kid. My responsibility. Everything you do affects me. When will you get that?"

"I need time alone out there as much as you need your church and sermon and prayer. When will *you* get that?"

She shook her head, her expression implying she was sickened by my presence. "Sometimes, Alice...sometimes." She released a smug chuckle.

"What?" I snapped. "Say it."

"Sometimes you sound just like your father," she snapped back.

"So."

"So, sometimes you're too much like him for your own good. You need to stop idealizing him. It's unbecoming."

The anger squirming inside my chest clawed its way up my throat, and I made no effort to restrain it. "I'd rather be like him than you any day!"

I snatched the two biscuits off the plate and marched out the back door. After getting my fishing pole and tackle box from the detached garage and reattaching the two strips of tape on the top of the door, I glanced at the kitchen window on my way across the yard and the light was off. A minute later, as I exited the garden and strode across the plains, pushing through shin-high prairie grass, I heard the truck's engine fire up in the distance.

9

The bend in Regreso Creek was about a ten- or fifteen-minute walk from the house. The sun rose directly ahead of me, warming my face and ironically cooling my nerves. Dad had not been a church goer. I remember him attending service with us each Easter and two or three Christmas Eves, but that's it. He spent nearly every Sunday, even ones in the winter when the water had frozen over, at the creek. "I hear God better there," he'd always said. "It's quieter. Easier to think. Besides, if God had wanted me to talk to him in a church, he would've created *that* instead of the creek, right?"

Mom hated having to explain to Pastor Lewis and others why he hadn't attended yet again, and she really hated the times he insisted I go fishing with him instead of to church with her. I loved everything about those mornings: the walks along the bank, the fragrance and trickle of the water, skipping stones, catching horny toads, fishing, our conversations, quiet moments, secrets shared, promises made, lessons learned.

Out there with Dad, I felt safer, more content, and freer than I did anywhere else on earth. And after he passed, I felt closest to him there, too.

Wary butterflies sprung to life in my gut as I approached the bend. My grip on my pole and tackle box tightened as I appraised the shade and vegetation along the creek, searching for Karl. I paused, held my breath, watched, listened. The greenery danced with the warm breeze. Tree leaves jittered, rustled. Lithe branches swayed. Shadows shifted.

The unseen creek water rippled. Unseen birds chirped. But there was no sign of Karl Wagner.

I made my way to the giant elm, checked the cavity in the crook, and found Dad's emergency stash gone. Karl had taken it. But had he stayed?

"Karl," I called out in my normal voice. "Are you here?"

No response.

Scanning the swaths of thick bushy areas along the bank downstream, I walked to Dad's lucky spot on the water's edge and set my pole and tackle box down. I hollered Karl's name again, louder this time, but other than silencing the birds, nothing changed. In one last effort, I shoved my pinkies into the corners of my mouth, curled my lips inward, and let loose a shrill whistle that would've made Dad proud.

That got a response.

Karl jumped to his feet in a clump of knee-high foliage about fifteen yards away. He stared at me, dazed, frightened awake, ready to bolt. Dad's blanket draped sloppily off his shoulders. I held up my hand to help mollify him, fingers spread wide like the night before. It took a few seconds, but eventually recognition dawned on his face, and his hand copied mine.

His focus stayed on me as he balled up the blanket, scooped up the canteen and rag the crackers had been wrapped in, and headed my way. He stopped ten feet away and patted the blanket-rag-canteen wad wedged under his right arm. "Thank you for this. Tell your papa I'm sorry I ate his crackers." He tilted his head at the giant elm. "You want me to put it back?"

I shook my head. "Keep it for now." I glanced at my tackle box and pole, the water, looked back at Karl. "My dad's dead."

He nodded solemnly. "Mine, too."

I sucked in a deep breath. "You fish?" I asked. Dad had called the question the perfect test of character. *"Anyone who says 'no' isn't worth the effort, Ali."*

Karl smiled, nodded again, and his gaze flicked to the creek. "Me and Mama used to fish the Traun all the time." The way he spat out the word Traun spoke to a foreign location. The same rich accent that crimped his English fit the word like a glove.

I pointed to my right. "There's an old pole somewhere in the grass behind that crooked oak tree with the damaged bark. The tip is snapped off, but it'll work. If you want to grab it, I got plenty of line and hooks in my box."

I sat in my regular spot on the bank and baited a hook with stale corn while he retrieved the pole. He sat a little out of arm's reach to my right, my tackle box and the blanket-rag-canteen wad in between us. Once he had his pole strung and baited and we'd both cast, I gestured at the two biscuits in the tackle box.

"You can have those," I said.

He thanked me and shoveled them into his mouth one after the other, practically swallowing them whole. Then took a drink from the canteen, and we watched the creek in silence for a moment, listening to the quiet flow of sun-dappled water.

"How'd your dad die?" I asked, keeping my attention on the creek. "Was he a Nazi soldier, too?"

"No." He looked my way and didn't continue until I made eye contact with him. His earnest gaze told me I'd hit a nerve. Whatever he wanted to say was important to him. "He was never a Nazi. He wasn't even German. He and Mama were both Austrian. They traveled back and forth across the border sometimes to find work, but they hated the Third Reich and joined the Austrian Resistance shortly after the Anschluss."

Confused, I scrunched my eyes and tried to pronounce Anschluss the way he had.

He repeated the word for me. "It's what we called Germany's annexation of Austria in 1938."

I nodded as though I understood way more about European affairs than I did.

"We were living in a small village south of Salzburg when the Nazis openly pushed into Austria and started rounding up all the Jews and Gypsies and sick people and shipped them off to work camps," he continued. "And anyone who tried to help them hide or escape were labeled traitors and hunted down and killed. Some died proudly, but others cooperated to try to save themselves. We had been part of a chain of people funneling 'unfortunates' out of Salzburg, and someone turned us in."

He aimed one of his palms at me. "Someone who'd also told them they'd heard rumors about a blue-eyed teenage boy who could heal people." Guilt rose in his eyes as his hand fell. "They came after us like a pack of hungry wolves after that, and Papa forced Mama and me to leave without him. We ran east, deeper into Austria, riding in the backs of trucks and covered wagons mostly, hiding with the same people we'd been helping. Word reached us four days later that he'd been killed in the streets of Salzburg where he'd been caught and refused to talk. We were told he was shot in the head, then shot twenty more times after he collapsed. We were also told the soldiers took everything from his pockets and kicked and spat on his body as they forced locals to get rid of it. We have no idea where he was taken." His focus shifted back to the water, and he drew in a shaky breath. "My papa wasn't anything close to a Nazi soldier."

I followed his lead and moved my attention to where my fishing line pierced the water as he dragged his thumb under his eyes, wiping away tears. There were so many follow-up questions I wanted to ask, so much I wanted to know, but I knew better than to ask. I may have been independent to a fault sometimes, but I understood his pain. For eight months, I'd understood. We'd boarded at different times, but we were passengers on the same ship, tossed around and damaged by the same choppy seas. His dad had been murdered by Nazis, just like mine. Died alone with no loved ones there to comfort him. Shot down for doing the right thing—being a decent human, a good husband, a protective father. On top of that, it was clear Karl also carried a heavy weight on his shoulders about the role he and his ability played in his dad's demise. He needed a moment to decompress. My questions could wait. I simply told him I was sorry and watched the water.

He broke the stillness a few minutes later by offering me the canteen. "Want a drink?"

My eyes landed on the faded name DOUG painted in green around the silver rim, and I shook my head. "Nazis killed my dad, too," I said, and we met eyes. "That's why I attacked you when I saw you in our garden." I pointed at his arm. "When I saw those, I was so angry I lost control."

He nodded considerately. "How long has he been dead?"

"Eight months. He was shot last December. In Italy."

"He was a soldier?"

"He joined after Japan attacked Pearl Harbor. He thought it was the right thing to do. That's just how he was." The memory of the last time I'd talked to Dad surfaced in my mind, and the same easy smile he'd flashed me as he walked out of my bedroom materialized on my own face. "In his heart, he wasn't anything close to a soldier, though. He was a fisherman." I swished my hand through the air like a magician's assistant revealing something magnificent. "This was his place."

"What was his name?"

"Doug," I said. "Douglas Allen Mayes."

Karl lifted the canteen in toasting gesture. "I wish I could've fished with him."

Over the next hour or so we exchanged stories about our dads while we fished. We were on a wave.

Karl told me how his papa (Franz) was a carpenter and loved the smell of fresh timber. How he'd climbed to a rooftop to serenade his mama (Anna) with a guitar and self-written lyrics as she walked to work the day after he first laid eyes on her. How he'd created elaborate scavenger hunts for his only child each year on his birthday that led to a handcrafted gift. How he'd mix the French, Italian, English, and German he'd learned from his own well-traveled father into mealtime conversations in order to teach Karl and Anna the languages as well. How he'd often broken into song and dance spontaneously. How he loved to garden with Anna, woodwork and share Toblerone candy bars with Karl.

I told him a couple of Dad's wild fishing adventures, including the time he (supposedly) "wrestled for hours" to reel in a forty-pound kingfish in the Gulf of Mexico as a teen. I told him how Dad had loved horses, was obsessed with the Pony Express, and had taught me and Mom to ride. How he'd listened to every St. Louis Cardinals baseball game on the radio and would hoot and holler and run around the house giving out high-fives when Stan "The Man" Musial smacked a homer. How he'd sometimes hide notes in my pockets with silly messages (I farted!) and accompanying silly stick figures that I'd find while sitting in class at school. How he'd regularly jumped out of closets or sprung around corners growling with his hands held high to scare me or Mom. How he'd loved lifting us off the ground in bear hugs and spinning us until we begged him to quit.

It was energizing and cathartic to tell someone about Dad who hadn't known him, talk about more than just the war. And based on Karl's demeanor, I believe he felt the same.

We caught three small catfish—two by me, one him—then switched to wooden lures and stood on the bank, hoping to snag a smallmouth bass. They were a rare catch in late summer on the Regreso, especially with the heat we'd had, but not impossible. We meandered up and down the bank, casting and reeling. Thinking. Talking.

"I'm guessing the Nazis eventually caught up to you and your mom or you wouldn't be here," I said.

"It took years, but yes, they did catch us." He wagged his arm. "That's how I got these. They used Mama—" He paused mid-reel, glanced at me. "They tortured her in front of me until I admitted I could do what they'd heard I could and showed them. She didn't want me to, but I had to. She…" He shook his head, continued reeling, re-cast. "Then they marked me with the swastikas, and I became their property."

"How long ago was that?"

"I'm not sure. Not long, though. Maybe half a year ago. The days mixed together. We traveled a lot—south I now know based on where we were captured—and they kept me blindfolded and gagged most of the time. The only time I was allowed outside was when I was used."

"What'd they do? Make you heal soldiers?"

"Soldiers, plants, trees, animals, bugs. Over and over and over. Then they'd demand I tell them how I did it and beat me when I didn't have an answer. I overheard them arguing after almost every test session. Two of the three officers who watched the tests wanted to keep me secret, make me their own special safety net, use me on their troops only. After all, I was 'their discovery.' The other one wanted to ship me back to Berlin, to Hitler and the other leaders, take credit for finding a true member of the master race. I never saw that one again after they had a heated argument one night. I spent my last few weeks in a medical tent with an SS soldier holding a gun on me all day and night. I was forced to heal soldiers nonstop as the Americans got closer and bullets flew outside. They brought in animal after animal, plant after plant, and even brought in…" Karl looked skyward and whispered something. "Jews and Gypsies and made me…" He shot me a desperate look. "I wouldn't have done it if they hadn't had Mama."

I nodded sympathetically, as if I knew what he'd done. "I believe you."

"From the very beginning they said Mama was being held nearby, that she was safe, and I'd be able to see her again once the war ended if I did what they said. After I threatened to stop eating and kill myself if they didn't let me talk to her, they gave me letters from her every now and then to prove she was alive, and I knew they were from her. They were written in her perfect straight handwriting and addressed to My Dearest BZGH."

"*BZGH?*" I asked

"*Brücke Zwischen den Händen Gottes.*"

Confused by the thick mess of consonants, I shook my head and shrugged my shoulders.

"In English…Bridge Between God's Hands."

"Right." My realization came out reed-thin.

"There's no way they could've known she called me that. She would've died before she told them. So I knew she was alive, and the letters were from her. I'm sure they told her what to write, to say everything would be okay if I did what they said, but I'm equally sure she only did it because they threatened her with my life the same way they did me with hers."

I almost asked if he believed she was still alive but thought better of it. "Are you trying to get back to her?" I asked instead. "Is that why you broke out of Camp Hutchinson?"

He nodded. "It's the only hope I have. I have to try."

"What if you just turn yourself in and tell the military everything you've told me? Maybe they'd—"

"No, they won't," he interjected, and held up an arm. His voice was laced with distrust, eyes steady with conviction. "These tattoos insure they'll never believe me. I'm a Nazi to them. Now and forever.

Nothing more, nothing less. And if they learn what I can do, they'll take me away to a hidden lab faster than you can bat an eye. They'll test me and question me and use me just like the Germans did. They'll never help me find my mama. If I turn myself in, I'll never see her again. I'll never know if…"

He returned to the tackle box, dropped his pole, sat down and hugged his knees to his chest. I continued to cast and reel, sorting through what I'd learned, fitting the pieces together, trying to find a way to help. When I returned to my spot on the bank, he looked at me.

"Was Hans the SS soldier who held you at gunpoint there at the end?" I asked. "Is that how he knows about your ability?"

His brow and mouth tightened as he nodded.

"I take it you don't care much for him?"

He shook his head. "He's been right by my side ever since we were caught, threatening me. Saying he knows exactly where Mama is and will send word and have her killed if I don't do exactly what he says. He acts like I'm still his prisoner. Like he owns me. He's a true Nazi. He enjoys inflicting pain and watching people beg for mercy."

Karl pointed to a pink scar on his bicep. "He put more than one cigarette out on me." He lifted his shirt, exposing a slash scar above his navel and raised his eyebrows. "He liked knives, too." Then he opened his mouth and pushed his tongue through a gap in his bottom row of teeth. "And using the butt of his rifle as a hammer."

"How'd you get away from him?" I asked.

"I pretended while we were at the camp, knowing there was little I could do and also fearing he might tell someone else about my ability. When a couple of the others had a plan to make a run for the train, I told him we should do it. After we hopped off the train and hid, I watched him all night, waiting, but he never fell asleep. The next afternoon, he finally did, and I snuck away. That's when I broke into that girl's house looking for food." He chuckled to himself. "I would've loved to have seen his face when he woke up and I was gone. I imagine he was very mad. I'm sure if we ever cross paths again, he'll let me know about it in more ways than one. I bet he's dreaming about what terrible things he'll do to me when he finds me. That's Hans."

"Where did you two hide that first night?"

"Under a pile of old wood and torn tarps in a shack behind a long building, a little ways from where the train stopped."

"Merriman Hall is probably the long building," I said to myself as much as to Karl. "If he was there yesterday afternoon, I bet he's still close by. Since then, people have been watching the streets like hawks." My eyebrows shot upward. "What if I tell Sheriff Bennington—he's one of Mom's good friends—that someone told me they saw him over there. Maybe they'll go search the area real good and find him. Then you won't have to worry about crossing paths with him anymore. Or him getting word to anyone about your mom."

He twisted his forearms back and forth. "What if he tells them about…you know…?"

"They won't believe a word he says. He's a Nazi, right? Like you. Nothing more, nothing less. They'll think he's saying whatever he can to save his own ass. And let's say he does and then they catch you; you don't have to do anything you don't want to do."

"I don't know." He drew out the *knoowwww*, betraying his uncertainty.

"What can it hurt? If they find him, he's out of the way and your chances to get home in one piece and finding your mom are better. And if they don't find him, or won't look, then I will."

I flashed a playful, head-cocked smile, but the look he shot me told me he knew I wasn't totally joking. "You can't," he said with a note of worry in his tone. "I don't want you or anyone else getting hurt on account of me. I've dealt with enough of that already. Promise you won't go look for him."

"I promise," I assured, and started rummaging through the tackle box for matches. I held them up like I'd unearthed a long-lost treasure. "Now, let's get a fire going and cook up the fish. I'm starving."

We talked little as we built a small fire inside the rock-ringed pit Dad and I had always used, heated the fish on found sticks, and ate with our hands. And what we did say involved the small pleasures of cooking and eating fresh fish. As we passed the canteen back and forth and watched the creek flow and the fire fade to ashes, Karl questioned me, asking my age and full name (he'd heard Robert call me Alice the night before) first.

"Alice Lucille Mayes, sixteen years old and full of vinegar and piss, according to my mom," I said with a sarcastic arm flourish and head-tip.

He laughed. "According to my mama, I'm twenty-three going on fifty."

I joined in on his laughter, then he asked more about my mom—if that was her in the kitchen window the night before, what she did for work, how she was dealing with dad's death, how close we were—and I told him the unfiltered truth, ending with the fight Mom and I had earlier in the morning.

"Was the boy who came looking for you in the garden last night your boyfriend?"

"Robert," I said. "No. He's not my boyfriend. Just a friend."

He gave me an *I-know-better* smirk. "A friend you kiss like a lover?"

"I just did that to keep him away from you."

"If you say."

I bit my bottom lip to fight back the joy wanting to explode on my face. It didn't work. "Okay," I said, feeling compelled to confess. "I wanted to kiss him, too. He's a great guy. He's smart and funny and caring. My best friend. But he's not my boyfriend."

"Not yet," Karl said with a wink.

I reached over the rock-ringed pit and smacked his arm, eliciting an over-the-top painful squeal and expression from him. When he reached back across the pit and nudged me, his hardened blue eyes shone like a kid's. He looked relaxed, really relaxed, and I really liked that. For the first time in a long while, if only for a brief moment, I think he wasn't worried about Nazis, or his ability, or tattoos, or his mom. We were hanging out, like two regular people—nothing more, nothing less.

Dad had taught me how to calculate the time using my fists and the horizon and the sun, and as noon approached, I told Karl I needed to head back and packed up my tackle box.

"I don't think Mom would ever come out here herself," I said, propping my pole over my shoulder. "But if I'm not home when she gets back from church, she might send Sheriff Bennington or someone else out here to check on me. I know she's mad at me, but she'll be worried, too. You know, with the mess that's going on and her being my mom."

Karl nodded slowly, like my words were our final goodbye. "Do you mind if I stay a little longer? I'll be sure and put the canteen and blanket back when I leave."

"Stay as long as you like." I glanced in the direction of my house, then looked at Karl and thumbed that way. "If you want, you could come back to my house." I'd been contemplating the offer on and off all morning. "We have a detached garage next to the house. If you go in the back door and up the stairs, there's a storage room you can hide in. Mom put some tape over the top of the back door so she'd know if someone had snuck inside, but I can make sure and put it back...or tell her I forgot to this morning. Anyway, the room's packed with all kinds of old furniture and clothes and stuff. It's probably hotter than hell up there, and there might be a snake or mouse or two, but you'll be safe. No one ever goes up there. If you open the window at night, it might cool off a little, and there's a trunk with some of Dad's clothes up there, too. You are about the same size as him. You could change out of those prisoner clothes and put on something that'll cover the tattoos."

He looked indecisively over my shoulder toward the house.

"It'll give you a little time to rest at least," I said. "And I could bring you some food tonight after Mom goes to bed."

He surprised me with a quick hug. "Thank you. I'm glad you attacked me in your garden. You're one of the good ones, Alice Lucille Mayes."

I gave him my go-to mock curtsy, said, "At your service," and left.

I always had pep in my step when I headed home from the creek. No matter how long or short the stay, it always had that effect on me. Dad said it did the same for him. Regreso Creek, fishing on that bend in particular, always, if only for a little while, had the ability to erase worry, squash anger, uplift spirits, align thoughts, and give hope. And that day was no different. In fact, thanks in part to Karl, too, of course, I felt better than I had any time since Dad's death as I glided across the plains.

10

I formulated a plan on my walk home. I decided I'd tell Mom that Meredith Fletcher, a hefty home-schooled girl a few years younger than me, had called looking for Sheriff Bennington. I'd say Meredith tried the Sheriff's office but no one had answered, and she knew Ace regularly ate lunch at our place after church services, so she'd tried here. That she wanted to let him know she'd seen someone suspicious, someone she'd never seen before, lurking around Merriman Hall around eleven o'clock, going in and out of the abandoned buildings next to it. I hoped the lie would force Mom to call Ace, and that he'd immediately gather a group and search the area and find Hans. I also hoped they'd take my word for it and not question Meredith first. In my mind, it all seemed perfect. But in the real world my plan and hopes were blown out of the water when I stepped through the back door and found Mom wiping down the kitchen table, humming a soft tune. With her home, I couldn't claim to have received a call from Meredith.

She'd changed into her cleaning skirt and button-up shirt. She stopped humming, and a warm, apologetic smile spread across her face when she noticed me. Church had obviously had the same positive effect on her that the creek did on me.

Relieved, I smiled back.

"I'm sorry about earlier," she said. "But that doesn't mean I agree with you going out to the creek alone right now. Promise me that was a onetime thing."

Mom rarely apologized to me, and vaguely or with caveats when she did. Had I not just returned from the creek, I might've pushed her to specifically apologize for disrespecting Dad, for saying I was too much like him for my own good, to admit it was perfectly normal for me to be a little like both of them, but I had just returned, so I didn't. I had more pressing issues to deal with than my lifelong battle to gain Mom's unconditional approval. Like how to get Ace over to Merriman Hall.

"I promise," I said. "And I'm sorry, too." She kissed the top of my head, and when she resumed wiping down the table, I asked, "Was the church packed today?"

"Everybody and their dog were there. That Specialist Henning fella—you know, the military guy from the meeting yesterday who looks like a bird— showed up. And so did the District Attorney who arrived last night and is staying at the Desoto—Benjamin Tullos, I believe Pastor Lewis said his name is. I'm pretty sure they enjoyed the sermon even though I think they were just there to try and find out who all had helped chase down the prisoner in town square yesterday." She suddenly smirked as if pinched by a pleasant memory. "Pastor Lewis, whew—he was on fire today. He had us electrified." She slowly shook her head, turned and tossed the rag into the sink. "His message was spot on, exactly what we needed to hear with everything that's going on, you know?"

I smiled a close-lipped smile and nodded as if I'd listened to the sermon right alongside her. "Did you see who Specialist Henning and the Tullos guy questioned?"

"They were talking to Pastor Lewis, Garrett Show, and a few others on the front lawn when Ruth and I left. Why?"

"I don't know. I just hope no one gets in trouble for that prisoner dying, that's all."

"I wouldn't worry." She placed the backside of her hand to her cheek as if shielding her words from prying eyes. "From what I've heard, they don't want to blame anyone. Everyone agrees it was an accident, and the investigation is just a formality. For state records and all."

"Oh, I see."

Mom glanced at the clock hanging on the wall. It was a quarter after noon. "Are you hungry?" she asked. "I can make you a grilled cheese real quick, but then we need to get."

"I'm good. I ate some fish at the creek. Where are we going?"

"Well, I didn't know if you'd be home or not, so I asked Ruth if she'd help me clean the Methodist church this afternoon. Even with everything that's going on, I feel bad about putting it off yesterday, so I want to go take care of it. I promised Pastor Hughes the job would be done for Mr. Hodges's memorial service on Tuesday, and I can't afford to lose the business. I'm supposed to pick up Ruth at twelve-thirty. It should only take a couple of hours with all three of us working."

"Okay," I said.

"So, the fishing went well at the creek this morning, huh? How many did you catch?"

"Two catfish. They were small," I patted my belly, "but enough."

"Good." Her smile wasn't totally genuine but not totally false either. "Then hurry and go change into your cleaning clothes so we can get out of here. Pastor Hughes said he'll probably be there when we arrive, and Ace said he'd try to come by and check on us, too, but still, the quicker we get the job done and get home the better."

I nodded half-heartedly and gazed down at the floor.

"What's wrong?"

Since I couldn't lie about receiving a phone call or having spoken to anyone, I lied about Dad. It was the only time I've ever tried to use my grief to my advantage, and I'm not proud of it, but I don't regret it. I had to try something. "I was thinking about Dad a lot this morning, talking to him, you know?"

She laid a motherly hand on my shoulder, nodded when I looked up.

"And, I don't know, I felt like he was out there with me, trying to tell me something about the Nazis." As my own words hit my ears, I realized I sounded just like "Bible-thumping fortune-teller" Hazel Lewis, the woman I mocked for using her "feelings" to make predictions. I felt like a fake, a fraud, and my body reacted accordingly. My stomach squirmed, mouth turned to sand. "For some reason I kept seeing images of Merriman Hall in my head," I went on. "And then I started thinking about how close it is to the train station, and how it's empty and surrounded by abandoned buildings, and how if you jumped off the train, it'd seem like a good place to hide."

"Alice…I don't think…"

"I know it sounds crazy, Mom. And you know I'm not the type to buy into stuff like this. But that should make you believe me even more. Something strange happened out there. Something real. Dad put that image in my head, I just know it. He was trying to show me where one of those prisoners was hiding so I could make sure they're caught and don't hurt anyone else like they did him."

Mom's brow knit with sympathy. "I know you miss your dad, sweetheart, and I understand why you want to believe that the person responsible for his death has been living in that camp and is one of the escaped prisoners. But that's—"

"Foolish?" I blurted out. "But what if, Mom? What if? Can't we just ask Ace to look around over there? What could it hurt?"

She shook her head. "I can't ask him to do that. Do you know how busy he is right now with everything going on in town? Besides, the military men and local watch groups have been patrolling the streets all day. I'm sure there are people looking around over there right now."

"But what if they're not searching the buildings? Please, Mom," I begged. "If you don't believe me then do it to prove me wrong. Prove me wrong, Mom."

As we held eye contact, I thought of Dad's easy smile, of Karl's papa on a rooftop with a guitar, and emotions stirred in my chest, filling my eyes with liquid. Mom's head tilted sideways, and she eyed me with adoring pity, like I was five years old, her "little alligator" again, innocent and ignorant to the true nature of the world. She opened her mouth but closed it again before any words fell out.

"I remember one time you told Hazel you'd follow her to the end of the world if she needed you to," I said. "Can't you at least do this one thing for me? *I* need you to. Please."

When a tear fell from my eye, she pulled me in for a hug. "All right, all right. There's no need to get upset. If it's that important to you, I'll ask Ace if he or someone else can take a look around there, okay?"

I sighed, satisfied. "Thank you, Mom."

"You're welcome." She patted my back. "Now, hurry and change while I load everything in the truck."

By the time we pulled out of the driveway, a silken stillness had replaced the morning's breeze, and gray clouds were encroaching from the west, on a collision course with the sun directly overhead. The sight was a welcome one. As you know, late summer thunderstorms are few and far between in the panhandle. We hadn't had rain in three weeks and only a trickle then, when a rogue cloudburst clipped us. I rolled down the passenger door window and breathed through my nose, hoping to catch the first scent of moisture when the headwinds hit.

Ruth lived alone in a small, well-kept house the size of a modern-day efficiency apartment and was waiting at the door when we arrived. The dinkiest adult I've ever known, she barely reached five-feet tall with shoes on, might've weighed ninety-five pounds carrying a sack of potatoes. She'd met Mom through church shortly after she'd followed her boyfriend (Ray the Rat Bastard, Dad had called him) from Louisiana to Sunray when he landed a job in the oil fields during the boom. When he left her high and dry without so much as a note after being canned six months later, Mom stepped in to help her stay afloat.

Ruth had been raised by her late grandma who'd worked cutting and styling hair in Louisiana, and Ruth had been trying to make money doing the same since arriving in town. But with Dorothy Ginsberg having a firm hold on a majority of women's hair in Sunray at the time, and Bud Cantrell's barbershop servicing the majority of men, her customers were few and far between. Luckily for her, Sherry Davis, the woman who'd helped Mom clean the churches on weekdays the previous two years, had recently moved to Dallas to care for her ailing sister, so Mom had a job to offer. Ruth happily accepted and had worked with Mom ever since. Even after Dorothy Ginsberg moved to California and Ruth's haircutting customer base tripled, giving her the financial freedom to quit, she stayed working for Mom, scheduling cuts around cleans. I wasn't privy to all their conversations on the issue, but from the ones I gleaned information from, I know Ruth didn't bend her schedule out of guilt or debt. She simply valued their friendship and didn't want to give up the time they spent together.

Ruth locked her front door and hopped in after I scooted to the middle and straddled the gearshift. She had on the same blue and white checkered dress she always wore when she cleaned with Mom. A bright red kerchief held her wavy black hair at bay, and equally bright red lipstick colored her lips. She had applied her customary overdose of Chantilly perfume, saturating the cab with hints of rose, patchouli, and jasmine. She greeted me, patted my leg, and asked if I felt well, which I answered with a smile and nod.

The Methodist church sat on a small lot on the far eastern side of Ozmer Street, just shy of where the paved road turned back to dirt on its way to the train depot on the edge of town. Two-thirds of the shotgun shell-shaped building was dedicated to the sanctuary, the other third to a restroom, two tiny offices, and two Bible study rooms. Mom parked directly in front of the open front door, next to Pastor Hughes's Ford Coupe, and we carried the cleaning supplies inside.

Pastor Hughes, a gentle man with gray hair and horrible eyesight who broke into prayer at the drop of a hat, met us in the sanctuary. "Thank you for coming," he said. "I'm sorry for the heat in here. I cracked open the windows and have the back door propped open, too, but there's not much of a breeze pushing through right now. God willing, the rain will hit us soon and drop the temperature." He sounded hoarse, weak, like he'd spent a majority of his voice's daily allowance preaching that morning.

"That would be a blessing," Mom said, and then apologized for not having the place clean for his Sunday services.

He touched her arm. "Don't worry about it, Martha. Everything's a little sideways in Sunray right now." He promptly closed his eyes and started praying out loud, compelling us to lower our heads. He asked God to ease Mom's heart, to protect and strengthen us as we cleaned, and bring the rain our way. We joined him in a soft "amen" when he finished.

"I'll get out of your way now," he said, grinning. "I'll be in the office if you need anything."

For the next hour, we scrubbed and polished and swept as the sky darkened, the wind intensified, and the scent of coming rain invaded the church. Mom sent me to tackle the restroom and two smaller Bible study rooms while she and Ruth worked on the sanctuary. Normally they chatted the entire time they cleaned, sharing every secret tidbit of gossip they'd heard since last speaking, but with Pastor Hughes in his office with the door open, they cleaned as silently together as I did alone. I didn't hear either of them say a word until I finished scouring the bathroom floor and made my way to the sanctuary.

Ruth was hunched over polishing pews, but Mom was standing in the open front doorway with her back to me, whispering. Ace faced her, holding his hat down by his side. He said something to Mom and waved his hat in greeting when he noticed me. Mom glanced at me over her shoulder, but quickly turned her attention to Ace when I set down my bucket and waved back. She said something to him as I crossed the room, and he nodded, slipped his hat onto his pale bald head and left before I reached the door.

Mom spun my way.

"Did you ask him?" I said.

She put her finger to her lips, gestured at Pastor Hughes's office with her eyes. "Don't talk so loud. I don't want Pastor Hughes to hear us. It's unprofessional."

"Did you ask him?" I whispered. "Is he going to go look?"

She nodded, but I knew she was lying. She immediately checked the bun on the back of her head and then straightened her shirt and skirt afterward. That was her liar's tell. Dad had teased her about it all the time. When she lied, she couldn't stop organizing, straightening, or aligning anything within reach. I guess it was her way of counter balancing the inner disorder lying created inside her.

I pushed a little. "Is he going over there right now?"

She nodded again, barely making eye contact with me, obviously placating me, wanting me to accept and move on. She'd probably told Ace I was being dramatic, overly emotional, and never mentioned Merriman Hall. "Now let's go help Ruth. It's not right to make her finish the pews on her own. And we still need to vacuum the carpeted aisle. We can talk about this when we get home."

My youthful impulse was to push harder, call her a liar loud enough to bring Pastor Hughes out of his office. But I shoved that down. I knew starting a fight with her, embarrassing her, wouldn't help my cause at all.

My attempt to get Ace involved had failed, but I still had one option.

Foolish or not, I had the option of me. Merriman Hall was only a couple of blocks northeast of the Methodist church. I could sneak out the back and be there in less than five minutes. I could find something to protect myself with, anything I could swing, then take a quick look around, flush Hans out into the open and scream for help if he was indeed still hunkering down in the area. Mom would fly off the handle no matter the outcome, probably lock me in my room for a year, and I'd be breaking my promise to Karl, but I had no other option. It was the right thing to do. I'd deal with the consequences later as they came.

I helped Mom and Ruth for ten minutes before telling them I needed to go to the bathroom, held up two fingers, and wrinkled up my nose.

"Alice." Mom exhaled sharply. "It's already clean. Can't you hold it? We'll be done in ten or fifteen minutes."

I put my hand on my lower abdomen and shook my head.

"Fine." She pointed at the bucket of cleaning supplies I'd used earlier. "Take that and re-clean the pot when you're done."

11

Wind-driven drizzle greeted me as I crossed the overgrown lot behind the church. But, in the minute or two it took to sneak across Jasper Street and zigzag between a series of homes and sheds in order to avoid watch patrols and skeptical eyes, the drizzle had escalated to a steady rain.

By the time I sprinted down an alley, traversed several backyards, and snagged a length of baseball bat-sized oak from the scrap pile behind Sam DeShields's wood shop, the steady rain had escalated to a downpour, thirty-mile-per-hour wind gusts and startling thunderclaps included.

When I reached Helton Drive and Merriman Hall came into view, I slipped between two abandoned shacks directly across the street to catch my breath and scan the roadside. A dozen scenarios flashed through my mind as my eyes roamed: I found Hans. I didn't. He ran and was caught. He got away. I attacked him. He attacked me.

I glanced down at the length of splintered wood in my hand as the magnitude and absurdity of the moment—the realization I'd stepped into one of my revenge fantasies—washed over me.

I was standing in the pouring rain, drenched head to toe, holding an impromptu weapon, hiding from people I'd known my whole life, searching for a Nazi I'd never met, literally risking my life, hoping to help another Nazi I'd only known for a day—a Nazi who wasn't really a Nazi and could magically heal people like the Son of God himself. All while I was supposed to be taking a dump in a Methodist Church bathroom and scrubbing my own shit stain out of the toilet afterward.

I released a nervous pop of laughter and scanned the roadside again. I hadn't seen a soul since arriving. The rain must've driven everyone indoors.

What am I doing? I thought. *This is crazy.*

I wished I had my dad's fish-gut shorts on.

"It's the right thing to do," I encouraged myself. "So let's go."

Most of the shacks in east Sunray had been built in Mercy by the Coffman Construction Company and were brought in at the behest of Sunoco Oil and Aster Petroleum during the boom. They were thrown together fast and cheap for the purpose of providing temporary sleeping quarters for oil field workers who would skip town the second the wells ran dry. Other than slight variations in materials here and there, they were carbon copies of Ruth's home: rectangular in shape, a slightly pitched roof, a single electrical light in the center of the ceiling, front and back doors separated by twenty feet and lined up perfectly with each another, small square windows on the walls perpendicular to the doors, an outlet below each. A short countertop ran beneath one of the windows, a mirror and a couple of cupboards above. About half had makeshift walls thrown up to create separate rooms. There was space inside for three or four cots, an equal number of chests or dressers for clothing, a potbelly stove, and maybe a small table and a few chairs.

A majority of the ones surrounding Merriman Hall were abandoned. Some had been placed on small lots between "proper houses," others packed side by side like sardines on larger lots. Strong winds had collapsed a couple, but most lived on, crookedly, sparingly, reeking of piss and feral animals, filled with scrap and trash and debris. Only a handful stood tall and proud, empty for the most part, eager for someone like Ruth to purchase and modernize. I knew I wouldn't have time to search them all, so I decided to follow my gut, circle Merriman Hall and check the ones I was drawn to, the ones I'd choose if I needed to hide to save my life.

The ones I chose to enter, I entered with the piece of oak held high, poised to swing like Stan the Man. As I stepped inside each, I hollered, "Hey! Get out of here!", hoping to scare anyone or anything hiding out into the open. And I continued yelling things like "I see you!" as I checked around dark corners, behind fallen walls, and underneath piles of debris.

The downpour continued as I circled the entire perimeter of Merriman Hall, searching, hunting. Water pooled in low areas, and the dirt roads turned to mud. I crossed paths with hissing cats, startled plenty of mice and rats and centipedes, but other than broken beer bottles and a couple of mattresses purposefully stacked in the corner of one of the shacks for either a comfortable night's sleep or a quick adventure with a prostitute, I discovered no signs of recent human activity.

Slightly crestfallen, I slipped back between the two shacks where I'd begun and eyed the last place I needed to check: Merriman Hall itself.

Before the air-conditioned Morley Theater was built, Merriman Hall had served as Sunray's hub. Small court cases, elections, town meetings, school dances, and basketball games were all held in the huge auditorium. Since then, the building had been converted into the town overflow for the most part, the four smaller rooms and attic stuffed with boxes of paper work, outdated furniture, the Sunray volunteer firefighters' supplies, and God knows what else. The auditorium was the only area left vacant, used for occasional roller-skating parties and livestock shows. I'd hoped I wouldn't have to venture into the building because it was the riskiest to enter, but my gut insisted I go. With the back doorway boarded up years earlier, and the front door always locked, the only way in and out was through one of the windows.

I snuck around to the backside of the building where six of the eight windows dotting the auditorium wall were hidden from view by a row of juniper trees. The first window only lifted about six inches before sticking, but the second slid up as easy as horse hooves on ice. I stuck my head into the opening, surveyed the spacious auditorium, then climbed through the gap.

Inside, the structure's frame wailed in response to the strong wind, and the relentless rain on the felt rag roof provided a sonorous background beat to the building's vocals. My Keds added flare to the song, squeaking on the wooden floor as I headed for the hallway located near the front door.

I cocked my weapon as I stepped into the dark hallway. A closed door stared back at me from the opposite end. Three open ones to my right allowed faint light to spill into the hall at even intervals.

"Hans!" I hollered as gruff as my DNA allowed. "We know you're here, you rat bastard."

I held my breath, listening, eyes on the doorways. If he was nearby, I wanted him to think I wasn't alone, that *we* knew exactly who and where he was. The sooner he acknowledged his presence, the bigger head start I'd have to reach the window. I waited, and waited.

"Hans!" I tried again, but heard nothing, so I moved on.

I stopped in the first open doorway and appraised the room. Boxes and loose papers were stacked five-feet high in places from the center of the room to each wall. A thin path parted the stacks and branched off in two directions at the back of the room. One way led to the window on the far wall, the other to the closet in the corner. I followed the path and stopped at the fork, head swiveling back and forth.

To my right, water leaked in around the window and had obviously been doing so for a long time.

To my left, the closet had no door, and a leaning stack of boxes blocked the entrance, waiting for a reason to crash down.

I backpedaled out of the room and made my way to the second doorway. It looked as if someone had stood in the center of that room and tossed junk in every direction, careful only to leave a short path back to the door. Hoses, pipes, crates, wagon parts, suitcases, fabric, shingles, you name it, it was probably buried in there. The closet door was closed, the clutter in front undisturbed. The rest of the junk appeared untouched as well. I marched to the center of the room anyway and spun in a circle, slamming my length of wood down again and again to no avail. I was halfway back to the doorway when I heard a loud crash.

I froze. It felt like I stood there for hours, motionless, unable to breathe, before another, lighter crash rang out followed by what sounded like quick footsteps in the hallway.

It's him, I thought. *He was in the first room, in the closet behind the leaning stack of boxes.*

I hurried to the doorway and peeked down the hall. Hans wasn't there. No one was. I waited, watched, listened to rainfall, distant thunder, creaks from gusts.

He's getting away. He's probably already gone.

The thought lit a fire in my chest. I clenched my teeth, raised the length of wood into swinging position, gripping it with both hands, and rushed to the end of the hallway. When I stepped into the auditorium, he attacked. He'd been waiting on the other side of the doorway with his back against wall.

He grabbed the length of wood and tried to wrench it free. I fought his efforts, twisting when he twisted, pushing when he pulled. I swung my head aside and thrust my shoulder into his face when he tried to head butt me, then stomped down on his bare foot and ground my heel into the skin, peeling a chunk loose. He yelled something in German, let go of the weapon, and backhanded me on the side of the head with his fat knuckles. A white flash exploded behind my eyes. I stooped, staggered, and he kicked me in the hip, knocking me onto the floor.

"Stupid girl," he said, and jerked the weapon out of my hands. His heavy accent resembled Karl's, but his annunciation of the English words paled in comparison.

My head was swimming. I scrabbled at the wooden floor to put distance between us as he propped the chunk of wood on his shoulder and eyed me with cold amusement. I stopped when I reached the wall and looked across the room at the open window I'd entered through.

Hans acknowledged the window with a quick glance, too, and then flashed me a cocky grin. Lightning flickered, brightening his face for a moment, giving me a good look. He had chiseled cheek bones, a firm chin, and dark, arrogant eyes. Handsome, definitely, but in an almost-diabolical way. Like he was made of wax or plastic.

"I hear you come in," he said. "You come alone." He spat on the floor near my arm, spittle splashing up on the back of my hand. "You know my name. Only one way you know that. You know Karl, yes?"

I refused to answer, spat back at his feet.

He clicked his tongue three times as though disappointed and swung the wood chunk at my leg. The jagged tip grazed my shin and pinged off the ball of my ankle as I rolled to the side. Hot barbs of pain knifed up my calf. I pulled both knees up to my chest, wrapped my arms around them like a shield, and fought to keep the pain from showing on my face. It didn't work.

He smirked. "Hurt, yes?" The smirk instantly morphed to a scowl. "I will not miss so much again if you don't tell me where is Karl."

"I don't who you're talking about," I shouted over the top of my knees. "I don't know a Karl." I forced out the name with disgust, like a massive clearing of the throat, mocking his accent.

He clicked his tongue three more times, and I squeezed my eyes shut and hugged my legs tighter, bracing for another blow that didn't come. When I opened my eyes, his gaze rested on me, and he squatted.

"Hear me, tough girl," he calmly said. "I question hundreds of men and women and children tougher than your dreams, so I know a lie. It's easy for me now. I see it." He aimed two fingers at his own face. "In the eyes." He rose and pointed the wood at my head. "I see it in you." He readied the weapon to strike. "I don't like lies. Tell me truth, or I promise I smash your head like I do other liars." His eyes flared with desire as though vocalizing the option to crush my skull had aroused him.

I had no doubt he would've loved nothing more than to watch my brains spill out onto the floor right then and there, and the prospect scared the shit out of me, but I didn't buy his lie detector nonsense. That sounded learned, copied, like the karaoke version of a favorite song. He hadn't been in charge of anyone or anything in the SS based on Karl's story. He wasn't an interrogator or body language savant. He was a guard, a watch dog. A bully. And in standard bully protocol, he was trying to project authority and knowhow beyond his means.

"All right, all right," I said. "I'll take you to him."

A quiver of a grin touched the corner of his mouth, and he pushed the tip of the wood chunk into my cheek. "No tricks, tough girl."

"No tricks," I repeated, staring into his eyes with every ounce of sincerity I had to offer. "I swear."

He shoved the wood harder against my cheek bone, forcing my head sideways. I didn't resist. "Where?" he asked. "How far?"

"Right outside." I pointed at the open window. "In one of the little shacks."

"Which? How far away?"

"I don't know exactly. There are so many, and they all look the same. I'll show you, though. It's hidden well. No one will see us if we go now while it's still raining. But after that, you have to promise to let me go home. No tricks."

He scrutinized me with a long, judging look, and eventually nodded. He couldn't hide his lie any more than he could read mine. He had no intention of letting me live. It was written all over his face.

"Up," he ordered. "Go to window. You run, you die."

I slowly levered myself off the floor and fingered the throbbing spot on the side of my head where he'd backhanded me. He stepped behind me and pressed the length of wood against my spine.

"Move."

I limped forward, favoring the ankle he'd whacked. My head was hung, eyes angled up at the window. As the rain and thunder and lightning raged on, I walked progressively slower, exaggerating my limp as we crossed the auditorium. About ten feet from the window, I stopped, bent, and put my hands on my knees. Staring down at the same wooden floor on which I'd once been deemed the "Roller-Skate Limbo Queen," I waited for Hans to push, which didn't take long.

He tapped my back with the piece of wood hard enough to sting. "Move."

"Give me a second," I said, and dropped to a knee. "Please. You hit me so hard. I feel like I'm going to faint."

One Mississippi.

Two Mississippi.

Three Mississippi.

Four—

"Enough." He tapped my back again, harder. "Up. Move."

"Please," I whispered. "Please. I'll do whatever you want." I craned my neck and caught a glimpse of his lower legs before closing my eyes, bowing my head, and holding up a submissive hand. Hoping the submissive pose tickled his ego enough to bring his guard down some. "Please, just give me—"

I kicked out my right leg and spun on my opposite heel, like a skater making a crouched turn, slicing my foot into his knees. His left leg buckled inward, smashing into his right, and he crashed onto the wooden floor with a sickening thud. The chunk of wood bounced out of his hand, rattled, and settled. I reared back and kicked him square in the chin as he squirmed to rise. His head flew back, and he rolled away from me, reaching for his face. My eyes jumped to the weapon, my thoughts to picking it up and bashing his head, but when he screamed out in German and began to sit up, I hightailed it to the window.

I didn't look back as I climbed into the gap, but I could hear him coming. I was halfway through when his hands grasped my thighs. With my lower abdomen and hips digging into the sill, I flopped and kicked like a fish out of water as he grunted and tugged. My feet connected with his face and chest and shoulders multiple times, eventually loosening his hold enough for me to throw my weight forward. His nails scraped trails into the skin on the backs of my legs as I slid down the brick wall onto the muddy ground.

I frantically crawled toward the junipers, jumped to my feet, and glanced back. He was maneuvering quickly through the window, rain washing away the blood flowing from the gash on his chin as soon as it appeared. Absolute anger contorted his face, leveled his gaze. He paused when we met eyes and spat German words at me. I don't know what he said, but his hatred came across loud and clear.

I turned and bolted between two junipers and burst out into the clearing behind them. I sprinted twenty yards and spun around, knowing I had at least five shacks and at least two proper houses within eyesight and earshot of my location.

Hans emerged from the junipers and stopped when he saw me. A rope of tension lassoed us together. We faced each other like two gunfighters in a street duel, shoulders square, eyes locked.

East of town the storm raged, the sky black as night. But, to the west, the clouds grew thin, sunshine on the verge of busting through. Thunder rattled in the distance, and in an instant, like a dimmer switch had been turned, the wind calmed and the loud rain faded to a quiet trickle. A sign from above if there ever was one.

"You're a fake rat bastard, and I hate everything about you!" I hollered.

He yelled back in German but added "tough girl" in English at the end. Then he ran toward me.

I knew I couldn't outrun him in an open sprint or beat him in hand-to-hand combat, but I could do what I'd planned on doing from the get-go once I had him out in the open: summon attention and keep him at bay until help arrived.

Glaring at him, I thrust my chin upward in defiance, opened up my mouth, and screamed as loud as I could. My entire body clenched as every ounce of hatred, anguish, disgust, and pain rooted inside me ripped loose, soared up my gullet, and flew into the air. I wanted everyone with a decent set of ears within half a mile to think the doors to Hell had opened up. I wanted them to hear torture manifest. I wanted them to be unable to hear and not come.

Hans stopped dead in his tracks ten yards from me. He looked over my shoulder as my scream faded. I followed his gaze and saw the back door to the Schmidt house wide open, two figures looming in the doorway, another crossing the backyard. Two shacks over, the Pearson's back door was open as well, and Top-Heavy Bill stood on his porch in overalls, a rifle in his hands. I looked back at Hans, inhaled a solid breath, and let loose a second dose of emotion, this time formed into the word Nazi and shrill enough to drop insects from the sky had there been any.

Hans briefly caught my eye, the fierce look he gave promising retribution, then turned and ran. I looked back over my shoulder as he looped around the row of junipers. Top-Heavy Bill was trotting my way. Mr. Schmidt followed close behind. I hoped at least one of their wives, kids, or someone else within earshot was already near or on a phone, notifying the sheriff's office or watch group members.

When I turned my focus back toward Hans, he was cutting between a shack and Merriman Hall, headed for Helton Street. The prospect of him reaching a secluded hiding spot, of him not being caught, of my failure, kick-started my legs. Yelling "Nazi" again and again like a tornado siren, I chased after him, refusing to let him out of my eyesight.

Mud colored my Keds brown and splashed up onto my calves as I went. He slipped and fell in a puddle when he tried to turn onto Helton, allowing me to make up ground. I continued to scream "Nazi" and followed him west on Helton, past a group of shacks, then north between two homes, down an alley, through a series of yards, across Fifth Street, an overgrown lot, Fourth.

He paused and frantically scanned his surroundings—including back at me—each time he changed directions. Curious onlookers emerged from buildings, slowed in their cars. I think he knew it was only a matter of time before others joined the chase.

As we approached north Main Street, he sprinted between two bars—The Oasis and the Night Cat—and then stopped dead in his tracks in the center of the paved road. The post office was directly to his right, the Garrison's black Whippet we called Old Whipper one of two cars idling in front. The driver's door was open, and Jasmine was leaning in, handing Benny a wad of envelopes. He sat in the passenger's seat, Nancy in the back.

Hans raced up behind Jasmine, wrapped his hands around her waist, and lifted her off the ground. She was a foot shorter than him and maybe half his weight, and he tossed her aside like a ragdoll.

Running toward the car, I hollered, "No!" The passenger door flew open and Benny hurried to his mom as Hans hopped in the driver's seat. I grabbed onto the open door with both hands before he could close it, and he punched the gas. Nancy screamed in the backseat as Old Whipper took off south, heading toward town square, two blocks away, pulling me along with it.

I held on for a good ten yards, the road tearing into the skin of my lower legs, before letting go. Then I immediately jumped up and ran after the car. I didn't feel any pain from the wounds or consider breaks or blood loss. That came later, when the adrenaline faded. I just ran, eyes glued to the back of Nancy's head, yelling "Nazi" over and over and over. People began appearing on each side of the street, from every building. Some rushed out onto the road and joined the chase just like with the first Nazi a couple of days earlier.

To avoid hitting a car backing away from a liquor store, Hans swerved Old Whipper up onto the adjacent walkway, narrowly missing three well-dressed women before curving back onto the road. The car sped up, seesawed on the slick pavement, shrugged off a man who tried to jump on the hood from the right, and zipped past Fulton's Grocery Store, scraping the back end of every car parked in front. Then it broke into a sideways drift when it reached the roundabout in front of the Sunoco filling station, skidded onto the grass in the Heart of Town Square, and mowed down the young red oak tree, barely missing the Texas-shaped, SUNRAY 1930 monument.

Hans corrected the slide and gave the engine all it could take. Old Whipper shot west down Ozmer Street and sped out of sight when I was in front of Fulton's. Many of the men who were chasing the car were faster and passed me as we approached the roundabout. I slowed when a crunch sounded in the distance and completely stopped when I rounded the curve and my eyes landed on Old Whipper. It had flipped onto its side at the intersection of Ozmer and First Street. Hans had tried to make the turn off the paved road and onto the dirt one too fast.

By the time I reached the wreck, twenty people had swarmed the car. I watched Deputy Putnam—who wasn't in uniform—and scrawny Sunoco gas pumper Ronald Faraday pull Nancy out of the car and carry her to the sidewalk where she was instantly surrounded by five or six others. I pushed through the people and knelt, calling out her name. A little blood dribbled from her nose, but there was no other obvious sign of injury. She had her eyes closed but was breathing, and making little moans.

"Is she okay?" I looked at Deputy Putnam, pleading for assurance. "She's just knocked out, right?" I touched her arm and said her name, told her to open her eyes.

Mr. Fulton took me by the shoulders and forced me to my feet. "Alice. Look at me. Alice." He twisted my shoulders and made me face him. His forehead and cheeks were sheeted with onion-scented sweat, and he was short on breath. I imagine he'd run from his store to the crash site, which was probably the farthest he'd run in years. "She's going to be okay, Alice. We need to give them space to check her and get her over to Dr. Mobley, okay?"

I started to nod, but my attention snapped to the Whippet when someone called out, "Ready over there, Garrett? Everyone out of the way?" A bunch of men had gathered on the top-end of Old Whipper, arms propped on the black metal, positioned to upright the car.

Garrett Show, donning a pressed suit, bowtie, and bedraggled hair-do as usual, stood on the underside of the car, holding onlookers at bay with his outstretched arms. His black mutt, Spade, was on all fours by his side. "We're ready," he answered.

"Okay, men," an older guy I didn't recognize in Camp Hutchinson military garb said. "Here we go. Push on three. One. Two. Three."

The car rocked forward a little and came back.

"Push."

Rocked farther, almost, and came back.

"Push."

The third effort tipped Old Whipper onto four wheels with a mud-squelching clack, eliciting gasps and moans from onlookers. That's when I saw Hans. His upper half dangled out of the driver's side window. The back of his head was split jaggedly down the center, like a watermelon dropped from a rooftop. Brains and blood oozed from the crack. His arms and neck hung at odd, broken angles. I couldn't see his face, but based on the expressions on the faces of the men and women who could, I knew it wasn't pretty.

"He must've flown out the window as the car flipped," someone behind me said.

"Yeah," someone else commented. "It smashed him real good."

"Serves him right."

Mr. Fulton gingerly touched the top of my back. "Come on, Alice. Let's go. You don't want to see that."

In shock, I allowed him to escort me away from the wreck, and he gestured at my legs as we crossed the street, heading toward town square. "Looks like you have some pretty nasty cuts there. Are you all right?"

I glanced down at my shins with disinterest and nodded.

"Good, good," he said. "Where's your mom? Did she come downtown with you?"

I could feel his worried gaze looming on me, but I kept my eyes aimed straight ahead, my legs pumping. "She's at the Methodist church with Ruth," I said. "Cleaning."

"Oh. Well, tell you what. If you come with me to the store, I'll give her a call and let her know where you are. Mary can get you something to drink and help you clean up those cuts, too. Sound good?"

"That's not necessary," I said.

"Are you sure? I don't feel—"

"I'll be fine," I insisted as we looped around the north end of the roundabout, both eyeing the fallen red oak. "I want to walk alone, please."

He slowed to a stop in front of the Sunoco and reluctantly allowed me to continue down Ozmer. I'd walked two blocks, well out of sight and earshot of the chaos when I saw Mom's truck heading my way.

We met up in front of an abandoned shack, and Ruth pushed the passenger door open and scooted over so I could get in.

12

Mom whipped a U-turn without saying a word, never laying eyes on me or the mess I'd caused around town square. She stared straight ahead, radiating anger, choking the life out of the wheel, lips pressed into a thin line, until we reached Ruth's house. She thanked Ruth for her help after Ruth hopped out, apologized for "everything," and told her she'd call her later. Then she resumed her livid driving stance, and we rode home in absolute separation. No eye contact or words whatsoever.

She stopped the truck in the driveway with a jolt, jumped out, slammed her door shut, marched to the house, unlocked the front door, stepped inside, and slammed that door shut, too. She'd given me the silent treatment many times before, for days on end sometimes, but rarely with such aggression.

I buried my face in my hands, closed my eyes, and sat there for a long while, breathing and crying. I felt fractured. So much had happened in such a short amount of time. My thoughts were scattered. Conflicting emotions warred inside me. Part of me wanted to run back to the scene, to Nancy's side, and apologize forever. Another part wanted to lash out at Hans and kill him more. One second, I wanted to crumple down on the floorboard and sob like a baby. The next, I wanted to run as far away as possible and never come back. In the end, though, I did what I knew I had to—I went in to face Mom.

I found her in the kitchen, standing next to the table, staring at the ringing phone. Her secret bottle of Southern Comfort sat on the counter for all to see. A quarter-full tumbler hung from her finger tips down by her side. I paused in the doorway and waited. She finally looked at me when the ringing stopped, her gaze condemning, crucifying, burying me on the spot.

"What in God's name were you thinking, Alice? Lying to my face. Sneaking out of the church and running off like that. It's unacceptable, and you know it. When are you going to grow up and stop all this nonsense? Do you have any idea what you put me through? And Ruth? And Pastor Hughes? We thought one of those Nazis had taken you. Or killed you. We ran around the church, and up and down the street, looking for you, screaming your name. We were terrified. Then when we went inside and called the sheriff's office, and Deputy Weber told us someone else had just called him and said they saw you running toward downtown, yelling like a crazy person. Do you know how scared and confused and embarrassed I was? Do you care? I can't take much more of you, Alice. I just can't." The phone started ringing again, and her eyes left mine for the first time. She took in my damp dirty clothes, scraped-up legs, mud-caked shoes. "What the hell happened to you?" She gestured at the phone with her tumbler. "What do they know that I don't? I want to hear it from you first. Where did you go? What did you do?"

I waited a beat to make sure she was finished before answering bluntly, in typical sixteen-year-old-Alice fashion. "I went to look for Nazis around Merriman Hall since Ace wasn't going to."

"*What?* I told you I talked to him about it. You saw us at the church."

"Yeah, I saw. I saw the guilty look on your face when I came into the room. I saw you hurry him away. And I saw all your…" I patted my hair and pretended to tidy non-existent buttons on my shirt like Dad sometimes had. "When I asked if you'd told him."

She wagged a finger at me. "Don't mock me, Alice. I won't stand for it." She jammed the same finger down on the table, the little joint curving with the force of her conviction. "I did tell Ace that you were upset after you went fishing this morning." She lifted the finger and jammed it down again. "And I did tell him you had a feeling you knew exactly where the Nazis were hiding and were convinced they were somewhere around Merriman Hall."

"But did you ask him to go look over there?" I pushed.

"No, I didn't," she admitted. "I didn't need to. He said people had been patrolling that part of town since yesterday like I tried to tell you this morning." She finished her whiskey, set her tumbler on the table. "But I did ask him if he thought you'd had your mind on your dad for too long and were just getting carried away with one of your foolish Nazi ideas like I did, and he said yes."

I answered her jab with an uppercut. "I found one of them, hiding in Merriman Hall. His name was Hans. We fought in the auditorium, and once we were outside, I chased him and started yelling so other people would hear and help. I didn't want him to get away."

She cut her eyes upward, tilted her head back as though the blow had hit her square in the chin, and whispered something to God.

"When we got to Main Street, he stole the Garrison's car," I continued, and she lowered her head. "Old Whipper. He threw Mrs. Garrison out of the way when she was about to get in." Shame filled my eyes with tears. "Benny was in the passenger seat and got out in time, but Nancy was still in the backseat when he took off. I tried to stop him. I grabbed the door but couldn't hold on. I…" I looked down and to the side as the image of the back of Nancy's head in the car window surfaced in my mind.

"Did something happen to Nancy?"

I nodded without looking up. "I tried to keep up with the car, but I lost track of it after it hit the oak tree in town square. I didn't see it flip over."

"*Flip?* Is she okay?"

"She had her eyes closed when they pulled her out of the car. I touched her arm and tried to talk to her, but she didn't say anything." I met eyes with Mom. Tears spilled. "If I could take her place, I would."

Her eyes softened, but only for a second. "That doesn't matter, Alice. I've told you a thousand times you can't go around doing whatever you want whenever you want. Didn't we already talk about this once today? When are you going to get it through your thick skull that your actions affect other people?"

"I know they do," I shot back. "But you only seem to think I affect people in bad ways. All you do is look for the bad. You never see the good in anything I do unless I do exactly what you tell me to do, or do it exactly how you want me to do it."

"Name one thing good that came out of what you just did." She put one hand on her hip and shot up an index finger with the other. "One. One thing. Because all I know so far is that you lied and ran away, which scared me, Ruth, and Pastor Hughes to death. Started a fight with a Nazi who could've killed you. Chased him through town, screaming at the top of your lungs, terrifying everyone who heard you. Got the Garrison's car stolen and destroyed, your legs all scraped up, and your friend Nancy hurt, maybe badly. From what I can see, nothing good came out of this. You didn't help anyone."

I imagined Karl sitting out by the creek, or maybe hiding in our garage, thought about everything he'd told me about Hans, how Hans had treated me in Merriman Hall. "The Nazi died when the car flipped."

Her eyebrows shot up, and she simultaneously threw her palms in the air. "Oh, great. So you're responsible for someone dying, too? That's not a good thing, Alice."

The phone rang, saving me from putting my foot in my mouth again and the argument from escalating into a screaming match. We held eye contact. The tense stillness between each ring seemed to last longer and longer. When the caller finally gave up, Mom turned around to refill her tumbler.

"I'm going to rinse off my legs," I said, and marched out the back door to the water pump.

I stole glances at her through the kitchen window as I painfully scrubbed the mud and blood off my shins. She remained where I'd last seen her, still as a statue, gazing down at the refilled tumbler, seemingly waiting for the perfect time to down it. I also stole a couple of glances at the garage, wondering if Karl had already come and I needed to reattach the tape above the door, hoping he might be looking down from the second-floor window and give me an encouraging wave, a little validation (*You're one of the good ones, Alice Lucille Mayes*), a sign that I hadn't royally messed up. But the tape was still intact.

An engine roared onto our street as I was taking off my shoes to clean them, and I immediately recognized the source: Ace's truck. His exhaust pipe had been on the verge of rusting off for months, which created a distinctive, smoky growl when he accelerated quickly. I watched Mom out of the corner of my eye as he pulled into our driveway and killed the engine. Seconds later, three rapid knocks sounded on the front door, and she disappeared from the kitchen window.

It had been at least twenty minutes since I'd left downtown—ages in Sunray time—so there was no doubt he'd already heard some of the story. He'd probably arrived on the scene shortly after I'd left. Probably already talked to Jasmine and Benny, Mr. Fulton and Top-Heavy Bill, maybe even Ruth and Pastor Hughes. I knew he'd have a ton of questions for me, especially after talking to Mom. I pumped a little water onto my shoes, rubbed them as clean as possible with my hands, wiped them on the circle of grass growing around the pump, and dropped them on the porch on my way inside.

I could hear Mom and Ace talking in the front of the house, so I eased the back door closed, crept to the doorway leading from the kitchen into the living room, and peeked around the corner. They were standing behind the couch, facing each other. Ace held Mom's right hand in his left, his sheriff-star-studded cattleman's hat in the other. She was telling him everything I'd just told her with a bite to her words, tears in her eyes. I waited for her to finish before stepping into the room. The more she said, the less I had to. They dropped hands and looked my way when the floor creaked beneath my bare feet.

"Ace needs to talk to you," Mom said, and stepped aside, giving him a direct line of sight to me.

"You want to sit down?" he asked, gesturing at the couch.

I shook my head.

"Okay." He glanced down, spun the star on his hat into proper position. When he locked eyes with me, he pushed out a breath. "I've known you since the day you were born, Alice. I love you like a daughter, and you know that. I also know how you are. You like things delivered cut and dry, so I'm going to be blunt with you." He glanced at Mom, looked back at me. "First off, I'm glad you're okay, and I'm real sorry about Nancy. I know you feel like shit about what happened to her, and so you know, I talked to Dr. Mobley, and he said she was awake and talking some. He was about to do some x-rays to see if he needs to send her to the hospital in Mercy or not. We should know soon."

An arrow of hope pierced my heart, and I nodded.

"But that doesn't mean I'm not pissed and don't think what you did was stupid and reckless. You *should* feel like shit. Not only about what happened to Nancy, but also for what you put your mom and everyone else through. You could've died. A bunch of people could've died. You should've come to me before you did something like that."

"I tried. I told Mom to ask you to look over there."

"You can't blame her," he declared, his eyes narrowing. He'd lectured me in the past about small things like manners, homework, and whatnot, but never with an ounce of anger in his voice like he had right then. In fact, I don't recall ever having a serious argument with him. Unlike Mom, he wasn't the arguing type. "She told me you had a feeling where they were, and I told her people were watching that area. You never told her you were going to go hunt over there by yourself, or she would've stopped you. You lied to her. This is all on you. If you want to make grown-up choices, you have to deal with the grown-up consequences."

The term grown-up triggered my reactive, teenage, piss-and-vinegar mechanism. "I know that," I snapped back.

He shook his head, and his gaze fell to his hat in his hands. He spun the star. Seconds stretched. "Do you not remember what happened to Lily?" He looked at me, the anger in his voice replaced by concern. His eyes, too. "Did you not hear Corporal Tanis tell everyone that the last two prisoners could be hiding together? Did you consider what would've happened if you stumbled across both of them? What they could do to you?"

"I did, and I was careful. I swear."

"I know you think that, Alice, but you're wrong. There was nothing careful about what you did."

Mom sidled up next to Ace and crossed her arms over her chest. "He's right. And your father would agree with him if he were here, too." They briefly met eyes, verifying an alliance against me.

"Don't," I said. "Don't try to use Dad against me. He would've told me to do what I thought was right if I truly believed in it, and that's what I did."

"Listen, I know you miss him and want to do right by him," Ace said. "I miss him, too. But I believe if he did send you a message down at the creek this morning—and I'm not saying he did or didn't—I don't think he wanted you to risk your life on account of it."

"Or other people's," Mom added. "He would never do that."

"Yes, he would," I countered. "That's exactly what he did when he joined the Army."

"He risked his life so you wouldn't have to," Ace said.

"No, he risked his life because he believed the cause was worth the risk. That's one of the last things he ever said to me. He *lost* his life defending that principle, and I don't care what you say, or how you try to spin it, he'd be proud that I'm strong enough to do the same."

"He was very proud of how strong you are," Ace agreed. "He was prouder of you than anyone else on this planet. He told me so more times than I can count. But he also told me to look out for you and your mom while he was gone. He trusted me to make sure you guys stay safe, healthy, happy—everything he would've made sure of if he were here—and that's what I'm doing. And will continue to do, whether you like it or not."

"You're not him," I lashed out as warm tears dribbled down my cheeks, unfairly directing my emotional chaos at him. "You can love his wife, marry her, move into his house, sleep in his bed, eat at his table, fish at his creek, yell at his daughter, but you still won't be him."

"Alice Lucille!" Mom yelled, using my name like a weapon, the words snapping like the thick leather of a belt. "How dare you!"

"It's okay, Martha," Ace said. He held his arm out as if to block her from rushing forward. "I do love your mom, perhaps more than you like, and we can talk about that later, if you want. But now is not the time. I want you to know right here and now, I'll never, ever try to be or replace your dad. I don't want to. I'm just trying to fulfill the promise I made to my best friend."

"You should be ashamed of yourself," Mom said. "Apologize to him this instant."

I knew I should. I felt it in my chest. He didn't deserve to take the brunt of my emotional instability. He'd been nothing but kind and helpful to me and Mom, and it really didn't bother me that they were falling in love. I'd known for a while, with their quick hand drops, furtive smiles, secret giggles, soft whisper conversations in dark corners, but we'd never talked about it. Maybe there had always been a spark there, the whole two kings and one queen thing, but I don't think so. I hadn't noticed a change in their relationship until a couple of months earlier, about six months after Dad had died, which made sense. They were good friends, the same age, laughed at the same silly jokes, prayed to the same God, and more importantly, as Dad's two best friends, had shared and were working through their loss together. They needed each other.

When I caught Ace's eyes, I tried to convey my regret without words. The look on his face assured me he understood, and when I opened my mouth to voice the apology, he cut me off by holding up his hand.

"Don't worry about it," he said. "There's no need to apologize."

"Yes, there is," Mom insisted. "She can't say things like that to you."

Ace turned to Mom and touched her forearm. "It's all right, Martha. It really is. It's been a rough day, and we're all emotionally charged right now. We just need to cool down for a little bit, catch our breath, and we can talk about this more later if we need to." He thumbed toward the front door. "I need to get over to the office, anyway. Specialist Henning and D.A. Tullos are going to want answers now that we have two dead prisoners on our hands."

Mom nodded, and he faced me. "I'm going to tell them everything that happened, including what you told your mom, but they're probably going to want to hear it from the horse's mouth, anyway, so don't be surprised if they show up later to talk to you. When they do, be honest with them."

I nodded. "I will."

He slipped on his hat, smoothed his thick mustache. "And please promise me one thing."

"What?" I asked.

"Promise me, feeling or not, you won't do anything like this again. That guy with the swastika tattoos on his arms is still missing, and I don't want to get a call about how someone saw you chasing him through town, or beating the shit out of him in town square, or anything like that, okay?" He patted his chest. "I don't know if this old ticker could take it."

I nodded again. "I promise."

13

Mom walked Ace to his truck, and whatever he said to her while they were outside must've been exactly what she needed to hear. When she returned, she didn't break into a lecture about respect or honor or manners like I'd expected. She simply gestured at my clothes as she passed by me on her way to the kitchen and said, "Get out of those before that dirt settles in and go fill the tub. I'll get you a towel and some hydrogen peroxide while you wash up. You don't want those cuts to get infected." Once out of sight, she added, "I'll get a comb, too. Your hair is mess. Scrub it good so you can get the tangles out."

I did as I was told. The phone rang two separate times while I bathed, but Mom ignored the noise. Once clean and dry, I doused my wounds, ran a comb through my hair, and headed upstairs to my bedroom for a fresh change of clothes. Well, a fresh t-shirt and undergarments. I suppose fish-gut shorts wouldn't qualify as fresh to most people. Not long after I shut the door, the phone rang again, and this time Mom answered.

Craving a good dose of comfort, a good dose of Dad, I took a big whiff of the creek water and Red Man tobacco fastened to the shorts before slipping them on and tightening the leather belt that lived in the loops. The resulting warm sensation that seeped through my body instantly relaxed my insides. Exhausted on all fronts, I flopped face-first onto my bed, closed my eyes, and instantly fell asleep.

I woke with a start when Mom opened the door and said my name. I felt like I'd been asleep for days, but the sun had only partially set, still casting faint light through my window. No more than a few hours could've passed. I sat up, wiped the drool from the corner of my mouth. Mom's eyes looked alcohol-softened.

"I just got off the phone with Jasmine Garrison," Mom said. "I wanted let you know that Nancy won't have to go to the hospital in Mercy right now. She has a concussion, a broken nose, broken pinky finger, a cracked rib, swollen wrist, and plenty of bruising, but nothing that won't heal. Dr. Mobley said it'll just take some time. He's allowing her to rest at home and said he'll check on her daily."

"Is she in a lot of pain?" I asked.

"Jasmine said she was pretty bad off before Dr. Mobley gave her some medicine, but she's doing better now."

"Can we go see her?"

Mom shook her head. "She needs to get as much rest as she can. Dr. Mobley told Jasmine he doesn't want her to have any visitors for at least a day or two."

I clasped my hands together between my legs, looked out the window, back at Mom. "Did you tell Mrs. Garrison how sorry I am, and that I didn't mean for this to happen? Did you tell her to tell Nancy, too?"

Mom nodded. "I told her everything, and she said to tell you that it's okay and asked you to please pray for Nancy."

I puffed out my cheeks and pushed out a breath. The positive news didn't fully alleviate the pressure built up inside my chest, but it helped a little. "Thank you."

"You're welcome," Mom said. "Hazel, Robert, and Thomas came by, too. Hazel said Pastor Lewis had called her from Mayor Wilson's office and told her what he knew, so she wanted to come and check on us. They stayed for a while, and we talked about everything that happened. Robert and Thomas came up here, hoping to talk to you, but they didn't want to wake you. They brought some chicken noodle soup for us. It's downstairs if you're hungry."

The phone rang again, and Mom glanced back over her shoulder at the staircase. "I better go see who that is. Ace is supposed to call when he gets home and tell me what Specialist Henning and D.A. Tullos said."

In my doorway, I paused and listened to her answer and start telling someone other than Ace what her daughter had done, then closed the door and returned to my bed. There was no way I could eat. My mind was racing. I rolled onto my side and curled into a fetal position facing the wall, thinking about everyone and everything in sporadic, unrelated spurts, waiting for night to fall.

I pretended to sleep when Mom finally came upstairs, opened my door, and entered my dark room. She touched my back, flicked on the overhead fan, and pulled the door mostly closed as she left. I flipped over where I could see the light coming from her bedroom lamp in the hallway and listened to her prepare for bed. The light went off ten minutes later, after she whispered her nightly Lord's Prayer and personal requests to Jesus. I stayed put until I heard snoring, then waited ten minutes more before creeping downstairs.

In the kitchen, I fished Dad's work thermos out of his lunchbox in the back of the pantry and filled it with Hazel's chicken noodle soup. When Mom asked, and she would (she documented food supply in the house as diligently as the state did land taxes), I'd say I woke up hungry in the middle of the night and came down and ate some. She'd never notice Dad's missing thermos as long as I put the lunchbox back where it went, and I did. Then I snuck outside and headed to the garage where I found the tape removed from the top of the door.

Alice Lucille Mayes, one of the good ones.

14

"Karl?" I whispered as I opened the door to the storage room at the top of the stairs. Trapped humid air from the rain hit me in the face. Bright moonlight shone through the window to my right, but the blue-tinged hue didn't reach too far into the room. I flicked on the flashlight I'd grabbed off the workbench garage when I'd entered and swam the beam back and forth. A thin film of dust had settled on the surface of the junk. Cobwebs clung to the rafters and trailed up the corners of the room. "Karl, are you still here? It's me, Alice."

My heart hitched when he popped up from behind Nana's old couch a few feet in front of me and held up a finger-spread hand. The hitch wasn't because he'd surprised me, but because for a split second I thought he was Dad. When the beam stopped on him, it only highlighted him from the neck down. He'd switched out of his prisoner clothes and into some of Dad's—clothes I hadn't laid eyes on since Dad left for boot camp. He wore Dad's green cotton long-sleeved undershirt and what Dad called his going-out jeans. With his face too shadowed to discern specific features, my brain filled in the gaps and tricked my eyes into buying that truth for half a second.

"I see you found Dad's trunk of clothes," I said, and closed the door behind me. I kept the light on him as he stepped out from behind the box-covered couch. His eyes appeared rested, the knot on his head from Lily's frying pan whack darker in color but less swollen. He had a content, almost happy look on his face. "They fit you good."

He glanced down at the clothes, ran his hands over the shirt, shot me a grateful look. "Yes. They do. Thank you."

I held out the thermos. "Hope you like chicken noodle soup. It's not much, and it's cold, but it's all I could get."

He took the thermos and thanked me again. "With this and the fish this morning, I might as well be royalty."

I smiled, and realizing he was squinting due to the flashlight shining directly on his face, turned it off. Looking back now, I think I might've also turned it off because I subconsciously didn't want to see the peaceful look on his face disappear when I told him that I'd broken my promise and gone after Hans. But at the time, the thought never crossed my mind. And it didn't work, anyway. I saw. We moved closer to the window, and as he unscrewed the lid and took a sip of the soup, my eyes adjusted to the moonlight enough for me not to miss the change.

"I need to tell you something," I said. "I broke my promise."

He lowered the thermos, and the change happened. Concern creased his brow. Worry emerged in his eyes.

Sick butterflies sprung awake in my belly, infecting me with unease. In one messy info dump, I told him what I'd done—my failed attempt to have Ace search the area, lying to Mom, finding Hans, what he'd said, how he'd died, the chase, Old Whipper, Nancy, all of it.

When I finished, he closed his eyes, began massaging his forehead with his index finger and thumb and whispering in German—curse words, I'm pretty sure. When he stopped, he made eye contact with me. "Why? Why did you do it? Did you not hear me? Did you not care?" His foreign accent had thickened with frustration. "I said I didn't want anyone getting hurt because of me. You promised." He shook his head, seemingly disappointed with himself as much as me, and whispered a harsh German word. "I shouldn't have told you about Hans. Or shown you what I can do."

"Please don't get mad," I said, my eyes welling up for the umpteenth time that day. "I can't take someone else telling me how wrong I was right now. I feel horrible about what happened to Nancy. I love her like a sister and would kill anyone who wanted to hurt her. And like I told my mom, I would take her pain away in a heartbeat if I could." I inhaled a shaky breath and wiped the tears from my eyes before they could fall. "I did it because in my heart I believed it was the right thing to do, okay? My gut told me it was worth the risk. I didn't want Hans to be able to hurt you or anyone else ever again."

He sighed. "I'm sorry." The frustration was gone from his voice. "I'm not mad, I promise. I know you were trying to help. I'm just…just…" He lightly shook his head. "Where is Nancy?"

The question caught me off guard. "*What?*"

"You said she was at home. Where is her home? Is it close?"

"A few blocks away. What do…" It suddenly dawned on me what he wanted to do.

He lifted his free hand and the one holding the thermos up by his head. "I can take her pain away right now. In a heartbeat, like you said—if you take me to her, and we have something else alive to bridge with."

I'm not going to lie and say the thought hadn't crossed my mind while I'd lain in my room waiting for Mom to go to sleep, a wisp of a hope, but it didn't seem possible. "There's going to be people watching the streets all night, and even if we get over there without being seen, I don't know if we'll be able to get in the house. Everyone's locking their windows and doors now. And what if Benny and her parents are awake? Or in her room? Her dad has a lot of guns, and I'm sure after what happened today, he's keeping one handy."

"I don't know if we'll be able to do it, or what might happen, but I want to try. I feel like we have to." Before I could agree, he placed his free hand on his abdomen and added, "My gut says it's worth the risk."

His words killed what remained of the sick butterflies in my stomach and brought a warm smile to my face. To me, his words spoke to more than just his desire to help Nancy. They spoke to his trust in me. They spoke to similarity, understanding, unity, an alliance. "Let's go," I said, and led him downstairs and into the starry, full moon night.

The Garrison's home was three blocks north on Temple Street, the second house on the left if you turned west off of Main, which, of course, we didn't. Streetlights lit Main from the north tip of Sunray to the south, and Ozmer from east to west. Most of the other downtown streets and neighborhoods were lit, too, but many of the residential streets on the outskirts wouldn't be lit until years later when more development warranted the spending. Temple Street was lit, but the two streets between my house and it were not, giving us a fairly secluded pathway to the house as long as we stayed away from Main Street.

We moved cautiously, using only hand gestures for communication, and kept as far away from houses as possible. That far south, they were scattered, so it wasn't a chore. We hid in the darkest available shadows and scanned for watch group members, paranoid eyes in windows, and passing cars before darting across each road. Other than one car that pulled into a driveway a good distance away from us, the two lit windows on the backside of the Gunther's home (the one upstairs cracked open with upbeat swing music trickling out), and a couple of barking dogs, we didn't encounter any signs of life.

In the Garrison's backyard, we crouched beneath the redbud that stood in the center of the yard like a beach umbrella and surveyed the house. It was a small, one-story, three-bedroom brick home with a big front porch but no garage. A streetlight lit the front yard and driveway. There were neighboring houses on either side and one across the street, but each lot was an acre in size. The distance plus the sheds, hedges, fences, and trees, and the dilapidated shacks some of homeowners had allowed to be built on their land in exchange for cash, provided adequate isolation for our purpose. All the visible windows on the Garrison's home were dark. I pointed to the one on the far-right corner of the house.

"That's her window," I whispered. "Benny's is the one directly to the left, closest to the porch."

"Is her bed near the window?" Karl asked.

"Unless they've moved it, which I doubt, it's in the corner of the room, and the room is pretty small. If you stick your hand through the window and reach right, you'd be able to touch anyone on it." I scanned the area beneath the window, imagined Karl reaching inside, touching Nancy. "There's nothing close enough for you to bridge to." I shot him a sidelong glance. "Can you use something that's not in the ground?"

He nodded. "As long as it's still alive."

I gestured at the mess of wild, bushy sunflowers to our left, growing three-feet high, half-dollar flowers abound. They were growing on either side of the Garrison's padlocked shed, which held all of Pete's plumbing supplies and the tools he didn't keep in his truck. "Will those sunflowers work?" I asked.

He looked that way and whispered, "If I use enough." His eyes narrowed as they skipped across the sunflowers, calculating. "They look strong…thick stalks and bright flowers with a lot seeds…so…yes…I think if we get six or seven of the big ones…yeah." He looked at me. "Seven or eight should work."

"Then let's get ten," I whispered, eliciting a smile from him. "Five each. You go right, and I'll go left."

"Get as much of the root as you can," he whispered. "And try to not to damage the leaves or flowers. They'll start to slowly lose energy as soon as they're pulled up. And if they're hurt, they'll be weaker."

I nodded, and after taking a quick appraisal of the Garrison's house and surrounding area, we hurried to the shed. Sunflowers, particularly the wild types, have shallow root systems, and combined with the rain-softened soil, that made uprooting the plants with minimal damage quick and easy.

We met back under the redbud in the center of the backyard. I tossed my loot at the base of the trunk. "I got eight."

He laid his on top of mine. "Nine."

Our attention moved to the house, and I whispered, "I'll go see if her window is unlocked."

As expected, it wouldn't budge, so I hurried back to Karl. "Okay," I whispered. "Plan B." Plotting, I looked at Benny's window, and Karl followed my gaze. "I'm going to knock on Benny's window. Hopefully, he's awake. If not, his bed is close to the window and maybe I can wake him without scaring him." I met eyes with Karl. "If he opens the window, I'll apologize and ask if I can please see Nancy. I'll say I feel horrible and want to tell her I'm sorry, which is one hundred percent true, so convincing him won't be hard. Then, if I get in her room, I'll find a way to unlock the window. I'm not sure how, but I will." My attention moved to Nancy's window, to the shed. "You'll be hiding behind the shed so Benny won't be able to see you, but you have to keep your eyes on her window. If I get in, and if you see my hand flutter the curtains, you know it's unlocked. Count to ten…no, twenty, just to be sure…then hurry over to the window with the sunflowers, do…your…you know…close the window, and meet me back behind the shed." I looked at Karl. "What do you think?"

His brow rose, a quirky grin ghosting his lips. "Did you think of that just now?"

"Not all of it," I whispered, smiling. "I've been thinking about it since we left. You think it'll work?"

"It will if Benny opens the window and lets you in and no one catches you."

I held up my crossed fingers and Karl copied me.

"All right," I whispered. "Let's do it. You go over behind the shed, and I'll go knock." I gestured at the uprooted sunflowers. "You should probably take those so you don't have to come back over here."

Karl nodded, scooped up the bundle of plants, gave me a firm nod, and took off. As he looped around the shed, I made my way to Benny's window and ducked. Once he was out of sight, I stood, tapped lightly on the glass, and whispered, "Benny. It's, Alice."

He peeked out of the side of his curtains almost instantly. His bushy black hair was bedraggled, expression blank, but his canted eyes were alert. We locked eyes, and when I held up my hand, he disappeared. Anxiety immediately wormed into my thoughts. *He blames me. He hates me. Nancy hates me. They all hate me. He ran to get his parents. They'll never talk to me—*

His hand parted the curtains and flicked the lock. Then the window slid up about a foot—enough for his head to fit in. The curtains flanked his face. He looked happy to see me, not angry in the slightest. "Sorry," he whispered, unintentionally calming my nerves. "I shut my door. I think my dad's still awake. What are you doing here?" He scanned the yard behind me. "Did you sneak out?"

I nodded. "I couldn't sleep. I had to come apologize. I'm so sorry for what happened. To you, your mom, Nancy, Old Whipper…I didn't mean for…" Emotion overcame me, and I paused to swallow it down.

"It's okay," he whispered. "I know it wasn't your fault."

"Do your parents blame me?"

Trepidation touched his eyes. "I don't know. Sort of, I guess. They said what you did was stupid and reckless, and you're lucky no one was killed, but then later they said you're brave for jumping on the car door like you did to try and stop him, and that you're the best type of friend to have. I don't think they'll hold it against you. I just think right now they're upset about Nancy." He glanced over his shoulder at his door.

I understood. When he looked back at me, I nodded. "Do you think she'll be all right?"

"Dr. Mobley said she would. It'll just take a while."

"Do you think she'll hate me?"

He chuckled as though I'd told him a lighthearted joke. "No way. You know how much she loves Wonder Woman and is always comparing you to her. She's going to think what you did was straight out of one of her comics." A knowing smile formed on his face. "You know how much she likes to draw. Give her a month in bed and I bet she'll have a full comic of her own called *Alice the Amazing* ready to go."

I simpered at the thought but hoped a month of healing wouldn't be necessary. All Karl needed was a minute, seconds even. "Do you think you could sneak me in and I can see her?"

His head tottered in indecision. "I don't know. She's not awake. The drugs knocked her out." He glanced over his shoulder at his door again. "And Mom's asleep, but Dad might—"

"Please. Just for a few seconds. Just long enough to hold her hand and let her know I love her and I'm sorry. I'll be super quiet." He glanced again. "Like Wonder Woman," I added with a light smile.

"Hold on," he whispered, and left, the thin curtains wafting in his wake.

Turning toward the shed, I saw the silhouette of Karl's head and gave him a thumb's up. He did the same, and I moved my attention back to the window. Benny returned a second or two later, leaving his bedroom door open behind him, a good sign.

"My dad's nodding on and off but not fully asleep," he whispered. "He's sitting in the rocking chair in front of the window with his rifle on his lap. The lamp and radio are on, and their door is half-shut, but you know how close their room is to Nancy's, so we'll have to be careful."

I nodded, he raised his window another twelve inches, and I climbed in.

With Benny in the lead, we tiptoed down the hall to Nancy's room, the sound of KGNT reporter Opal Felton's southern drawl growing louder as we went. Nancy's door was wide open, her room dark save for the moonlight seeping through the veil of a curtain covering her window. Mr. and Mrs. Garrison's bedroom was directly across the hall, and orange light from their lamp cut across the gap between the doors, reaching a few feet into hers. Keeping his eyes on his parent's room, Benny stopped in front of her door and motioned me inside.

I made my way to Nancy's window and faced the bed. She was lying on her back, arms by her side, sheet pulled up to her chin. Her chest moved steadily up and down in step with the soft hiss coming from her open mouth. I couldn't see much, but I could see that her nose had swollen to three times its normal dainty size, and the nostrils were packed with gauze. Her silky black hair was splayed out around her head on the pillow like bird wings. Her eyes were closed, but obviously swollen as well. The lids appeared on the verge of popping. I wanted to touch her, caress her face, but knew better. I settled on touching her shoulder. "I'm sorry," I whispered, and leaned down by her ear. "You'll feel better soon."

Benny looked my way, his eyes screaming hurry, and motioned for me to get out. When his eyes moved back to his parents' room, I slid my hand behind the curtain, unlocked the window, and made sure to jostle the curtain as I slid my hand back out. I was stealing one last glimpse at Nancy when I heard fat footsteps coming from across the hall. Benny's head jerked my way, and he waved his hand up and down, telling me to get down. I dove onto the wooden floor and rolled under Nancy's bed. Holding my breath, I started silently counting. I'd told Karl to count to twenty before opening the window.

One Mississippi.

The lamplight grew as Pete opened his bedroom door and stepped into the hall, rifle in one hand, empty glass the other. "What are you doing out here?"

Two Mississippi.

"I was having trouble sleeping," Benny said. "So I came to check on Nancy."

"How is she?"

"Sleeping like a baby."

Pete touched Benny's shoulder. "Don't worry. She's going to be all right, son."

Six Mississippi.

"Okay," Benny said, and gestured at the empty glass. "Do you want me to get you some more?"

No, Benny! Nine Mississippi.

"No. I'm good." Pete handed the glass to Benny. "Just put it in the kitchen for me, then I want you to go to bed. You need to get some rest. You're going to be responsible for Nancy's chores starting tomorrow."

"Yes, sir."

Thirteen Mississippi.

As Benny walked out of sight, Pete walked over to Nancy's bed side, looked down at his daughter, and adjusted her sheet.

Sixteen Mississippi.

Seventeen Mississippi.

Pete yawned, then made his way back to his bedroom.

Nineteen Mississippi.

He pushed his door half-closed, lessening the lamplight and muffling Opal Felton's voice, and I rolled out from under the bed. I paused in the doorway when the window slid open and Karl's hand poked out from behind the curtain. His fingertips danced around the pillow for a second before landing on Nancy's cheek. I wanted to stay and watch. I wanted to know if I'd be able to see it happen. Would her body lift off the mattress? Would there be a glow? A spark? Anything? But I couldn't take the risk. Besides, movement teased the corner of my eye and I snapped my head and saw Benny standing in front of his bedroom door, frantically waving me to him.

I followed him into his room, and he shut the door.

"That was close," he whispered. "Do you feel better?"

"I do, thank you." I gave him a hug, told him I'd come by tomorrow to see Nancy again and apologize to his parents, then climbed out his window.

I noticed a pile of ashes beneath Nancy's window on my way to the shed. Karl was waiting, smiling like a little kid. He nodded when we met eyes, and I smiled. He held up his ash-grayed hand and I high-fived him, coloring my hand gray as well.

We took the same path home that we'd taken to get there, and although we moved quickly and cautiously, we moved with confidence rather than anxiety. With a sense of victory. Smiling so big and wide that if our teeth had been neon, we would've lit up the town. I felt twenty pounds lighter, like an invisible cross had been lifted off my shoulders. My world was as right as cake and pie, as Ace liked to say.

15

In the storage room above the garage, we propped open the door and raised the window to flush out the warm air, cleared the boxes off of Nana Mayes's old couch, and sat down. The full moon stared down at us through the open window, casting a bright, elongated rectangle of light on half of each of our bodies.

Karl had Dad's thermos between his thighs, and I had the flashlight I'd left behind in my lap. I told him what had happened inside the Garrison's house with Pete, and we marveled at the close call. That led to a conversation about the Garrisons in general—their moving to Sunray from the Houston area when the twins were seven, Pete's start-up plumbing business, Jasmine's nationality, the prejudice after Pearl Harbor, funny stories about the stupid stuff Benny, Nancy, Robert, and I had done around town. When the steam ran out on that topic, a calm silence filled the air.

"Thank you for what you did for Nancy," I said, fiddling with the flashlight as he chugged chicken soup.

"My pleasure." He tipped the thermos back, tapped the bottom to knock the last dregs into his mouth.

"I'm sorry for being so prejudiced in the garden that first day, too." I looked at Karl as he lowered the thermos, hoping he registered the awakening and remorse in my eyes. "I treated you the same way people around here treated the Garrisons. I hated those people for doing that, but I did the same to you. I should've given you a chance to explain yourself before I tried to kill you."

His eyes read mine, and he patted my thigh. "Don't worry. I know how hard it is to separate the good ones from the bad ones sometimes." He twisted a swastika tattoo my way. "Especially if they remind you of people who destroyed your life."

We held eye contact for a moment, an understanding passing between us. I wasn't wise by any means, but I knew he wasn't just talking about me. He was talking about himself, his life in Europe, people he'd crossed paths with I'd never know about. When he looked toward the window, I followed suit, and we sat with our own thoughts for a while.

I eventually broke the silence. "When did you first know? You know, that you were a bridge?"

I pulled my legs up into crisscross-apple-sauce position on the couch and waited for him to look my way. When he did, a pleasant smile of recollection formed on his face.

"I personally don't remember the first time, but I heard Mama tell the story enough times to have a memory nonetheless. She said I was about eighteen months old. I was crawling around in the backyard garden, and she was watering plants nearby. She said she turned around to check on me and saw me sitting on my bottom with my hands at my sides, grasping the grass. She said my eyes rolled up in my head and she thought I was having a seizure or something. As she ran toward me, she said the grass in my right hand wilted to ash, and the grass in my left doubled in height and thickness. By the time she scooped me up, I was more than alert and giggling uncontrollably."

Smiling in awe, I asked, "Did it start happening a lot after that?"

"No. Mama said it happened a couple more times over the next few years, but it didn't start happening a lot until I was six or seven and started learning how to control it. I think that first time I flipped the switch—or lowered the bridge as Mama came to say—it was a reflex. Maybe the ability awakening inside me. I don't know."

"And neither of your parents could do it?"

He shook his head.

I realized I'd never asked: "Do you have any brothers or sisters?"

He shook his head again. "Mama and Papa had tried to have kids for almost twenty years before I came along. Mama lost five and almost died a couple of times. Even before we learned what I could do, she called me her miracle child." He chuckled at the irony, and I did, too. "Afterward, when I got older, she always winked at me when she said it around people who didn't know what I could do, who was everyone except Papa and a couple of their close friends. The rumors didn't start spreading about me until I was twelve, after I healed a few people who'd been injured when a church collapsed during a storm. I had learned to control the switch by then." He looked upward wistfully, as if traveling back in time, overseas, back home. "The church was down the street from our house, and some of our neighbors had gone inside when the wind picked up. When the roof fell in, we heard the crash from our living room. Once the storm quieted, we ran down the street and Mama and Papa dragged the injured ones into the forest so I could help them." He shook his head, looked at me, and shrugged. "I guess some other people saw. After that, the rumors started, and secret requests started coming in."

"How'd you learn to control it? Was it hard?"

"Practice. Mama and Papa helped me practice. Once I started realizing what I could do and Mama caught me experimenting on my own, she started taking me out into the garden every morning after Papa left for work and we'd practice. I don't know exactly when she figured out what I was actually doing, but at some point she realized I was somehow passing energy from one living thing to another. She'd have me put my hands on two plants in the garden, close my eyes, and try to do it. It didn't take long for me to learn how to consciously raise and lower the bridge." He glanced down at his hands as though they weren't his, twisted them in the blue moonlight. "That part was easy. The hard part was learning how to control the direction and speed of the flow. It took years to learn how to only pull and push as much as I wanted, and in the direction I wanted. In the beginning, it was all or nothing. I killed hundreds of plants, and only after I mastered that, and after Papa insisted Mama let me try, we moved onto insects. Then small animals. Then, one day after Mama burned herself while cooking potatoes, she held out her hand, pointed at the ivy on the table, and I healed the burn. She was the first human I helped."

"She sounds like a great mom," I said. "I think a lot of parents wouldn't have known how to handle a kid…well…like you."

He smiled a pure smile. "She is. She—Anna… Did I tell you her name is Anna?"

I nodded. "You did."

"She's the smartest, most selfless person I know. She believes we're all put on Earth for a specific purpose, and she has always told me that ever since that first instance with the grass in the garden, she's known her purpose was to make sure I understood mine." He chuckled to himself. "The only selfish act I remember her indulging in was when she made me enhance the stargazer lilies in her garden to twice their normal size when they bloomed every summer. Stargazers were her favorite, but they were also our neighbor's favorite. Mama and Frau Geiger had an unspoken competition each year over whose were the best, and every year Mama lost until I learned how to properly bridge."

I laughed. "I hope I get to meet her someday."

"Me too," he said. "I think you two would get along. She's a lot like you. She's tough. Resilient. Thinks for herself, does what she thinks is right. When she sees a problem, she does everything she can to fix it. When she believes something—like, for instance, how my ability makes me unique but not better than anyone else with a good heart—she preaches it from the mountain tops. When she sees someone in need, she's there for them no matter what." He shook his head in disbelief. "You wouldn't believe the things she's orchestrated. The hope she's given."

As was the case every time (though few) I was with Karl, questions bombarded my mind. I had a thousand queued up, locked and loaded missiles ready to direct his way, some about his mom and some not. But I held back. I could tell he was enjoying talking about his mom, traveling back in time to when they were together, and I didn't want to interfere with that.

"After Papa died," he continued, "she grieved, but never in front of me. Sometimes I'd hear her crying and whispering to Papa at night when she thought I was asleep. But she never allowed his death to slow her down. She was determined not only for us to stay free and survive, but also to continue helping others do the same. Like we'd been doing when we lived in Salzberg, remember? Helping the unfortunates?"

I nodded. "I remember."

"During the first year, as we moved from village to village, traveling under blankets in the backs of cars and trucks and wagons, hiding in homes of those in the Austrian Resistance, sleeping in basements and behind trash bins, Mama found ways to sneak into the villages and make money. She never told me exactly what she did, and I'm not sure I want to know. She did what she had to, plain and simple. Eventually, she had enough to buy an old truck, and we took off on our own. That's when we changed our last name from Hoppler to Wagner. Hoppler had been my Papa's last name, and the name the Nazis knew us by. Papa had come from a line of German grape growers and wine makers, and at one time a heppe was the name of the tool used for harvesting grapes, a hoppler one who used it. Mama chose Wagner because in German it means 'delivers with wagon,' and that's what we called our truck—*Der Wagen*.

"For the next few years, we traveled up and down the Traun River, from where it hits the Danube in Linz all the way to the southern border. There were pockets of farmers up and down the eastern side of the river who were secretly a part of the resistance. Mom befriended the ones she found trustworthy, which were few, and we—well, I—began helping them double their crop output. Using my ability, it only took minutes for their plants to produce the same amount of cabbage, beets, potatoes, or whatever that it normally took months to make. I healed people when I could and when needed, but our main purpose became delivering food to families harboring unfortunates. We'd load up the back of *der wagen* as full as we could on the farms, then, posing as merchants, we'd travel to the small rural areas near the Traun. We sold some of the food to Nazi supporters to maintain our cover, but most of our food (and the money we made off of Nazi supporters) went to people in the resistance.

"After a while, the people in the villages began to anticipate our arrival every couple of months. We were the wagon merchants with the sweetest apples, largest tomatoes, crispest greens. Our produce was twice as fresh and twice the size as others." Karl paused and took a deep breath. The onslaught of reflection had filled his eyes with tears. Happy and sad ones both, I figured. "Yes, Anna Hoppler Wagner," he said. "She's one of the good ones." He patted my thigh, flashed me a weak smile. "Like you."

Right then and there I knew I had to try to help him get home. He spoke about his mom in the present tense, with love and reverence. He had hope she was still alive, that he'd see and hug and smell her again. He had the hope I no longer had when it came to my dad. Hope I would've given anything to get back. I knew Little Alice Mayes in Podunk Sunray, Texas could never escort him all the way to Europe, but I had to try something. I wanted to keep his hope alive. I wanted to help give him the chance I'd lost—the chance to see his mom again.

"Thanks," I said. "But I can't hold a candle to her. Everything she's gone through and done. How strong she is." I looked at the moon, back at Karl. "I want to help you get back to her somehow. I think if you hide up here for a few weeks, until everyone assumes you're no longer in town, I can keep bringing you food and we can come up with a way to—"

I stopped when he shook his head. His eyes spoke to gratitude despite the objection. "I can't stay that long. There's no way. I'd go crazy hiding up here, safe, day after day after day, wondering where she is, imagining what's happening to her, regretting that I am not doing anything to help. No, I have to find a way out of here as soon as possible. I have to try to get home someway." His eyes searched mine for a moment. "And please don't think I'm putting this on you. You've already helped me so much, done more than I could've hoped for. It's just the longer it takes me to get home... I'd never forgive myself if I found out I could've done more. You understand?"

"I do," I said, and he gazed longingly out the window.

Seconds stretched to minutes. Quick looks passed between us but no words. I fiddled with the flashlight in my lap, feeling sorry for him. I wanted to assure him that his mom would be okay, that I'd do everything I could to help him see her again, but I knew the silence was his to break.

When he finally did, he asked, "Do you think Nancy felt what happened while she was sleeping?"

The question lightened my heart. "Absolutely," I said, embracing the change of topic. "She might not be able to explain it or fully recall it, but I think part of her will always know something special happened. Do you?"

He nodded. "I hope so."

I thought about how his mom had said he giggled uncontrollably after the grass incident when he was a toddler. "How does it feel for you when you do it?"

"Probably close to what it felt like when I healed you. Some people have told me how it felt to them, and my experiences are similar. The physical feeling has lessened over time, but it still comes. I've just gotten used to it." He fluffed the hairs on one of his forearms. "My skin still tingles, but my hairs don't stand anymore." He touched his stomach. "My gut still shakes, too, but I no longer have to smile or laugh if I don't want to. And I don't lose control of my bladder like when I was a kid, either." We both chuckled, and he twirled his finger in front of his eyes. "The bright light that used to blind me is dimmer now, too. But..." His eyes widened, and he tapped his chest. "The happiness in my chest has grown as the physical sensations have faded. You know...the sense of fulfillment."

I nodded in understanding. "I know it may be a dumb question, and I'm sure you've been asked it a million times, but can you heal yourself?"

He shook his head. "I'm just the bridge."

"Between God's hands," I added, remembering what he'd told me that night in our garden: *A bridge between God's hands is what Mama always says.* "BZGH."

"Right." He wiggled his fingers. "BZGH."

The conversation shifted to simpler, surface topics after that. I asked him if he'd had any girlfriends, and he told me about a few girls he'd "gotten close to" when on the run with his mama, and the first girl he'd kissed while living in Salzberg when he was ten. Katrina was her name. She had blonde hair and her lips tasted like celery. He asked me more about my relationship with Robert, and I told him stories about the entire Lewis family, who had moved to Sunray from Paola, Kansas twelve years earlier. We talked about clothes and favorite foods, hairstyles and dancing (he even forced me to my feet and tried to teach me his favorite German dance). We teased each other, laughed at stupid things, and recalled pointless events we otherwise might've forgotten. Like when I'd snuck a garter snake into church and it had escaped during Pastor Lewis's sermon, and when Karl had tasted sheep poop on a dare from a friend.

After a couple of hours, I told him I needed to go inside. Mom always woke before dawn, and I needed to be in my bed when she passed by my room and glanced inside to check on me, and have the tape back in place on top of the door if she came outside to check. We agreed to meet in the storage room again the following night to discuss ideas on how to get him on his way as soon as possible. I told him if I had the chance, I'd bring him some food and water during the day, too.

Downstairs, I put the flashlight back on the workbench and reattached the tape on the door before hurrying to the house.

The clock in the kitchen read four-fifteen when I snuck through the back door, barefooted after leaving my Keds on the back porch. I returned the thermos to Dad's lunchbox, crept upstairs, peeked into Mom's room and found her snoring, then went to my room and fell fast asleep with my clothes on.

PRESENT

3

As Alice had aged, particularly after having the bursa sac in her left hip removed at eighty-one, which also required a bone grinding procedure on the joint after an infection, she'd placed wooden chairs at random spots throughout the garden. Elderly rest stops, she jokingly called them. Places for her (and later Emily and others) to escape the sun for a minute, rest, cool down, hydrate, eat a snack or sandwich if needed. The oak chairs had been handcrafted by Sunray born and bred S.D. Junior, the grandson of Sam DeShields—the man whose wood pile Alice had taken the length of oak from when she went searching for Hans. Alice had purchased the chairs from S.D. with the knowledge of that afternoon in mind. For her, secretly linking the past and present, tying generations together, strengthening the invisible small-town web that connected them all, added to the richness of the garden and gave her satisfaction little else could.

The chairs were simple and unpainted, most undiscernible from aged bark. They were hard to notice unless you were looking for them.

Because of Alice's continuous need to pause while speaking, and Emily's desire to be fully engulfed in the tale and visualize as she listened, they had stopped and sat in two of the chairs beneath a peach tree. The tree stood in the center of what they called Avocado Circle and cast a westward shadow due to the rising sun. They'd moved the chairs out into a fat section of shade, angled toward each other. Wildflowers carpeted the ground around their feet, the flowery scent enhancing as the morning air warmed.

Alice had planted the peach tree—along with twenty others in random spots throughout the garden—in '74, a year after she'd planted the ring of fourteen avocado trees that made up Avocado Circle. Avocado trees are supposedly impossible to grow in the Texas Panhandle, and she'd lost two early on, but after creating a north wind barrier—a C-shaped crop of juniper trees wedged tightly together—and then fully encircling it and Avocado Circle with more English hedges that were now ten feet high or more, the trees took to the soil and grew fast like most things in the garden did. They weren't spaced in an exact circle shape, only roughly so. The secluded area was one of Alice's favorite resting spots. She had slipped off her shoes and socks and had planted her bare feet in the mess of wildflowers. Had she been able, she would've lain down with her hands behind her head, shirt knotted and pant legs rolled up, fully immersed in the vegetation. That's what she used to do when she needed a break—in a different lifetime, it seemed.

Emily had taken off her backpack and hooked it around the back of her chair. The shovel handle rested against the pack. She sat cross-legged, eyes on Alice, and looked like she was about to burst with curiosity. "Wait...so, is Nancy Garrison the same Nancy I met about seven or eight years ago? The lady you introduced me and Juan to when we were harvesting pears? You said she was one of your oldest friends."

Alice smiled. "Yep." She loved seeing the sparkle in Emily's grass-green eyes when the dots connected. "She was in the panhandle, well, just passing through for business actually, and wanted to come see me and the garden in person again. That was the first time she'd visited since she'd come back for her mom's funeral nearly twenty years earlier."

"Why so long?"

"After high school, she and Benny both moved up northeast to attend the University of Virginia. She got a job in marketing up there after that, got married, bought a house, had three kids, the whole nine yards. We wrote letters over the years and exchanged pictures, but with her husband's family and most of her business dealings anchored up there, she had little time to visit. When you met her, she was on a cross-country trip, on her way to spend a week in California with one of her daughters and her grandkids. Her flight from Charlottesville to Sacramento had an unusually long eight-hour layover in Mercy, so she decided to drive down. That was a good day. It was the last time I saw her."

"Is she…"

Alice nodded. "Her heart gave out when you were living in Denton. Her oldest son called and invited me up for the funeral service, but I didn't see the need. She was already gone. My presence up east wouldn't have given me any more of a connection with her than I have here at home."

"Sorry," Emily offered.

"It's okay," Alice said. "She lived a good life. The life she wanted. She was loved and fulfilled and had no regrets when she moved on. That's the best any one of us can hope for."

"What about Benny? What happened to him?"

"Benny. He stayed up on the east coast, too. I exchanged occasional letters with him, but not near as many as I did with Nancy. Much to his dad's pleasure, he cofounded the Leak Finders plumbing chain. He died from prostate cancer when he was fifty, leaving behind his wife of twenty years, Clara. They never had any kids. They always said their dogs were their kids; they bred and trained Saint Bernards on a competitive level."

"The house," Emily said, "the second on the left off of Main where the Garrisons lived… I know that house. I think it's vacant now, but I remember trick-or-treating there when I was a kid because the lady who lived there had a fetish for lawn gnomes. There were about a hundred in the front yard, and they freaked me out. I always thought they were staring at me."

"That would've been Mrs. Burton," Alice said with a humorous sigh. "She loved those gnomes almost more than the kids she gave piano lessons to."

Emily snapped her fingers. "Mrs. Burton. Yeah. That was her name." Grinning with new knowledge, she shook her head. "I can't believe that's where Karl healed Nancy. That's so cool."

Alice beamed inside. She loved this part. The uncontainable intrigue on Emily's face was another sure sign Alice was making the right choice. As Emily absorbed the truth, Alice could practically see the gears churning in her young friend's head, processing the details, awakening to the idea that it's not the size or grandeur of a city that makes it big or exciting. It's the secret history, the protected stories, the private memories passed down only once every blue moon. Emily's vision of boring-as-fuck tiny Sunray was expanding right before Alice's eyes, morphing from black-and-white into color. Invisible additions were being constructed, short roads being stretched. Buildings like Merriman Hall (recently restored and now Sunray's official DMV) and the storage room above Alice's garage (now Emily's apartment), places like town square and the lucky bend in Regreso Creek where they'd fished hundreds of times, Main Street and Temple Street, were all changing without changing, growing without growing.

"Did you ever tell Nancy what really happened?" Emily asked. "I know you couldn't tell her about Karl then, but did she ever know?"

Alice shook her head. "That wasn't my place. I like to think she knows now, though. Assuming you get to learn the full truth of things when you meet your maker." Alice glanced down and smirked. "I can imagine the shocked look on her face when she was told, or got to see, or whatever. I wish I could've been there. I bet she would've socked me in the arm the way I did people all the time back then."

"How did everyone explain how she healed overnight when she had such bad wounds?"

"There were two separate camps on that. One believed the power of prayer had healed her. That God had performed a miracle to prove He was on the side of the American faithful and would always have their back against the Nazis. The other camp thought Dr. Mobley, who was known to mix liquor with his morning coffee, had been a little tipsy and misdiagnosed the extent of her injuries. People who claimed to have seen the x-rays said they were blurry at best. Others said they could smell the alcohol on him from a mile away."

Alice paused to clean her bifocals with her shirt bottom before going on. "Most people, including Nancy's family and my mom, were firmly rooted in the miracle camp. They believed their prayers had been answered, that God had definitely healed her. They didn't fully dismiss the idea that Dr. Mobley could've *maybe, accidentally* misrepresented the extent of her injuries. But they said even if he had, it was only by a smidge. They insisted he was too experienced and wise to have been that far off with a little drink in him or not. Besides, they said he was a lifelong Christian, and God was strong with him. So any mistakes he'd made were by God's design, anyway."

"The devout don't change much, do they?" Emily remarked with a weak headshake.

Seeing the question as more of a nod to Emily's personal experiences with the evangelical Bible-thumpers she'd crossed paths with than an actual question, Alice didn't bother answering.

"What did Nancy say when she learned about how you found Hans?" Emily tapped Alice's knee. "Did she compare you to Wonder Woman like Benny thought she would?"

Alice smiled. "She did. She never stopped actually. When I went to Virginia for her wedding and met her husband, and later when I met her kids, she introduced me as her friend Alice, you know, the one I told you about, the one who chased down that Nazi like Wonder Woman back in Texas." Alice chuckled softly to herself. "Her youngest daughter Leila told me I didn't look like Wonder Woman at all. She was six and had recently discovered Nancy's old Wonder Woman comics. 'Where's your star headband?' she asked me. 'Where's your red boots? If you're really her, show me the Lasso of Truth.' Nancy told her I'd left all of that at home."

Emily shot Alice an ornery smile. "Will you show *me*?" She pressed her palms together as if in prayer. "Please? I won't tell a soul."

"If I did, I'd have to kill you," Alice said, deadpan, and Emily laughed.

Alice glanced up at the peach tree when a bird tweeted overhead. The bird was bright blue, plump, sounding out from a nest on a sturdy branch. Her focus shifted to an obscure knot on the tree trunk she'd known for decades, the petals of a yellow wildflower she'd just met, farther out, past the avocado trees, to the small section of land seeded with bluebonnets. These small pleasures, the art and sounds of the country, were what she'd miss most about the garden. She really was her dad's daughter.

"Becca called me Wonder Woman once," Emily said, pulling Alice's attention back to her. "Remember when I was in the eighth grade and I beat up Eric Little outside of the Morley because he was bullying Juan and Becca for holding hands? Calling Juan a wetback and Becca a wetback lover?"

"I remember," Alice said. "Eric was like ten years older than you guys and had been out drinking with his buddies that night. He shoved Becca and spit on Juan when they told him to get out of their face, so you coldcocked him, right?"

"Broke his nose and blackened both of his eyes with one shot," Emily happily admitted. "He didn't sound right for months." She batted her eyes demurely. "I might've kicked him in the stomach a couple of times when he was on the ground, too."

"I think you're the one who needs to show me the Lasso of Truth?" Alice mimicked Emily's earlier prayer hands. "Please? Placate this old woman, won't you?"

Emily swiped at the air in front of Alice's hands. "I can't hold a candle to your Wonder Woman. Becca called me that once and once only. Besides, you can't be Wonder Woman without a Superman, and I've never had a Superman like you."

"*Superman?*"

"Karl," Emily said. "He's your Superman."

Emily proceeded to do what would come naturally to most people her age after learning Karl Hoppler Wagner (BZGH) existed. She was a young twenty-year-old struggling to find herself and come to peace with the size and complexity of the adult world, and having an ear handy, she gushed on and on, relating, making comparisons, reveling in marveled belief.

Alice patiently listened as Emily repeated the Hans incident and all things Karl, mostly in sentences beginning with "I can't believe you…" and "It's crazy that he…," making connections to her new truth as she went ("That's just like so and so…" and "He reminds me of…") Fact or fiction connections, it didn't matter. Believing Alice, believing in Karl, destroyed the barrier between those two worlds. Emily connected Alice not only to Wonder Woman, but also to Joan of Arc, Katniss in *Hunger Games*, her favorite politician Alexandria Ocasio Cortez, Idgie in "that green tomatoes movie" they'd watched on Netflix together. She connected Karl's mom to Linda Hamilton in *Terminator*—a mother willing to sacrifice everything to make sure her special son fulfilled his destiny—and Karl's whimsical, selfless father to Alice's. She connected Karl not only to Superman, but also to Jesus of Nazareth, "John, the big black guy," in *The Green Mile*, and her own adoptive grandad, Phillip Newel, a Dallas firefighter who'd saved anywhere from forty to fifty lives according to his colleagues and extended family but never once mentioned doing so.

When she finished reflecting, she wanted to know more. "What happened the next day? Did you come up with a plan to help him get back to his mom?"

Alice sighed sharply, her eyes surveying the greenery around the chairs. She knew it was only going to get harder from here, but she couldn't stop. Not now. The truth was the truth. The peach-tree shadow had shifted. Emily would soon be exposed to the sunlight. "Let's move the chairs so we stay out of the sun and have a sip of water, then I'll tell you."

PAST

16

Mom shook me awake the next morning. "Alice. Get up. It's late."

By the time my eyes focused and my consciousness reconnected with reality, she had walked to the doorway and was watching me with tired, impatient eyes. She was wearing one of her church dresses and her typical touch of going-out makeup. Bright mid-morning sunshine angled through my window.

"What time is it?" I asked.

"Almost nine o'clock."

I pushed loose hairs off my face, palmed my eyes. "Why are you wearing that?"

"Pastor Lewis is holding a special prayer service at the church this morning. He thinks it'll be good for everyone to get together and worship and pray for Nancy and her family after what happened yesterday. He called this morning and asked me to help spread the word. It starts at nine-thirty, and we're going, so you need to hurry and get cleaned up." Her eyes took in the clothes I'd slept in as I stood and stretched. "I'd like you to wear one of your dresses, and I'd appreciate it if you didn't fight me on it. I think you owe me that much after what you put me through yesterday and the position you've put me in. A lot of people aren't happy with what you did, which means they're not happy with me, either."

"Okay," I complied, extending an olive branch.

Foolish or not, I didn't regret following my gut (especially knowing Nancy would be fine and Hans was no longer a threat to Karl or anyone else in town), but I did feel bad about the unintended consequences and wanted to make amends for the hurt and anxiety my choices had caused Mom. I could tell my lack of resistance shocked her despite the subtlety of her reaction. Only someone who knew her as well as I did would've noticed the slight twitch of her brow.

"There's a bowl of oatmeal and a leftover biscuit on the table downstairs," she said. "So get a move on."

Mom had bought me two new dresses the previous Christmas after I'd shot up two inches and outgrown my others. They were identical knee-length, A-line dresses with puffed shoulders. One was blue, the other white. I choose blue because it matched my favorite Keds, and Mom was big on matching. She'd bought hair bows to match each dress, but I'd somehow misplaced those shortly after Christmas. After I changed, I ran a brush through my hair and pinned it up in a tight ponytail with my one fancy hairclip that had belonged to Nana Mayes. The spot on my temple where Hans had hit me was sensitive to the touch but not swollen enough to be seen, unlike the scrapes on my shins. The redness and swelling around the wounds had faded some, which made the developing scabs stand out even more.

In the kitchen, Mom had left the radio tuned to KGNT's weekday classical music hour, the volume low. Having not eaten anything since the catfish fish at the creek the previous morning, I devoured the oatmeal and biscuit, then rinsed out my bowl and hurried to the outhouse to pee. I continually glanced up at the storage room window—which Karl had thankfully remembered to close—as I crossed the yard on my way back to the house, fighting the urge to run up and check on him real quick. I kicked off the summer outhouse shoes on the back porch, slipped on my Keds, headed inside and found Mom waiting by the open front door with the Chevy keys in her hand.

"Did you lock the back door?" she asked.

"Sure did," I said, and followed her to the truck.

We took Main Street north, and as we moved through the roundabout and curved onto Ozmer Street, Mom surveyed the Heart of Town Square but kept whatever opinions she had about the missing oak tree and streaks of destroyed grass where Old Whipper had skidded to herself.

There were just as many cars lining the road and people standing on the Trinity Lutheran Church lawn smoking and chatting as on any typical Sunday morning. Mom pulled into a parking spot in front of the First Baptist Church across the street, killed the engine, and looked my way. Her expression indicated she had a lecture poised on the tip of her tongue, but before she had the chance to begin, Ruth walked up to the driver's side door and greeted us through the open window. The overpowering scent of Chantilly perfume wafted into the cab with her greeting. She wore the white hat with a lacy pink ribbon mom had bought her for her birthday some years prior and had curled the tips of her shoulder-length hair upward like big fish hooks. After complimenting our attire, she asked if we wanted to walk in with her, and Mom accepted.

When we stepped into the sanctuary and eyes landed on us, the buzz of *Have you heard?* conversations briefly lulled before picking back up. All the doors and windows were open, the fans whirring, circulating the warm, perfume-rich air. Some people sat silently in the pews, watching and waiting, but most were on their feet, gathered into small chatty groups. The Gideon twins, Anne and Greta, were standing with Pastor Lewis, Mr. Fulton, Mae Keats, Sally Cole, and couple of others up by the podium. Tessa Sanders was holding court in the center aisle at the back of the room, surrounded by a rapt audience of teenagers and kids including Robert and Thomas. Hazel and the other ladies with seemingly endless supplies of fancy hats lingered in front of the first row of pews, and when Hazel saw us, she waved us over.

Mom put her hand on my back. "Let's go."

I scanned the room, and most of the people who still had their gaze on me looked away as though caught ogling a nude picture. Robert didn't, though. He smiled when we locked eyes, raised his hand in the air, and started moving toward us with Thomas on his heels. When I raised my hand, too, Mom followed my eyes and looked their way.

"Go ahead," she said. "But be quick. I want you to sit up there with Ruth and me."

"Okay," I said, and approached Robert and Thomas as they rounded the back end of the pews. Dressed in identical black slacks, shiny black shoes, and white short-sleeved button-ups, and with their hair parted on the same side, they looked like two pieces of the same nesting doll.

Robert hugged me. "How are you?"

"I'm good," I said, wishing we were sitting in his room playing cards so we could really talk. There was so much I wanted to tell him, so much I could tell he wanted to know.

Thomas pointed at my shins matter-of-factly. "Your legs don't look good."

Robert nudged his younger brother's shoulder. "Don't be rude."

A slight smile formed on my face. I didn't find Thomas's remark rude at all. In fact, I found comfort in the normalcy of his reaction. I wouldn't expect anything less than unbridled honesty from him. That's who he'd always been. His sameness made the whole situation feel a little less awkward.

"Have you talked to Benny or Mr. or Mrs. Garrison today?" I asked. "Are any of them coming?"

Robert shook his head. "Dad went over to their house early this morning to pray over Nancy and invite them to the service, but they all wanted to stay there with her."

"Was she awake?"

Robert shook his head again. "Dad said she was sound asleep, which is good according to Dr. Mobley. The more rest she gets the better."

When I glanced at Tessa, who was still holding court about fifteen feet away, Robert and Thomas glanced, too. I hadn't heard much of what she'd said, but I'd heard enough to know she was talking about me. And if people could take classes on backbiting and character bashing, Tessa would've passed with flying colors. Top of her class. "What's she been saying over there?" I asked.

Robert met eyes with me but was reluctant to answer.

"I heard her say my name a second ago."

He glanced at Tessa, looked back at me.

"Just tell me," I said. "You know I don't care what she thinks."

Thomas answered for him. "She said what you did was the stupidest thing anyone has ever done and that she always knew there was something seriously wrong with you."

Robert flared his eyes at Thomas in an apparent attempt to shut him up, but Thomas continued anyway. "She also told Robert to be careful around you because you're selfish and don't care if what you do hurts or kills anyone else."

"But I told her that wasn't true," Robert added with conviction, holding my gaze. "And that she needed to stop spreading rumors."

Thomas chuckled. "Then she called him lovesick and naïve."

Robert blushed endearingly, and by the way his eyes briefly fell to my lips, I assumed the memory of our kiss had jumped to the forefront of his mind. The last time we'd seen each other was that night in the garden. "Which is ridiculous," he blurted out.

"Of course it is," I said, turning my palms upward in a sarcastic gesture of certainty. "Everyone knows you're too dumb to be lovesick or naïve."

Grinning, he lightly tapped my shoulder with his fist the way I normally did his, and grinning back, I rubbed the area as though he'd hurt me, the way he normally did. Like with Thomas's blunt honesty, the sense of normalcy, although the roles were reversed, felt good.

I stopped rubbing and snapped my attention toward Tessa when I faintly heard *"the one with those tattoos on his forearms"* followed by a couple of girly gasps. She had her left arm extended and was running her right hand over the top of it in the same spot where Karl had tattoos. Our eyes briefly caught, and she paused for a second before continuing to talk.

"What's wrong?" Robert asked.

"Shhh," I said, cocking my head sideways, angling an ear toward Tessa to catch more of what was being said.

"...sitting in the passenger seat when we were pulling away from Fulton's right before we got here, and that's when I saw him standing in the gap between The Mug and the Go Club. I know it was him. It had to be. He was staring at me like he wanted to attack me like he did Lily."

"Now she's telling them she saw the other prisoner this morning," I told Robert.

Confusion crinkled his eyes. "What? Where?"

"She's lying," I said.

"How do you know?" he asked.

Eyeing Tessa, I ignored the question, whispered, "That's not fair."

I honestly didn't give two hoots about what she thought or said about me. She'd been spreading rumors about me since second grade, and I didn't care if she continued doing so until we were old and gray. But I couldn't let her lie about Karl. The more fear she stirred up, the harder people would search, the more revenge they'd want. He needed things to calm down.

I glanced at Mom who was talking with Hazel, Ruth, and the others, took in a deep breath and held it. *If I confront her calmly, I can do this without causing a mess*, I thought, truly believing I could. And that I should. I pushed out the breath and headed Tessa's way.

Robert reached for my arm, whispered my name and told me to wait, but I didn't look back.

Tessa quieted and all eyes fell on me as I stepped between her two best friends (and two of the biggest ass kissers) Brenda and Eleanor. The three of them were what would now be called mean girls. They dressed and talked the same, hated and liked the same. All three wore similar A-line dresses, had similar long flowy hair styles, and smelled of the same perfume—Bourjois or something French like that. It was Tessa's favorite, and very expensive, as she'd let everyone know hundreds of times.

Tessa flashed a smile when we met eyes. Though she batted her eyes sweetly and greeted me with a soft, mousy voice, her smile wasn't innocent of cruelty.

I skipped the sarcastic curtsy I normally would've given her. "You need to stop lying," I said. "You didn't see that guy this morning."

"Who do you think you are? You have no idea who I did or didn't see."

"You're just going to scare everyone by saying stuff like that, so you need to stop. That guy's probably long gone by now, anyway."

She chuckled. "You're funny. We all saw just how much you care about not scaring people yesterday. Or hurting or killing them for that matter. So I don't want to hear it. All you care about is yourself."

I let the personal attack slide off my back. "Just tell the truth. Tell everyone you didn't see him."

"I did see him," she said, surveying the small audience around us, reading their reactions. She angled her chin up with an air of superiority when her eyes came back to me. "You're just jealous because you have some kind of sick fascination with those prisoners because of your dad and can't stand that I saw him and you didn't. It's not my fault you didn't get a *feeling* about where this one was." Her eyes sparkled with glee when her remark produced light chuckles from Brenda, Eleanor, and a couple of others.

"You didn't see him," I said calmly, although my pulse was escalating.

"You keep telling yourself that."

I glanced around the room to make sure no adults were paying attention to us, and they weren't. I crossed my arms over my chest. "What did he look like then? What was he wearing?"

She scoffed. "Like a Nazi, what do you think?"

I raised my eyebrows in doubt, calling her bluff.

"He had short hair and dark eyes and wore a shirt with numbers on the pocket just like the other two. Happy?"

"You're lying," I said, and took a step forward, closing the gap between us. "Just like you lied about meeting President Roosevelt in Dallas last year. And about getting a letter from Judy Garland. And about your parents owning a hotel in New York. I could go on if you want."

Tessa's nostrils flared and her lips tightened.

"If you saw him," I pushed, "why isn't there a search going on right now?"

She thrust her hands on her hips. "I didn't say anything at the time because my little sister was in the car, and I didn't want to scare her. He ran away right after I saw him, anyway."

"Your need to be the center of attention is pathetic," I said, and turned to leave.

"Says the boy..." She covered her mouth as though she'd accidentally let the word slip. "I mean, girl who wears her dad's ugly, stinky fish shorts all over town to remind everybody how he's dead and we should feel sorry for her and let her do whatever she wants."

She must've leaned toward me when she spoke because I felt her hot breath on the back of my neck. I clenched my fists and met eyes with Robert as gasps and chuckles sounded around me. I could feel the tick of my pulse in my neck, hear it in my ears. Robert shook his head, his eyes imploring me to stay calm, walk away. He put his hand on my shoulder as if to guide me away, and although he did it gently, and had good intentions, I jerked away. Then I spun around and directed my anger where it belonged, on Tessa. She was smiling. Cold amusement filled her eyes.

I wanted to punch her more than I'd ever wanted to punch anyone in my life. And I fully intended to. She'd crossed the line. I wanted to break her nose and ruin her pretty face with her own blood. I wanted to stand over her after she fell and scream in her face: *If you ever talk about my dad again, you'll be as dead as he is!*

But when I reared back, Robert saved me from myself. He wrapped his gangly arms around me and lifted me off the ground. I kicked and flailed as he backpedaled away from Tessa, yelling for him to put me down. Tessa's mouth fell open as if she was appalled, but delight twinkled in her eyes. Brenda and Eleanor rushed to her side and eyed me fearfully as they looped their arms around hers and urged her backwards. More gasps and a couple of surprised shrieks exploded from the onlookers. Some backed away from Robert as though he were carrying a bomb; others, the smaller kids, hurried to find their parents.

The commotion silenced the adult chatter and brought their attention our way. By the time Robert set me down, Pastor Lewis, Mom, Ruth, Tessa's Mom, and several other adults were rushing to the back of the sanctuary. Everyone who wasn't coming was watching. I shoved Robert when he let go of me and told him to stop although he already had. He lifted his hands in the air in submission.

"I was just trying to help," he said. "She's not worth it."

Angry tears filling my eyes, I looked at Tessa. Her mom, socialite extraordinaire Patty Sanders, was by her side, surveying her daughter as though she'd been mauled by a tiger. Tessa's gaze remained on me.

"What's going on?" Pastor Lewis asked, stepping in front of me with outstretched arms, one palm aimed at me, one in Tessa's direction. His attention bounced back and forth from me to her. When no one immediately responded, he locked eyes with his son. "*Robert?*"

Before Robert could answer, Tessa aimed an accusatory finger at me. "She attacked me."

"No, I didn't," I countered. "I didn't have the chance."

"Only because Robert stopped you," she snapped back.

Mom appeared next to me, and I reflexively jerked away when she put her hand on my shoulder. "Calm down, Alice." She spoke softly but harshly and close to my ear. "What are you doing?"

I glanced at her, and the embarrassment on her face made me feel the need to explain in a quiet tone as well. "She was lying about seeing the guy with swastika tattoos on his arms, Mom, and then she was saying stuff about Dad, and me, and my shorts, mean stuff, and I... I..."

"You saw the prisoner with tattoos?" Pastor Lewis asked, drawing everyone's attention to Tessa who nodded without hesitation. "When?"

"This morning, in the car, on Main Street," she said. "When we were on our way here."

"She's lying," I said.

She shook her head at the accusation. "I promise I'm not." Her gaze moved from her Mom to Pastor Lewis as a sad, helpless expression formed on her face, and Patty draped a comforting arm over her shoulder. In the presence of adults, she was putting on a show, casting herself as the victim. Which made me the villain. She made eye contact with me. "I saw him whether you believe me or not, and it scared me half to death. If anyone should sympathize with me, I think it would be you."

"Why didn't you tell me?" her mom asked.

She shrugged and then put her head on her mom's shoulder and pretended to cry, milking the situation for all it was worth.

"We need to tell Sheriff Bennington so he can go search the area," Pastor Lewis said.

"She's lying," I repeated as he walked toward Tessa, but my words fell on deaf ears.

"Take her to my office," Pastor Lewis ordered Patty. "And we'll call the sheriff's office." Then he looked at Mom. "I'm sorry, Martha, but you need to take Alice home. She's too emotional and fragile after everything that happened yesterday to be here right now." He spoke like I wasn't standing right there, as though his opinion were fact.

"I'm not *too* emotional," I insisted. "And if anyone is fragile, it's all of you for believing her lies."

"Don't be disrespectful!" Mom screeched.

Pastor Lewis acknowledged me with a frustrated glance. "I understand you're in a lot of pain about what happened to Nancy, Alice. But directing your pain at innocent people won't heal your guilt. That's between you and God. Now, please, go with your mom while we sort this out. And I suggest you spend some serious time in prayer."

"We will," Mom assured. "I'm so sorry." Grabbing my upper arm hard enough to leave finger marks, she led me up the center aisle as Pastor Lewis marched toward his office.

Robert caught my eyes and tried to touch my hand as we passed him, but he didn't quite reach far enough. Everyone stayed silent and cleared out of way as we moved, allowing us passage to the front doors, all eyes weighing down on our two person parade. The second our feet hit the bright sunshine on the porch, a buzz of chatter filled the room behind us.

In the truck, I didn't wait to see if Mom would give me the silent treatment, a lecture, or a scolding. I took initiative as she pulled away from the church. "I'm sorry, Mom. I didn't mean to cause any trouble. I swear. I was being nice to her until she started talking about Dad. And you should've heard all the horrible things she said about me before that."

She cut her eyes at me. "I don't know what to do with you anymore." She glared at the road ahead. "When's it going to stop with you, Alice? One minute you're sweet and nice, the next you're calling good people names and starting fights. In God's house of all places."

"Tessa's not a good person, Mom. She *was* lying so I wasn't calling her names. I was saying the truth. And I didn't start anything. She did. I just asked her to stop lying and scaring people."

Mom looked at me as if she didn't believe a word I said.

"What?" I asked. "You think I'm lying?"

"What do you expect me to believe?"

"I expect you to give your own daughter the benefit of the doubt."

"Maybe I would if you hadn't lied to my face yesterday and brought this whole mess on us. Why, for once, can't you just… I wish…" She shook her head as though she was either too tired to finish, or believed finishing would be worthless.

"Wish what?" I said. "That I was more like the beautiful and righteous Tessa Sanders? A proper young lady who fawns over dresses and makeup and sits with her legs crossed and bats her eyes and revels in social status and popularity?"

She cut her eyes at me again but didn't say anything.

"I know you've always wished I was more like her." I crossed my arms over my chest, and a lump formed in my throat, making it hard to say what I said next. "Sometimes I think you wish you'd never had me at all."

"I've never once wished such a thing, Alice, and you know it."

"I can tell by the way you look at me sometimes that I disgust you." I glanced out the passenger window at the passing shacks, looked at her. "And Dad told me how you'd always wanted a ton of kids, but the complications you had giving birth to me ruined your chances to have any more."

My admission, something Dad had told me to never mention to Mom because she was "sensitive about it," created shifting shadows of conflicting emotion in her eyes. I saw glimpses of hurt, anger, sympathy, sorrow. She forced an awkward swallow, like the lump in my throat was contagious, and she'd caught it. "You don't disgust me, Alice. I love you and wouldn't trade you for anyone else in the world." We briefly met eyes. "It's your bad choices that disgust me, and that doesn't make me a horrible mom. The day you find a parent who says they aren't disgusted by some of their kid's choices is the day you've found someone you can truly call a liar."

Her veiled confirmation that she believed Tessa ended our conversation, and we rode the rest of the way home in silence.

That was one of only two times in my life I mentioned to Mom what Dad had told me, and she never once brought the subject up herself. Not to me, anyway. I'm sure she discussed it with Ace at some point, though. They talked about everything.

The second time I mentioned it to her was after I had a miscarriage ten years later. I wasn't in a serious relationship at the time, the pregnancy wasn't planned, and to be honest, I'd never had a great desire like some women to be a mom. But when I found out I was pregnant, a hopeful feeling I think only new mothers can experience awoke inside me and dominated my existence. Without ever laying eyes on the person growing inside me or knowing their sex, I imagined their future—who they'd be, the great things they'd accomplish, how I'd be there to help them through all the ups and downs. When I miscarried what turned out to be a boy (Kevin Douglas

Mayes, I named him) during my fourth month, the pain I felt from the loss was just as strong as the pain I'd felt when Dad had died.

Of course the two losses were different. One was the loss of a person I'd shared actual experiences with while the other was the loss of the potential, and hope, and expectation of a full-lived life. But the depth of the hurt was equal. When I called Mom to tell her what had happened, which was the first time we'd talked since I'd told her I was expecting, I brought up our conversation in the truck from all those years earlier and said how sorry I was for throwing what Dad had told me in her face. I told her I'd been stupid and selfish and didn't understand how hard it must've been for her to lose her hope for more children. Though all she said was, "You don't need to worry about that," before changing the subject to my well-being, I could tell it was genuine.

17

Mom turned on the kitchen radio and began wiping down the already clean countertops as the KGNT Story Connections woman with a sultry voice read an excerpt from her daily selection, *Gone with the Wind*. I stood at the bottom of the stairs for a minute or two, waiting for Mom to insist I clean something, too, but the order never came, so I went up to my room and shut the door.

I changed into the same t-shirt and fish-gut shorts I'd slept in the night before, grabbed my diary, and sat in my favorite spot on the floor in front of my open window. My intention was to write about Hans, Nancy's healing, and everything else that had happened over the past twenty-four hours, but my thoughts were too scattered. Tessa's accusation had created a distracting sense of urgency in me. I knew her lie would spark more fear and panic, which would intensify the vigilance on the part of the military, search groups, and sheriff's office, which would increase the likelihood of Karl being caught. The most I wrote without pausing, staring aimlessly out the window at our garden and brainstorming ways to help him safely escape, was about half a sentence. When the knock came on the front door an hour or so later, I'd barely reached the point of my story where I was chasing Hans.

I found my feet in an instant, slipped my diary back into the chest at the foot of my bed, and left my room. The kitchen radio went silent as I descended the stairs, and I followed Mom to the front door after she marched past me. Other than Ace and the Lewises, we rarely had unannounced visitors, so when Mom opened the door and I saw Ace standing there in full uniform with his hat in his hands, I wasn't surprised. I was surprised, however, to see Corporal Tanis and an older, wiry man in a black suit flanking him. I'd forgotten Ace had warned us they'd probably want to question me about Hans.

Ace held Mom's gaze for a moment before greeting her by name and introducing both of us to Corporal Tanis and District Attorney Benjamin Tullos. "I'm sorry I didn't call first," he said with an air of formality I wasn't used to from him. "But we came straight here from the church after talking with Tessa about her sighting this morning. Corporal Tanis just arrived in town and wanted to talk to Alice as soon as possible."

"Okay," Mom said and invited them inside.

She led them to the living room where Tanis and Tullos sat on the couch, Ace in the armchair to their right. She offered them something to drink and all three politely declined, then she instructed me to get two chairs from the table in the kitchen for us. I put them side by side in front of the fireplace, facing the couch, and Mom removed the vase of tall sunflowers from the coffee table in front of us to open a clear line of sight before sitting down next to me.

"I assume you know why we want to talk to you, Alice," Tanis said, focusing on me. He sat on the edge of the cushion, back as straight and stiff as the top of his silver crewcut. He wore the same military outfit he'd worn to the meeting and projected the same confident aura. Although he flashed me a cordial smile, it carried little warmth. Which made sense. At the town meeting on Saturday, he'd advised everyone not to do or say anything to make the prisoner situation more of a mess than it already was, and I'd done both. He'd wanted everything to be settled quietly, without leaving a stain on him, and I'd inadvertently jacked the volume all the way up to ten.

I nodded. "To talk about the prisoner who died yesterday."

"Correct," he said. "Sheriff Bennington already told D.A. Tullos and me everything he knows about what happened, but we'd like to hear it directly from you, too. We hope you might have some information that might help us locate the last prisoner still at large—the one Tessa Sanders saw downtown this morning. We know he was buddies with the one you encountered yesterday and believe they were hiding together at some point."

The rebellious urge to call Tessa a liar made its way to the tip of my tongue, but I swallowed it down.

"And I need a statement from you for my official report about the prisoner's death yesterday since you were a central figure in the incident," Tullos added in a brisk, definitive manner. "The more information I have, the better job I can do." His relentless frown, defensive posture, and unexpressive eyes suggested he was someone who was hard to please and averse to hugs. A lot like Nana Mayes had been.

"Before we get to all that, though," Tanis said, looking at Mom. "I'd like to offer you and your family our condolences on your husband's death, and thank you for his service. I didn't know him personally, of course, but I consider every soldier a brother. Rest assured, his sacrifice will never be forgotten."

Mom whispered a thank you, and his attention moved back to me.

"Now, Alice, we talked about this on the way over here, and we decided it would be best if you start from the time you woke up yesterday so we get a full picture of what happened."

An expectant hush fell over the room, and butterflies hatched from heavy cocoons in my stomach. Tullos pulled a notepad and pencil out of his inner jacket pocket and watched me over the top of his tiny glasses, poised to write. Ace's gaze moved back and forth from me to Mom as he nervously spun the sheriff star on his hat in his lap. Mom sat perfectly still, her head angled my way, and when I glanced at her, she waggled her eyebrows for me to get going.

The day before Ace had said to be honest if the military or D.A. questioned me about the Hans incident, and I was as honest as possible given the circumstances. I started with wanting to go fishing instead of to church and went from there. Lying about my Dad-inspired feeling and leaving Karl out of the story came easy because I'd already given Mom and Ace the same story. All I had to do was regurgitate. When it came to everything else, I gave generic details, brief descriptions, and no motives, which I could tell frustrated Tanis and Tullos. I'm sure guilt played a role in my perception, but the longer I talked the more convinced I became they knew I was holding something back, and I started sweating. Unbidden, Ace turned on the overhead fan, but the breeze gave little relief. I was burning up from the inside. From the pressure of knowing Karl was in the storage room above the garage fifty feet away, and the two men staring at me were hunting for him.

When I finished, Tanis spoke first. "So, to clarify a few things you were unclear about, you were alone at the creek all morning?"

"Just me and the fish," I said, stealing a page from Dad's playbook.

"Have you ever had any other special feelings like the one you had that day?" Tullos asked. "Feelings that inspired you to act out?"

I shook my head and gave him the same answer I'd given Mom when I'd first told her and she'd doubted me. "Never. Which is why I felt so strong about pursuing it." Then I doubled- down on my conviction, trying to squash any idea that I was lying. "And I don't care if you guys think I'm a little off my rocker, or a stupid, emotional, delusional little girl. I know what I felt, and it was real, and I know it came from my dad."

Mom put her hand on my knee as emotion surfaced in my eyes, and after she told me to calm down, Tanis and Tullos fell right back into their interrogation, intent on pulling specific details out of my story. Although they seemed to approach the questioning from different angles—Tanis on gleaning information that would help catch Karl before anything else crazy happened, Tullos primarily on investigating my role in Hans's death—they played off one another so well you'd have thought they'd worked together for years. I barely had time to breathe between questions.

Did you have a vision along with the feeling? Did you hear any voices? Why do you think your dad wanted you to go there? Exactly how many shacks did you search? Did you come across or talk to anyone else after you left the church? Why did you think you'd need a weapon? How did you know the window at Merriman Hall would be unlocked? Did you see or hear anyone else inside there with him? Did you search the whole building? Can you describe the details of the fight? How many times did he hit you? How many did you hit him? Did you want to kill him? Did he say anything to you? Did he try to touch you inappropriately? Are you positive he was alone? Do you think he wanted to kill you? Why did you decide to chase him after you got out of the building? Did he seem to have a specific destination in mind or did he run aimlessly?

I maintained eye contact and answered all their questions, most truthfully, but gave short answers, replying with a simple *yes, no,* or *I don't know* when possible. I learned early on that my longer replies spawned deeper probes. The only lies I told were in relation to my "feeling" at the creek and my verbal interaction with Hans. I said he'd yelled some foreign words while we were fighting, but the only English words I heard were "tough girl."

By the time Tullos put his notepad and pencil back in his pocket twenty minutes later, the phone had rung two separate times, and my armpits were drenched with sweat.

"I guess I have all I need for now, Corporal," he said, scooting forward on the couch, seemingly eager to leave. "Do you have anything else you'd like to ask before we head downtown?"

Tanis shook his head and stood, bringing everyone else to their feet. He extended his hand across the coffee table and shook Mom's hand. "Thank you for your time, Mrs. Mayes. I'm sorry we had to meet under these circumstances."

"Me, too," Mom said. "I hope you catch that last prisoner soon so this will all be over."

"We will," he assured. "Specialist Henning, Deputy Putnam, and Deputy Weber are canvasing the area downtown where he was spotted this morning as we speak. And along with making sure the roads in and out of town are monitored, I've already requested permission to bring twenty more soldiers up from Camp Hutchinson tomorrow morning to help do a thorough sweep through town if he's not found by then. For such a small town, there are a lot of places to hide in Sunray, but I'm confident he'll be in custody by nightfall tomorrow."

The news of a full-on town search escalated my sense of urgency to help Karl get out of Sunray into pure panic. As Tanis extended his hand toward me and I shook it, the number of butterflies swarming in my stomach multiplied tenfold.

"Thank you for your help, Alice" he said. "For what it's worth, I do believe your dad is watching out for you from above." He glanced at Mom. "And although I don't think he would've wanted you to risk your life like you did, I think he's proud of the courage you showed. Let us know if you remember anything else, and we'll keep your friend Nancy in our prayers."

I managed a soft "thank you," and Tullos shook my mom's hand, then mine. He gave each of us a single nod but no words, reinforcing my belief he was a hard man to please, and unlike Tanis, either had no social skills or didn't care to use them on us.

Ace bid us a casual farewell, and as Mom saw the three men out, I darted upstairs to my bedroom and shut the door. My mind was racing, hands trembling. I felt like I was going to puke. I paced back and forth from my bed to my window, whispering to myself, hating Tessa for lying and sparking more panic, paranoid that Tanis and Tullos thought I knew more than I'd said, fearful a thorough town search would expose Karl. I knew if I didn't come up with an idea, and quick, his chances of escaping Sunray were slim to none.

Luckily, or fatefully, one sprouted in my mind within seconds.

18

Mom called me down for lunch around noon, and by the time I finished eating the egg salad sandwich she'd left on the table for me, my idea had grown into a simple yet elaborate plan. She'd left me to eat alone and was in the spare bedroom needlessly cleaning and rearranging. Keeping an ear out for her, I threw together a sandwich for Karl, wrapped it in a rag I found in the pantry, and quietly hid it on the back porch in an empty plant container. Then I headed back up to my room and started phase one of the plan: concocting a way to get out to Karl and run the plan by him to see if he objected.

The back right hinge on the chest at the foot of my bed had been loose for years. The cedar chest was made by Sam DeShields and had been a gift from Ace on my tenth birthday. *"You're a double-digiter, now. Every double-digiter needs a good chest."* It housed my underwear, bathing suit, diary, the little cash I'd saved, my personalized Bible (also a birthday present but from Mom), a couple of old dolls and toys, and the stack of letters Dad had sent me while he was in the Army. I raised the lid and wiggled it in directions it wasn't meant to wiggle, jerked on it, adding extra weight and pressure on the loose hinge. When the screws attaching the hinge began to pull away from the base, I twisted the lid harder, until they eventually broke free and clacked on the wooden floor. Leaving the lid askew for Mom to see if she came to check, I scooped up the screws and headed downstairs.

Mom was hunched over in front of the closet in the spare bedroom, digging through an old suitcase stuffed with papers. I stopped in the doorway and held up the screws. "The hinge on my chest finally gave out."

She turned my way, and her relaxed expression and soft gaze—the polar opposite of how she'd looked most of the morning—suggested she'd been sipping from the bottle of Southern Comfort she kept hidden in the dresser in the room. Which was fine by me. Not only did I know it would give her some much needed relief, I also knew the earlier she started drinking, the earlier she usually went to bed and the sounder she slept. As long as she made it to her bedroom before passing out, which I could help make sure happened, it would be easier for me to sneak out of the house at nightfall.

"I'm going out to the garage to see if I can find some fatter screws and a different hinge," I said. "I think Dad had hinges in a box somewhere out there."

She nodded. "Watch out for snakes...and be sure to put the tape back on top of the door before you come back in. You might have to put new pieces if it's not sticking well."

"I will."

As I passed through the kitchen, the phone rang, and Mom hollered for me to answer.

"Hello."

"Alice. It's Benny." He sounded upbeat and eager, happy I'd answered instead of Mom. "You're not going to believe this."

The corners of my mouth pulled upward. "What?" I asked, though I already knew the answer.

"When Nancy woke up a little while ago, she felt way better. Like, miracle better. The swelling around her face is totally gone, and even though she hasn't taken any of her pain medicine this morning, she says she isn't sore. She says she doesn't feel tired or groggy or anything. Can you believe it?" He spoke without pausing for punctuation. "And Dr. Mobley just left and said our prayers must've been answered because he doesn't understand how she could've healed so quickly. He left the splint on her wrist and pinky and the wrappings around on her rib cage but wants to take more x-rays, so we're going to his office in an hour." His voice lowered to a hand-cupped whisper, but the relentless pace of his words continued. "When I told her you came by last night to check on her and that you felt guilty, she asked me to call you and tell you that she's not mad at all, and that she can't wait to talk to you about what happened, and that she loves you. She would've called herself, but Mom and Dad are being overly cautious and don't want her to do too much yet."

I closed my eyes and inhaled deeply through my nose to fight back happy tears. "I'm so glad, Benny. I can't wait to see her. Tell her I love her, too, and I'll come by as soon as I can."

"Okay. I better go. Mom says she wants to use the phone. I'll talk to you later."

I heard Mom walk into the kitchen behind me as I hung up the phone.

"Who was it?" she asked.

I told her, and after she learned the good news, she looked upward and whispered, "Thank you." Then she hugged me, short but heartfelt. "Oh, what a relief. What a blessing for her and her family. God is good."

I nodded. "I'd like to go see her tomorrow if we can."

"We'll see," she said. "It depends upon what's going on with the search and all that mess. But if we can't go tomorrow, we'll go the next day. That'll give you plenty of time to make her a card and help me bake them a cake or muffins or something."

"Nancy's favorite is Lazy Daisy cake," I offered.

"Lazy Daisy it is then. I'm pretty sure we have all the ingredients. If not, we'll figure something out."

I thumbed at the back door. "I'm going to go look for screws and a hinge."

"Okay. Grab some paints for the card while you're out there. And don't forget the tape."

"Okay."

As I stepped out onto the back porch, the phone started ringing again. I paused in the open doorway and listened to Mom answer, greet Hazel, and say, "Yes, I heard. What a blessing," before closing the door, slipping on the summer bathroom shoes, retrieving the sandwich I'd made for Karl, and heading to the garage.

19

The air inside the lower level of the garage felt a good deal warmer than the near one-hundred-degree temperature outside, and it grew warmer and warmer the higher up the stairs I climbed. I was already on the verge of sweating when I pushed open the storage room door and an even warmer wave fell out. The sunshine shooting through the window lit the room significantly more than the moonlight had the night before.

"Karl," I whispered. "It's Alice."

My heart didn't hitch when he popped up from behind the couch dressed in Dad's long sleeve white shirt and going-out jeans like it had the first time I'd met him up there. His face was slick with sweat, shirt untucked, sleeves pushed up to the elbows exposing the markings on his arms. The bruise on his forehead from Lily's frying pan looked darker than I'd noticed the night before, but he looked rested and had a smile on his face—a smile big enough to reveal the gap in his bottom row of teeth where Hans had knocked some out.

We met in front of the window, and I handed him the sandwich. "It's egg salad. Sorry I couldn't bring water, too."

"Thank you." He removed the cloth and took a huge bite.

"Listen," I said. "My mom knows I'm out here but thinks I'm looking for screws and a hinge and some paint, so I don't have a lot of time. But I have a lot of stuff I need to tell you, so I'm just going to plow through it as fast as I can. Stop me if I'm not making any sense."

I told him the bad news first. About Tessa's lie and how her accusation about him had stoked the town's collective fear. About Tanis's and Tullos's interrogation, how I feared they were on to me, how they were searching specifically for him right now and had requested more guards to come in and conduct a thorough town search tomorrow.

Karl's chewing slowed as I spoke, and by the time I said, "You're the last prisoner still on the loose, so the focus is on you and you alone now," he stopped all together.

"But there's some good news, too," I said. "I know it doesn't help with any of the other stuff, but Nancy's brother called and she's feeling fine now just like we knew she would."

In contrast to the defeat tugging at his eyes, he forced down the partially chewed food in his mouth and flashed a pleased smile.

I touched his arm. "And I think I might have come up with a good way to get you safely out of Sunray tonight without arousing much suspicion. It may not be perfect, or get you super far, but it's better than nothing. After that, it will be up to you what happens. I would love to help you get all the way back to Europe and find your mom, but that's just not possible."

He nodded for me to go on.

"There's a town the same size as Sunray about twenty miles east of here called Antler. I figure if you can get there, you could hop on a train, hitch a ride, pay for a ride, or even steal a car…I don't know. But I think as long as you are wearing fresh clothes when you get there, your tattoos are hidden, you have a clean-shaven face, a little cash, and a driver's license, you'll have a good chance to get to Dallas or Houston, where it'll be easier to blend in and increase your options to get all the way home. With Dad's old clothes and stuff, I can manage everything including getting you a compass so you'll know which direction to go. The only thing you'll have to decide is how you travel there. I thought of three possible options. You can't take a car because there are checkpoints set up on all the roads in and out of town, so that leaves walking, a bike, or a horse. I say a horse is best. At least for a majority of the trip."

He arched an inquisitive eyebrow.

"Like I told you," I said, "my dad was obsessed with the Pony Express, so I know quite a bit about the endurance of horses." I held up my hand as if to prevent him from attacking although he showed no such signs. "And I know you said you were around horses a lot when you were little, too, but just let me run it by you so you know where I'm coming from and see if you agree." I glanced out the window to make sure Mom wasn't coming before continuing.

"Dad always said a well-conditioned horse can trot, with a few walk breaks, around fifteen miles without too much strain. He also said the Pony Express horses averaged about 10 miles-per-hour, and the riders had to switch out their horses every 12 to15 miles to keep them fresh. You could ride for the first ten to fifteen miles, ditch the horse on a farm, or near a dirt road, or anywhere you think it would be found quickly, and then walk the rest of the way to Antler. It's all pasture and farmland between there and here, and there's only one highway you'd have to cross, but you could do that way south of town, and there shouldn't be many cars out that late at night. If you leave by one in the morning, you could easily be there by sunup. If you walked the whole way, it would take at least twice as long. And there are a couple of old bikes in the garage, but trying to pedal a bike across the open plains with any amount of speed is a fool's errand."

"Do you have a…what did you call it…well-conditioned horse?"

I bit my lip, shook my head. "No. But there are more than enough on the Chase Ranch just southwest of town. And a couple of them are high quality horses owned by rich assholes who pay good money to have them stabled there. I'll borrow one of those. Remember, my dad worked at the ranch when he was younger and used to take me out there to ride, so I know my way around the place really well. I can stay south of town where no one will see me and be over there and back in forty-five minutes or less. Those horses are well trained and used to running on the plains."

He smirked. "*Borrow?*"

Feeling a smile rising on my face, I dipped my chin and cut my eyes up at him. "*Yes. Borrow.* It's not stealing because we wouldn't keep it, and when you ditch the horse somewhere and it's found, feelers will be sent out, and it'll either be returned to its rich asshole owner, or someone else will adopt it and love it."

He inhaled and looked down at the floor for a long moment, seemingly deep in thought.

"You don't think it's a good idea, do you?" I asked. "I know it's not the best, but it's all I…"

I quieted when he made eye contact with me. "I think it's a great idea," he said, appearing on the verge of tears. "Ten times better than anything I could've thought up. I just would've run with nothing and nowhere to go. Thank you." He hugged me, careful not to smash the sandwich into my back, and when we separated, set his free hand on my shoulder. "We will borrow a horse, and then I'll—"

"Get your hands off her!"

The command came from the doorway behind me, and when I spun on my heels, I saw who my ears had told me I'd see—Robert. He'd switched out of his church clothes and was in a t-shirt and shorts, hair loose and flowing rather than slicked down. His normally gentle and accepting eyes were wide with concerned anger and aimed at the swastika on Karl's forearm. When he rushed toward us, I threw my hands out to stop him. He took my movement as a gesture for protection, seized my wrist, and tried to pull me toward him.

"No, Robert," I said, jerking free from his grasp. "It's not what you think." I shoved his hands away when he tried to grab me again. "Stop. He's not trying to hurt me."

Robert stared at Karl as Karl raised his hands in the air and slowly backpedaled. He clenched his bony hands into tight fists, the tendons in his neck as taut as piano wires.

"Robert,' I said. "Look at me." When he didn't, I cupped my hand around his chin, forcing his attention my way. "I know what it looks like, but he's not like the others. He's not a real Nazi. He was kidnapped and forced to work for them."

His eyes flitted back and forth from me to Karl who had stopped in front of the couch with his hands still in the air. "Is that what he told you? He's lying. Trying to trick you. That's what they do. The

Devil's Disciples, remember? We need to go get help." He pointed at Karl. "You stay right there."

"You don't understand," I said, and glanced at Karl, silently pleading for his okay to tell Robert the full truth. When he gave me a nod of confirmation, I locked eyes with Robert. "Do you trust me?"

He scrunched his eyes and shook his head as if my question had been in a foreign a language. " *What?*"

"Do you trust me?" I asked again with more force. "Do you believe in me?"

Long seconds passed. "Of course, but—"

I covered his mouth with my hand. "Then please listen to me." I pointed at Karl. "He—Karl—has a special ability, and the Nazis were using him. He's a bridge. He can heal people." I held out my arm and touched it where Karl had healed me. "He healed a cut on my arm. Like magic. And Nancy...the way news spreads around here I imagine you've already heard about Nancy...about how she woke up feeling miraculously better today. Right? Totally healed?"

It took a few seconds, but he eventually nodded.

"That's because Karl healed her. We snuck over there last night, and Benny let me in her room because he thought I just wanted to see her, but I secretly unlocked her window so he could reach in and do it. You know how bad her injuries were. There's only one way she could've healed that fast—a miracle. Ask Benny. He'll tell you I was there." I pointed at Karl again. He'd lowered his hands and had slid his shirt sleeves down to cover his tattoos. The egg salad sandwich was still in one of his hands. "He's the miracle. And all he wants to do is go home and find his mom who is being held and tortured by the Nazis."

Robert's incredulous gaze moved to Karl.

"I know it sounds crazy, but it's true," I said. "You have to believe me."

"I'll show you if you want," Karl said, offering what I'd hoped he would.

Robert looked at me, and when I gave him an encouraging nod, he nodded, too.

"Did you knock on the door and talk to my mom?" I asked. "Does she know you're out here?"

"I knocked," he said hesitantly, as if he were unsure if that was a good or bad thing. "She knew I was coming. My mom asked her if I could come and talk to you when they were on the phone, and she said that was fine. She said she'd washed the pot we left last night, and I could pick that up, too. When I got here, she was on the phone with someone else and told me you were out here looking for hinges and paint and I should come help you."

"So she was in the kitchen?"

"Yeah. Sitting at the table."

"Good," I said, knowing she couldn't see the right side of the backyard from there. "I'm going to go grab a knife from the tackle box downstairs and a weed or something from the yard real quick. You two stay here."

When I came back with a knife in one hand and two good-sized pigweeds in the other, they were still standing in the exact same spots. Karl was talking about Hans, his egg salad sandwich re-wrapped in the cloth and resting on the couch behind him. Robert's hands were no longer fisted, but the look on his face told me his guard was still up.

"All right," I said, hurrying over to Karl and handing him the pigweed. He put one on the couch beside his sandwich and clutched the other.

I flipped the pocketknife blade free, ready to slit my arm exactly where Karl had healed me before, and looked at Robert. "Come closer so you can see it happen," I told him, and he did. "Watch the plant and my arm."

Butterflies swarmed to life in my stomach as I cut my arm deep enough to produce a thick blood flow. I felt like an alcoholic who'd just popped the cap on their first beer in days—eager with want, giddy for the elation I knew was about to surge through me. My anticipation trumped any pain my torn flesh tried to produce.

Holding the pigweed next to my arm, Karl took me by the wrist, closed his eyes, and it started. Just like the first time, an indescribable pleasure poured into my arm and trickled throughout my body. My hairs stood on end, time slowed, and my senses magnified. The room grew brighter, edges of objects and features on faces more defined, crisper. I could feel every individual cell in the skin around the wound rippling, tickling with an electrical energy. The smell of old furniture and dust and sweat—three unique scents from three different people—hit my nose like a punch. Robert's amazed gasp as his eyes moved from the gash on my arm to the shriveling pigweed sounded like a chorus of gasps. His eyes grew impossibly wide as the wound sealed and the pigweed turned to ash, cascading to the floor in a mixture of a thousand grays and with an audible poof.

When Karl opened his eyes, Robert uttered, "How did…? What…?"

Karl and I both smiled. "Touch it," I told Robert. "It's fine."

He rubbed his hand over the smooth skin, smearing the fresh blood, and rubbed his red fingertips together. "That was…"

I offered him the knife. "You want to feel it?" I glanced at Karl. "Is that okay?"

Karl nodded and picked up the other pigweed.

Robert eyed the knife.

"You don't have to," Karl said.

"I think you should, though," I added.

Robert took the knife, and after I hurried to the window to make sure Mom wasn't coming and hurried back, he squeezed his lips together and ran the knife along his skin. His cut wasn't as deep or long as mine, but good enough to bleed and need repair.

When Karl closed his eyes and lowered the bridge, Robert closed his eyes, too. Both jealous of him and happy for him to experience it, I smiled when Robert's eyes popped open and were filled with pure wonder. And my smile grew so big it hurt when I saw not only the hairs on his arms standing on end, but also the ones on his head, making it look like he'd stuck his hand in a socket.

Elated and beaming ear to ear after the wound was healed and the weed disintegrated, he fingered his own perfect arm like he had mine. He'd not only lowered his guard, he'd buried it deep underground. "That was…"

"Amazing," I filled in.

"Yes…amazing." He looked at Karl. "Surely if you turned yourself in and showed them what you could do then—"

"No," Karl and I interjected at the same time, stopping Robert dead in his tracks.

"That's not an option," I said.

We spent the next five or ten minutes hovering near the window, sweating, watching for Mom, telling Robert exactly why that wasn't an option. Karl and I alternated talking like an old married couple, rivaling the rhythmic flow Tanis and Tullos had had during the interrogation. I could tell Robert was being overloaded with explanation, buried in information, and I felt bad, but we didn't have time to field the questions his eyes screamed to ask. We dumped everything on him, all at once. We told him a truncated version of Karl's life in Europe and experiences with his ability, about BZGH (*Brücke Zwischen den Händen Gottes*, Bridge Between God's Hands), about Hans and the Third Reich, about his desire to find his mom and his fear of what would happen if anyone knew about his ability—a Nazis', a liar's, a Devil's Disciples' ability that had been used against American forces.

"I don't trust them," Karl said. "They'd never believe me."

"They'd lock him up and test him for God knows how long," I added. "And he'd never have a chance to find his mom."

Then we told him about the plan to help Karl escape. Antler, the horse, all of it, again in one massive dump of information.

"It gives him the best chance to get home as quickly as possible," I said. "And it puts his life and fate in his own hands." Karl smiled, wiggled his fingers at me, and realizing what I'd said, I nudged his arm. "I didn't mean it that way."

As Karl's smile faded, he looked at Robert. "I couldn't live with myself if I don't try to get home." He gazed out the window at the horizon, at the land that would become the Garden of Sunray, and Robert and I followed suit. "I know my ability is a gift from God, and I know I have a purpose. My mama taught me that since I was old enough to listen, but she also taught me there was a time and place for everything." He met eyes with Robert. "This is not the time or place for me to show everyone what I can do."

"I understand," Robert said, his natural empathetic nature overriding the fact that he was still obviously trying to process everything. He glanced at Karl's hands. "BZGH, I like that. I really like that."

Pure joy sprung to life in my chest, and I took his hand in mine and gave a firm squeeze. It felt good to have my best friend by my side, to have someone else to share the experience of Karl Wagner with.

He gave a solid squeeze back. "I have a little money I can pitch in, too. And if you want, I can sneak out tonight and help you steal the horse."

A mischievous, knowing look passed between Karl and me, and then we both chuckled.

Curious, Robert shrugged. "What? The more eyes we have to watch out for people the better, right?"

"You're right," I said. "It's not that. We're just laughing at something we talked about earlier. I'd love to have your help. But, just so you know," I cut my eyes at Karl, "we're *borrowing* the horse, not stealing it."

Before Robert and I went downstairs to look for the paint, brushes, screws, and a hinge, I helped Karl find a suitcase and told him to take any of Dad's clothes from the trunk he wanted, make sure all the shirts were long sleeved and to pack them up. I told him there were a couple of pairs of newer, nicer shoes in the chest with Dad's clothes that he should take, too. Standing at the top of the staircase, I told him I'd gather everything else he'd need for his journey and come out to the garage after Mom fell asleep.

"Be sure and finish your sandwich," I said as Robert and I descended the stairs, sounding exactly like my mother. "You'll need all the energy you can get for tonight's journey."

Robert and I found the screws, paints, and brush quickly but didn't find a hinge. After we put the knife back in the tackle box, closed the door, and reattached the tape, we walked to the shaded area on the side of the garage and faced one another.

"Thank you," I said, rising up on my tiptoes and kissing him. "For what happened at the church earlier." I thumbed at the garage. "And this. I'm sorry I didn't tell you about Karl. I wanted to, I swear I did. But...well...you know. I couldn't."

He smiled. "It's okay. I get it now. It all makes sense. Meeting him explains a lot. I thought it was strange when I heard you were insisting that you'd had a *feeling* about where Hans was hiding. You've never believed in things like that." He chuckled to himself. "You hate things like that. And now I also understand why you went after Hans so hard, and why you cared so much about what Tessa was saying at the church. Usually, you don't give two flips about what she says."

"That was a one-time thing," I said, smiling, and our lips were about to touch again when the back door opened, and Mom stepped out.

I backed away from Robert, and he winked, whispered, "Tonight, out here, as soon as I can," and we headed toward the house.

We met Mom on the back porch. "I was just coming to check on you guys. Did you find everything?"

I held up the can of paints, brush tips sticking out. "Found the paints and brushes."

Robert opened his fist, revealing three fat screws. "And screws."

"But we gave up on trying to find the box with hinges in it for now," I said.

"Yeah, there's just so much to look through." Robert confirmed. "And it was getting too hot in there. I told her I'd come by in the morning and we'd look again when it's cooler."

"That's smart," Mom said, and then motioned us toward the back door. "Speaking of cool, come on inside, and we'll get you guys something cool to drink. You two are beet red and sweating like pigs."

On the way inside, once Mom's back was turned, Robert gingerly side-kicked me in the backside as I slipped off the summer bathroom shoes, and then I smacked him in the upper arm.

20

For the next thirty minutes, we hung out in the kitchen with Mom, drinking sweet tea and skimming the surface of Sunray's trendiest gossip topics—Nancy, the power of prayer, Tessa, Nazis, and so on. Mom did most of the talking, needlessly wiping down the counters, table, and stovetop as she rambled. What little Robert and I said aloud we said to Mom, agreeing with her. Between us, we spoke silently, exchanging furtive looks and knowing grins. Despite the magnitude of our situation, I'm glad we were still young enough to overlook the potential consequences of our plan and simply relish our secret knowledge, revel in the thought we were smarter than the adults who governed our lives, were scheming on a level and part of something bigger than they could ever imagine.

At the front door with his mom's pot in hand, Robert promised Mom he'd thank Hazel again for the chicken noodle soup and that he'd come back in the morning to help me continue the hinge search. When Mom went back to the spare bedroom to "finish up," I grabbed the paints and brushes and some paper and headed up to my room. I wanted to give her as much alone time as possible, hoping more alone time meant more sips of whiskey.

By the time she had migrated to the kitchen, turned on the radio, and started making the Lazy Daisy, I'd caught my diary up to date and started on Nancy's I'm Sorry/Get Well Soon/I Love You card. I painted a cluster of sunflowers gripped in a hand on the front because...well...you know why. On the inside, I painted a cross because I knew that would please both Mom and Nancy's parents, and I painted a rainbow arching over it because I couldn't think of anything else. I also painted a little blue butterfly on the bottom right corner because she loved butterflies and blue was her favorite color. The message I penned was short and to the point:

> *I'm so sorry about what happened, Nancy! We love you and hope and pray you get well soon!*
> *Love, Martha and Alice*

I went down to the kitchen around seven o'clock and showed Mom the card, after I'd finished all of it but the butterfly. The tumbler and bottle of Southern Comfort were nowhere to be seen, and she didn't act drunk at all, but she did have a carefree way about her I knew was the result of the alcohol. Swing music, her favorite, played on the radio, and she swayed to the beat as she stirred and mixed. I made a sandwich with the leftover egg salad and asked her if I could eat in my room, saying I wanted to eat while I added a few finishing touches to the card. She gave the okay, and I rushed back upstairs with the plate and card.

I put the sandwich in the chest at the foot of my bed, underneath my bathing suit, then crept out into the hall and down to Mom's room. The straight razor Dad had used for shaving was in a leather bag on the shelf at the top of the closet. His wallet with his typed-out driver's license was up there, too, in a cigar box with some of his old family pictures, dog tags, and a couple of other personal items that were special to him and Mom. I slid the chair Mom kept in the corner by the window over to the closet, stood on the seat, retrieved the two items I needed, shoved them in my pocket, replaced the chair, and snuck back to my room unseen.

I hid the license and razor in my chest with the sandwich, and as I sat on my bed painting the blue butterfly, the phone rang and Mom answered. Ten minutes later, I headed down to return the plate and show her the butterfly I'd added to the card and found her off the phone and taking the cake out of the oven. The aroma of fresh baked cake sweetened the air. I showed her the card, and after she read the message aloud again, she smiled and assured me Nancy would love it.

"Who called?" I asked, hoping it had been Benny or one of Nancy's parents with more good news.

"It was Greta Gideon."

I puckered my face like my spit had suddenly turned to lemon juice. "What did she want?"

"To make sure I was still coming to clean her house tomorrow morning." As she poured milk into a pot to start making the icing for the cake, she asked me to grab the canister with dried coconut from the pantry.

"What time are we going?" I asked, setting the canister on the counter.

She held eye contact with me for a moment, the alcohol-relaxed look in her eyes slightly diminishing. "I'm going to call Ruth and ask her to help me instead of you."

"Why? I always help you clean the Gideon's in the summer."

She pushed out a breath. "Apparently, Greta and Anne were on the sidewalk talking to Mrs. Collins when you chased the car down Main Street, and they were almost hit."

Guilt tightened my throat. I hated the Gideon twins, cleaning their house, the pompous way they acted, the demeaning way they treated Mom, but I knew Mom valued the job. And I liked Mrs. Collins, a lot. She was a single, thirty-year-old woman who lived in a small house next to the school and taught English, math, and science for grades eight through twelve. She had a sarcastic sense of humor and outspoken liberal viewpoints on women's roles in the war effort.

"I'll call and apologize to them if you want," I offered.

She sucked in the corners of her mouth and flashed a tiny thankful smile. "That's okay. You know how they are. It wouldn't do any good. They thrive on grudges. Their forgiveness will take time. I'll just have to deal with it. I'm just glad they didn't fire me."

I apologized again, promised I'd feed the chickens and water the garden in the morning while she was gone, and asked if she would call Nancy's parents and ask if we could go over tomorrow after she finished cleaning the Gideon's house. She said she would, and when the phone rang a few minutes later while she was finishing up the icing, I answered. It was Ace, checking in. He told me there were no updates on the last prisoner's whereabouts and that the following day's town search was a go for 9:00 a.m., and then I passed the phone to Mom and headed back upstairs.

I switched into the over-sized t-shirt that doubled as my nightgown to appear ready for bed whenever Mom came up, and then knelt in front of the chest at the foot of my bed. I dug out the paper sack in the bottom, dumped out the coins I had squirreled away over the years, and counted the money. It turned out to be $1.42, which equals about $20 today. Not a lot, but not nothing, either. I figured Robert would bring enough to at least double it, probably more. I scooped the coins back into the sack, rolled it up, slid it into the pocket of my fish-shorts, and then put those, and the t-shirt and socks I planned to wear that night, in the chest. Before closing the lid—as much as I could close it with the damaged hinge, anyway—I took out the stack of letters tied together with twine, the ones Dad had sent me while he was in boot camp and overseas.

I didn't have many, sixteen to be exact, but I'd read them countless times each since December, enough to wear the folds thin. They were simple letters written in his horrible handwriting on paper that smelled faintly of gasoline for some reason, but I didn't care. What I cared about was that my name was on the envelope they came in (Mom got one of her own each time) along with a little silly sketch on the back (Mom's didn't have a sketch), that he began each one with *Dear Ali*, and that when I read, I heard his voice loud and clear in my mind.

He wrote about some of the day-to-day movements he made, but never mentioned anything about war or death. Most of what he wrote was about the guys he'd met and "worked" with, particularly the ones he thought I'd find strange and interesting. He usually wrote about two or three people per letter, a couple of sentences on each guy, promising to elaborate more when he got home. There was a Bob who'd grown up in Utah with five moms and twenty-six siblings. A Ted from south Texas who was cross-eyed but could somehow hit a bullseye from two hundred yards out like clockwork. Johnny from Louisiana with six toes on each of his feet. Grover from New Mexico who'd had a perfect circle of white hair on the side of his head since birth and a mole the exact same size on his left cheek to match. On and on it went. Over the years, I've often wondered what ever happened to those men, to their families, if they remembered Dad and wrote about him to their loved ones, too. I always told myself I'd write a book with them as characters someday, a comedy or something, but someday never came, I guess.

Dad ended each letter one of two ways.

One: a reminder of a life lesson he'd taught me about patience, resilience, self-reliance, dealing with loss, or following my gut. The reminder was usually expressed in an extended fishing metaphor, followed by a nonsensical rhyme.

> *Don't forget, you don't stop casting just because the line snapped and the fish got away. You re-string your pole, bait the hook, and cast it again. In the same spot.*
> *See you soon, tadpole.*
> *Hopefully not upside down in a hole.*
> *Love, Dad*

Two: a reminder of how proud he was of me and how much he loved me, followed by a nonsensical rhyme.

> *Always remember, if you close your eyes and listen hard enough, you'll always be able to hear me cheering for you. You're the biggest star in my show.*
> *Take care, redbud.*
> *Steer clear of snakes and stinky mud.*
> *Love, Dad*

Similar to the fish-gut shorts, depending upon my mindset, the letters had the ability to either encourage me or sadden me. That night,

I needed courage, needed to know he had my back, and that's what those letters gave me. Like a boxer psyching themselves up for a championship fight, I read them all in order, put them away, and then flicked on my bedside lamp. I lay there with my hands behind my head staring at the whirring fan overhead, waiting for Mom to come upstairs, thinking about what I needed to remember to grab before I left the house. I imagined the layout of the Chase Ranch stables, the location of the best horses, the weak spots in the barbed-wire fences. Karl heading east toward the creek with hope and a chance. Mrs. Collins had always said if you write down the steps you needed to take to achieve a goal, or saw yourself doing it in your head, you were more likely to make it come true. If she was right, I didn't want to squander that knowledge.

When I heard Mom coming, I sat up and watched the door. When she appeared, I stretched and gave her my best tired eyes. She looked truly exhausted. *Perfect*, I thought.

"Been a long day, huh?" she asked.

"It has," I said. "Did you talk to the Garrisons? Did they say we could go visit Nancy tomorrow?"

"Yes. In the evening sometime. Hopefully after they find the last prisoner."

I slid my legs under my sheets and covered a fake yawn with my hand. "You going to bed, early, too?"

"I am." As if my yawn were contagious, she yawned, too. "Did you say your prayers?"

I nodded.

She glanced at my window to make sure it was closed, told me good night, and went to her room. I turned off my lamp, rolled onto my side, facing the door, and patiently waited. It took about an hour for her light to go off but only five minutes after that for the snoring to commence. Like the night before, I waited about ten more before easing out of bed, peeling off my makeshift nightgown, quietly opening my chest, gathering my clothes, the license, razor, and sandwich, and creeping downstairs.

I put on my shorts, t-shirt, socks, and shoes in the kitchen, shoved the license in my pocket, collected a bar of soap and the tin box labeled Johnson and Johnson First Aid Kit—which included extra bandages and a few other items Dad had added over the years—from under the sink, and then snuck out the back door.

21

Karl was sitting on the bottom step in the garage with a suitcase between his legs when I removed the tape and opened the door. He smiled when the night air and bright moonlight touched his face.

"Ready?" I asked. "Did you pack everything?"

He nodded, stood, scooped up the suitcase and stepped out of the garage. He had changed into a clean long-sleeved green shirt but still had on Dad's going-out jeans.

I piled the first aid kit, sandwich, bar of soap, and razor on top of the suitcase. "Take these and go wait in the garden behind the chicken coop just in case Mom happens to wake up and come out here." I pulled the license and bag of coins out of my short pockets. "And here's Dad's driver's license so you have an ID and a dollar-forty-two in coins. Put them in your suitcase. Your name is Douglas Mayes now, and your birthday is December 1, 1905. He's a little older than you, but that shouldn't matter. You can just say it was a mistake or something if it comes up." I pointed toward the water pump. "I'll go get a bucket of water so you can wash up and shave."

I collected a bucket off the back porch, filled it at the pump, and when I met up with Karl behind the coop, he was closing his suitcase, the bag of coins, license, and sandwich no longer with the other supplies. I set the bucket on the ground, and he picked up the soap.

When he took off his shirt and began washing his chest and pits and face, I noticed the pink scars from cigarette burns on his arms he'd told me about. And knife-slice scars on his abdomen and back. He glanced at me, and I quickly turned away from him and looked skyward.

Embarrassed, I felt the need to say something. "Be sure and leave a little suds on your face to help with the shaving. And be careful, that razor's sharp as sharp gets." When he didn't reply, I added, "Sorry if I sound bossy. I think I've been spending too much time with my mom lately."

"Good joke," he said, chuckling.

I waited with my back to him and listened as he shaved his face and splashed water out of the bucket on himself. I faced him again when he asked, "What do you think?"

He still had his shirt off and his hands were out in ta-da fashion. With his face clean-shaven, he looked closer to my age than twenty-three.

"You missed a few spots on your neck," I said. "Give me the razor." He tilted his head back, and I cleaned up his neck. "There. Good as new. No one will ever know you've been hiding out in an old stinky garage for two days."

He glanced down at his arms, ran his fingers over the markings he'd been given. "Not new enough." His eyes searched mine. "I want to take them off. Not just hide them."

I shook my head. When discussing our plan, we'd never mentioned getting rid of the swastikas, only using the gauze in the first aid kit to cover them. He'd told me the first night we'd talked in the garden that he'd cut them off if he could, but I'd thought it was just a figure of speech, an exaggeration to prove a point. Maybe I was stupid, but posing it as an actual option had never crossed my mind.

"I don't know if that's a good idea. It'll really hurt. And bleed. A lot."

"I don't care about the pain or blood," he said. "I just don't want to have to say they are mine anymore."

We held eye contact for a long moment. I hadn't known him long—three days to be exact—but I knew him well enough to know he would do it whether I helped or not.

"If they are real wounds," he continued, "I won't have to lie about why they are covered. And if anyone wants to see them, they can. I'll also put one or two more cuts on each arm so it doesn't look like I did it on purpose. I think I'll have a better chance if I do it." He gestured at the land. "And I'll feel better in here." He tapped his chest.

Giving him a nod of solidarity, I handed the razor back to him. "We're going to need something to soak up some of the blood," I said, opening the suitcase. I flipped through the shirts he'd packed, found the dingiest one and tossed it over my shoulder. Then I opened the first aid kit, took out the antiseptic ointment, bandages, Aspirin, and safety pins, set them on the ground next to the bar of soap, and picked up the bucket of water. It was about a quarter full. "All right. I'm ready when you are."

I held my breath when he angled the blade above the half dollar-sized swastika on his left forearm and gave me a look that said, *here I go*. I sucked in a gasp when he dug the blade under his skin and smoothly swiped it sideways like he was fileting a fish down at the creek. His lips parted, exposing his gritted teeth as he groaned and dipped the blade out from under his skin. Ninety-five percent of the tattoo clung to the layer of flesh stuck to the blade, and he slung it onto the ground. Without hesitation, he cut off the remaining five percent, and then removed another smaller layer of skin closer to his wrist. Blood surfaced from the wounds like flowing lava, thick and red and glistening in the bright moonlight. Unable to peel my eyes off the wounds, I opened my mouth, wanting to ask if he was okay, but I couldn't find my voice. He switched the blade to his left hand and repeated the process on his right arm, this time making the second wound closer to his elbow rather than his wrist. He dropped the blade and held his arms out in front of him, blood running from the four fileted patches of arm, dripping onto the ground like rainwater from a rooftop.

I poured a little water over his arms, and before the blood had washed off his arm, new blood had arisen. "Grab the soap and rub it over them," I said.

He did, grimacing as he scrubbed.

I continued pouring water in small doses over each wound, until the bucket was empty. "Okay. I'm going to dry them now." I dropped the bucket, unslung the shirt off my shoulder, and he jerked when I started wiping away the water and blood on his left arm. "Sorry," I whispered, and moved to the right arm. "Here." I handed him the shirt, bent and grabbed the antiseptic ointment and bandages. "I'll do the left first so dry it as best you can."

After he dragged the shirt over the wounds, I squeezed a glob of ointment on them, but they were still gushing blood so bad most of it ran off or stuck to my fingertips. He dabbed the areas around the wounds again, drying the good skin, then I started wrapping tan bandages over them as quickly and tightly as I could. The wounds were close enough together for me to cover them both without wasting too much wrapping. I covered his forearm from the elbow to the wrist, three or four times over, using one of the three rolls of wrapping. Then I snagged some safety pins off the ground and secured it. By the time I was halfway finished lathering and wrapping his right arm, blood circles were visible on the left's dressings.

When we finished, he pulled on his green long-sleeved shirt but left the sleeves pushed up to the elbows. "Until the blood dries," he said. "I don't want to mark the shirt."

I knew he was in a lot of physical pain. He had to be with those wounds. But he didn't stop grinning as I put everything including the razor and bar of soap in the first aid kit. He looked relieved, like a hundred pound weight had been lifted off his shoulders. Or arms, I guess. I handed him the kit after I snapped the lid closed. "Put that in your suitcase and take it with you. When Mom notices it's gone, I'll tell her I left it down at the creek or something."

He picked up the wet, bloody shirt after wedging the kit in the suitcase. "What do we do with this?"

I took it. "I'll hide it somewhere in the garage in a second. I need to grab the compass for you, anyway, and it's in there." My eyes took in his bandaged forearms, then I looked into his eyes, and he gave me a full smile. "You feel better now?"

He twisted his arms out in front of him. "Good as new."

Smiling in disbelief, I shook my head. "I can't believe you did that."

He lowered his arms, and we both gazed at the moon. "Thank you for all you have done for me, Alice." We met eyes again. "I will never forget you."

"I'll never forget you, either," I said, feeling a lump forming in my throat, emotion swelling in my chest like it had when I'd told Dad goodbye the last time, not knowing when or if I'd ever see him again.

"You are one of the good ones."

"So are you," I said, and he hugged me, long and hard.

"If I have the chance," he said as we separated, "I'll introduce you to my mama someday, and we can all go fishing."

Warm happy tears flooding my eyes, I nodded. "I'd like that."

I inhaled a deep, calming breath and jiggled the wet shirt. I needed to stay focused. There was a lot to do yet. "I'm going to go hide this and grab the compass. Keep an eye out for Robert. If he's not here pretty soon, I'll have to go get the horse without him. He might not have been able to sneak out. Sometimes his dad stays up pretty late."

In the dark garage, I found the flashlight by feeling around on the workbench and turned it on. I maneuvered to the center of the room, stuffed the shirt in a box full of dirty rags and old newspapers, then made my way back to the work bench. Dad had a dozen or more tackle boxes. The newer ones were filled mostly with fishing gear, but the older ones he called mystery boxes. I knew at least two or three had compasses, I just wasn't sure where they'd be. I searched through one with no luck, then another, then another. When I pulled out the fourth, opened it and shined the light inside, I not only saw a compass, but also a smattering of bullets and the small pistol Dad had used to shoot rabbits in the garden. I'd forgotten all about the gun, hadn't laid eyes on it in over two years. I took that as a sign. I shoved a handful of bullets in my pocket, grabbed the compass and gun, put the flashlight back on the workbench, and reattached the tape to the top of the door when I left the garage.

Karl was standing behind the coop, gazing east.

"No Robert yet?" I asked. He shook his head, and I handed him the compass. "Here you go."

He examined it, spinning in a circle, watching the needle.

I pointed southeast. "If you go to the bend in the creek where we fished the other day and then head straight east, you'll be aimed right at Antler. And you should be far enough south to avoid any checkpoints when you cross Highway 86. Be sure and fill Dad's canteen with water at the creek and take it with you. It has your name on it after all."

He flashed a grateful smile, nodded, and shoved the compass in his pocket.

I held out the pistol. "I found this in the garage. You should probably take it, too. I forgot it was in there or I would've told you about it earlier. It might come in handy if you run into trouble. And not just with people. But with snakes or cows or coyotes or something. You never know what you might come across and need to scare off."

I dug the bullets out of my pocket. "It's probably loaded, but take these."

He extended his hand, I dumped them in his open palm, and he put them in the same pocket he had the compass. Then he examined the gun. "Looks old."

"I know it works, though. Dad used it to shoot rabbits in the garden and sometimes prairie dogs on the way to—"

I stopped when I saw Robert emerge from behind a small mesquite thicket on the edge of the yard, looking toward the dark house.

"There he is," I whispered, raising my hand in the air. "Over here by the coop," I whispered louder.

Karl and I met him in the center of the garden where the pumpkins and squash were plentiful, well-lit by the full moon and countless stars directly overhead. He had on the same t-shirt he'd worn to my house that afternoon but had switched out his shorts for jeans. He was smiling, though his eyes carried a heavy dose of seriousness—the look of a man on a mission. He greeted Karl, and as they shook hands, he noticed the bloodstained bandages on Karl's arm, the pistol in his other hand.

"You okay?" Robert asked.

Karl nodded. "Yes."

"What are the bandages for?"

"We got rid of his tattoos," I said.

Robert peered at the bandages again. "How did you…"

"With a razor," Karl said.

Robert's eyebrows shot up in dismay. "Oh, my…ouch." He rubbed one of his own forearms as though it ached. "That must've hurt. Can you not heal yourself?"

Karl shook his head, and I patted his back.

"You ready?" I asked Robert. "We need to get going."

Robert rubbed his hands together in anticipation. "Let's do it."

I turned to Karl. "Remember, if we're not back by the time the moon is behind the house, that means something bad happened."

We'd decided it would be best for him to wait at the house in case Robert and I were seen. Or worse, caught. "Just go back up to the storage room and hide and we'll come—"

"What's going on?"

The deep voice with a thick drawl came from behind Robert. And sounded close. Karl and I jerked our heads that way as Robert spun on his heels. My heart leapt up into my throat when a flashlight beam drifted across my face, and Karl instinctively aimed the gun.

Pastor Lewis was about ten yards away, his lanky six-foot-five frame marching toward us. He wore his usual outfit—black slacks and a short-sleeved black button up adorned with a clerical collar. As much time as I'd spent at the Lewis's house, I'm sure I must've seen him dressed in something else at least once, but I don't remember it. He slowed as he approached Robert, focusing the flashlight on Karl. He stopped when he saw the gun in Karl's hand. Then the beam of light bounced from one of Karl's forearms to the other, pausing briefly on the bloody bandages.

"You're him," Pastor Lewis said more to himself than us. He aimed the light on Karl's face. "The prisoner...the Nazi."

"He's not a Nazi," I said, holding up my hand to shield Karl's face from the light.

"Turn off the light, Dad," Robert said, reaching for Pastor Lewis's arm. "He's not who you think he is."

"Let us explain," I said. "Please."

Pastor Lewis knocked Robert's hand away and held the light steady.

I looked at Karl. "Put the gun down, Karl." Looked back at Pastor Lewis. "He's not going to hurt anyone."

"Then why does he have a gun pointed at me?"

"He's scared," I said. "Karl, please put it down."

"You don't understand, Dad," Robert pled. "We're trying to help him. He's...he's...a gift from God. Like an angel. He can...do things with his hands…" Robert rotated his own hands as though that would explain better.

"Is that the lie he told you?" Keeping his eyes on Karl, Pastor Lewis shook his head in disgust. "Preying on kids, tricking them, using God as a shield, is one of the evilest forms of deceit."

"I didn't lie to them," Karl said, lowering the gun down to his side. "I'm not using—"

Seizing the opportunity, Pastor Lewis dropped the flashlight and lunged at Karl, reaching for the gun. They struggled for control, shoving, grunting, stumbling back and forth, all hands on the weapon.

"Stop!" I said, trying to wedge myself between them.

Pastor Lewis's elbow caught me in the face, and as I staggered back, Robert shoved between them in my place. "Dad! Let him go! He won't hurt you!"

When Robert wrapped his arms around his dad's shoulders and jerked him away from Karl, the gun went off. Karl fell back on his haunches as Robert crumpled to the ground next to the gun. Pastor Lewis dropped to his knees next to his son and said his name. I knelt on the opposite side of Robert as Karl scooted backward, away from us, and stood.

Pastor Lewis twisted his son's limp head, revealing a bullet hole in his temple, blood seeping out.

I shook Robert's shoulder. "Robert, Robert, Robert. Wake up."

"Move," Karl said, bending over next to me.

I glanced at Mom's upstairs bedroom window when her light popped on, then looked back at Karl.

Pastor Lewis scooped up the gun, stood, and aimed it at Karl. "Get away from my son!" He straddled Robert's body as though defending it from scavengers.

Karl and I both rose to our feet. "I can try to help him," Karl said.

"He can," I agreed. "Let him…please, Pastor."

When Karl moved toward Robert, Pastor Lewis's face pinched,

and he fired a shot at Karl, the bullet hitting above his right hip. "Stay away from my boy, demon!"

Placing his hand on his side, Karl staggered back a step and fell to a knee, smashing a small, deformed pumpkin growing on a vine. Pastor Lewis moved toward him, holding the pistol with both hands, eyes screaming vengeance and indignation.

"No," I said, grabbing Pastor Lewis's arm. "Don't do it. You don't understand."

He struggled free from my grasp, shoved me to the ground, and re-aimed at Karl. I reached for his leg, begging him to stop, but he kicked my hand away and lorded over me. "He's deceived you, Alice. If you help him, you're just as evil as he is and deserve the same punishment. Do you want that?"

I reached out to Karl, catching his eyes and whispering his name. I think he took Pastor's question as a threat, my gesture as one for help. That coupled with his own self-preservation instinct is the only way to explain what happened next because I don't believe he had a malicious bone in his body, and you'll never convince me otherwise.

Karl bent forward, as though praying at Pastor Lewis's feet.

But he didn't pray.

He snaked one of his hands into the pumpkin vines on the ground to his left and wrapped his fingers around a vine. Then, as Pastor Lewis declared, "You'll never hurt anyone else ever again," Karl wrapped his other hand around Pastor's ankle, closed his eyes, and opened the floodgates.

Pastor Lewis instantly grew stiff, as though a rigor mortis spell had befallen his body. His eyes were the only part of him that moved. They widened, his pupils dilating in fear as his life, energy, chi, soul, everything unphysical that he was, began flooding out of his body, passing through Karl and into the pumpkin vine.

My face fell slack as my eyes bounced back and forth from the pumpkin vine to Pastor Lewis. I understood what was happening, but I still couldn't believe the sight of it.

Pastor Lewis's skin began to darken and wrinkle, like a time-lapsed video of rotting fruit, and what little hair he had atop his scalp turned white. Meanwhile, the pumpkin vine in Karl's other hand swelled to the size of my thigh. The leaves on the vine expanded to four or five times their normal size and little vines started branching off in various directions, sprouting new leaves. Some slithered over Karl's arms, others across the soil. Then, as Pastor Lewis's skin dried to dust and fell away, his eyeballs shriveled into petrified prunes, and his exposed teeth and bones began to turn gray and powdery. The four pumpkins clinging to the original vine that had been the size of cantaloupes seconds earlier grew insanely large. Discovery-Channel-Pumpkin-Contest large.

I flinched when the first of the four pumpkins ruptured, and then watched in awe as all the others swelled and exploded, casting chunks of pulpy orange, yellowish white seeds, and strands of gooey innards a few feet into the air.

The whole incident lasted only seconds but seemed to go on for hours. When it was over, the ripe stench of Halloween clung to the air.

As I crawled toward Karl, I noticed Mom's shadow hurry past her lit window, and I knew she'd be on her way downstairs soon.

Karl opened his eyes when Pastor Lewis's clothes collapsed onto his hand. He didn't look at Pastor Lewis's empty shirt and pants, the pile of ash they rested on, the gun beside the pile, or the tips of the shoes poking out of the ash. He looked at Robert's body, partially sprinkled in ash, and then briefly met eyes with me before putting a hand on Robert's chest. He still had a grip on the giant vine with the other hand. A circle of blood similar to the ones on his arm bandages colored his shirt on his lower right abdomen.

He closed his eyes and the vine began to shrink. Robert's back arched up off the ground as if lifted by an invisible rope and pulley, and his hair stood on end like it had in the storage room earlier that afternoon. He remained partially suspended in the air as the vine and all its foliage shriveled and grayed and turned to ash, but his eyes never opened. He didn't awaken. And the bullet hole on his temple remained.

Karl opened his eyes and gazed at me. If hurt and sadness could manifest into a uniform, physical shape, it would've been Karl's face. "It's too late. He's gone."

Hearing the truth drove a needle of pain into my heart, but before I had the chance to take a breath, the living room light came on and I jumped to my feet.

"Mom's coming," I said, helping Karl stand. I eyed his gunshot wound. "Are you going to be okay? Can you make it to the creek?"

He nodded, grimaced as he picked up the pistol, and then gestured toward the coop. "Grab the suitcase. We can't leave it there."

"Okay," I said. "But you get moving." I sprinted to retrieve the suitcase, and seconds before I caught back up with him at the edge of the garden, the kitchen light turned on.

I handed him the suitcase. "Hide and I promise I'll come out there as soon as I can," I said.

He met eyes with me. He was standing partially hunched over, favoring his right side, eyes pinched in pain. "I'm sorry, Alice. I didn't mean for this to happen."

I touched his shoulder. "I know."

"Tell them I attacked you and Robert. Tell them the Nazi did it. Tell them you never saw the pastor."

"I...I can't..."

"Please. For me."

I nodded.

He glanced toward Robert, the ash pile that was Pastor Lewis. "We need to hide the pastor's clothes and flashlight. It's the only way for—"

"Go. Go," I said. "I'll take care of it."

I sprinted to the center of the garden, picked up Pastor Lewis's clothes, shoes, and the flashlight, and as I quickly scattered the ashes with my feet, the porch light popped on. I rushed to the outhouse, dropped the bundle down the chute, and was running toward the house when the back door began to open. I stole one last glance over my shoulder as I hopped onto the porch to make sure Karl was out of sight, and he was.

Mom stepped outside with her pistol in her right hand, poised to shoot. "Alice. What's going on? Was that a gunshot?"

I threw myself into her, wrapped my arms around her, buried my face in her nightgown and shouted, "Robert's dead, Mom. He's dead." Saying his name aloud twisted the needle of pain in my chest, and I started sobbing.

"*What?*" Mom said, stroking my head with her free hand. "*Dead?* What happened? How did he… Are you sure? Are *you* okay? *Alice?*"

I couldn't answer. All I could do was sob, loud and ugly. For Robert. For Karl. For Pastor Lewis. For not being able to fix any of it. None of them deserved to be hurt. None of them deserved to die. We'd had a plan. A good plan. It had all gone wrong so fast.

Eventually, she forced me off of her. "Alice, calm down. You need to tell me exactly what happened. Where's Robert?"

I wiped some of the wetness off of my cheeks although tears were still streaming from my eyes. "We met in the garden and were talking about everything… That's all. We hadn't had a chance to talk since… But then the prisoner with tattoos came out of nowhere and attacked us." I faced the garden, pulled in a shaky breath. "Robert tried to defend me, and the man shot him."

Fear widened Mom's eyes. "You're sure he's dead?"

Hugging myself as tremors spread throughout my body, I nodded.

She put both hands on the gun and scanned the yard like seasoned officer. "Where's the Nazi?"

I pointed north, toward town. "He ran around the garage that way."

"Get inside," she ordered, keeping the gun pointed at the yard. "We need to call Ace."

22

Within an hour of Mom calling Ace, Robert's body had been moved to Dr. Mobley's office, which also served as the town morgue, Pastor Lewis had been reported missing, and McGee Street was packed.

Ace, Deputies Weber and Putnam, Corporal Tanis, Specialist Henning, the handful of other military personnel who'd been helping monitor the town since the escape, and a few locals including Mayor Wilson were all on scene, flashlights and guns in hand. They had positioned the sheriff's cruiser, Ace's truck, a military jeep, and Putnam's car so as to light the street from our house to the Lewis's. They searched in groups of two, Tanis directing who to search where. Weber and Putnam thoroughly searched our garage and house to make sure the prisoner hadn't snuck inside unseen, while others went to the Lewis's and Dalton's homes on either end of McGee. Other duos headed north, into town. A couple of others looped around the perimeter of our land. The soldiers who were scheduled to arrive the next morning were summoned by Tanis and told to head to town immediately.

Ace was the first to learn Pastor Lewis was missing. Shortly after arriving, as Tanis coordinated the search efforts, he'd demanded to be the one to tell Pastor Lewis and Hazel about Robert. After hugging a tearful Mom and insisting she not go with him, he walked down to the Lewis house. And after he talked to Hazel and Thomas, "breaking their hearts" in his words, he immediately returned to tell Tanis that Pastor Lewis was missing and to question me.

I learned that Thomas had seen Robert sneak out of their bedroom window, climb down the trellis, and head in the direction of our house. Ace said Thomas was afraid his older brother was in danger because there was still a Nazi on the loose. Their Mom had reiterated to him and Robert just before bed that she didn't have a good feeling about "the one with tattoos on his arms," so he'd gone downstairs and awoken his dad who'd fallen asleep in his office chair and told him what he'd seen. Pastor Lewis then woke Hazel and told her what had happened, grabbed a flashlight, and went to find his son. When Ace asked if I'd seen him, I told the worst lie I've ever told. I told him I'd only seen Robert and the prisoner, no one else. It wasn't easy then, and it's not easy to talk about now. I knew that never actually knowing what happened to Pastor Lewis would haunt Hazel and Thomas forever. But I also knew they wouldn't believe what actually happened, even if I told them. I also knew telling them the full truth would bring more questions, questions that would force me to betray Karl, and I couldn't do that. Foolish or not, I believed I could still help him. My body rebelled against the lie. My gut knotted up and tears rippled in my eyes as the words fell out of my mouth, but Ace believed me. Afterward, I sobbed and he hugged me like a father, assuring me everything would be okay.

In the hours approaching sunrise, the number of men and cars on McGee Street lessened as the search progressed deeper into town. The wind steadily increased, too, dispersing any ashes remaining in the garden. From my open bedroom window, I nervously watched four men loop deeper and deeper out into our land as the sky turned orange and the wind whipped up wisps of dry soil. Two went out as far as the dilapidated windmill about half a mile away before turning back with nothing to show for their efforts. Thank God.

Ace brought Hazel by the house around 8:00 a.m. She was a wreck. Her eyes were swollen and bloodshot and rimmed with dark circles. She was white-knuckling one of Pastor Lewis's handkerchiefs, the ones he used to obsessively pat sweat off his head. Ace had driven her and Thomas to Dr. Mobley's office to see Robert, and she wanted to stop and see Mom and me on the way home. Thomas stayed in Ace's truck with his head down, and Hazel and Mom bawled in each other's arms on the porch. When Hazel hugged me, I cried too, and apologized again and again for my part in something she'd never understand. Right then, in the emotion of the moment, she said she didn't blame me. But in the weeks and months to come, it was obvious in how she looked at me when we crossed paths and the things I heard she was saying about me behind closed doors, that she did blame me, at least somewhat.

Word about Robert's death and Pastor Lewis's disappearance spread through town like wildfire, lighting up our phone. When Ruth found out around 10:00 a.m., she immediately called to check on us, and when Mom choked up on the phone, Ruth headed straight to our house. Deputy Putnam pulled her over on Main Street, searched her car, and told her they wanted everyone to stay home until the entire town was cleared. But she refused to return, compelling him to escort her the rest of the way to our house, where she greeted Mom and me with comforting hugs and an open ear.

Tanis and D.A. Tullos knocked on the door an hour or so later, after the extra troops had arrived and already helped the others perform house-to-house, shack-to-shack, business-to-business, church-to-church searches of two thirds of town. There had been some vague, maybe, possibly sightings by locals and transients, but no definitive signs of the Nazi or Pastor Lewis.

They questioned Mom about her night first, then asked her to walk them through the house and account for all of our firearms since they still had no idea how the prisoner had come across a weapon or what type of weapon he had. She showed them her pistol and told them that shortly after she'd been awoken, she'd checked my room and found my bed empty, then retrieved the gun from her nightstand before heading downstairs to look for me. Then she showed them Dad's shotgun and two hunting rifles in the spare bedroom closet, all three in dust-covered cases and unloaded. When he asked if there were any firearms in the garage, it took her a second to remember Dad's old pistol. I shrugged when she asked me if I knew where he kept it (*"Didn't he keep it somewhere in the garage?"*) and then followed them out there and helped them search.

Mom headed to the storage room upstairs after we'd rummaged through pretty much everything downstairs, and that's when she saw the chest she'd had Robert and me carry up there months earlier was open, and some of Dad's clothes were missing. A deeper search revealed a possible missing suitcase, too. Mom couldn't be one hundred percent sure.

Back inside, Tanis and Tullos questioned me in the living room with Mom sitting by my side and Tullos jotting in his notepad just like the day before. But unlike the day before, after having me give my version of the events, which I did with as few details as possible much to their chagrin, the questions and comments they hurled at me were leading and based on speculation rather than fact.

It seems odd that the prisoner showed up in your backyard last night at the exact same time you and Robert were out there, too, don't you think? And that he had a gun and clothes from your garage. You knew he was in there, didn't you? Is that why you held back information yesterday? That would make sense. Did he convince you to go find his friend, and his friend got scared and ran? Is that why you chased him? We know how deceitful and manipulative they can be. How long was he staying in your garage? One day? Two? How long did Robert know he was up there? Did he just find out last night or was the three dollars he had in his pocket for the prisoner? How much money did the prisoner want? He'd definitely need money to stay on the run. You're sure you never saw Pastor Lewis? Hear him? There were an awful lot of pumpkins destroyed for just two people to have had a struggle out there. What do you think happened to Pastor Lewis, then?

Lying to them was easier than lying to Ace, Hazel, or Mom, but it still wasn't *easy* by any stretch. And I didn't want to do it. I didn't like lying to them. I knew they were only doing what they thought was right. They wanted to catch who they thought was a violent prisoner. But I had to do what I thought was right too, which was protecting Karl from them, helping him get home, keeping his hope alive, so I willed myself through it.

My gut knotted up and tears trickled down my cheeks as I denied everything other than secretly meeting Robert in the garden and being attacked by the prisoner. They seemed dead set on pulling what they thought I knew out of me, repeating the same manipulative questions two or three times in two or three different ways, but I held firm to my story. Before leaving, Tanis asked me one last time if there was anything else I knew, because if they found out later that I knew more than what I was saying, there would be "stark consequences." I assured him that he knew everything I did. They questioned me again at the sheriff's office with Ace, Deputy Putnam, and Mom present three days later to "reconfirm" my story and see if I "recalled anything I'd forgotten to tell them." But neither he nor Tullos ever stepped foot in our house again.

Mom, Ruth, and I spent the bulk of the afternoon sitting in the living room and around the table in the kitchen, waiting, taking turns fielding phone calls. Mom never scolded me about sneaking out or lectured me about the consequences. Our conversations were stop and start, and despite Ruth's many offers to cook or make tea, we ate and drank next to nothing. The radio filled the awkward silences with music and various programming, and each hour on the hour during the KGNT News Update, Opal Felton reported there had been a death in Sunray and another person was missing, both possibly linked to one of the escaped prisoners. No names or ages were given. When he started making the same announcement for the fourth time, Mom turned the radio off.

Many people like the Garrisons, Keats, and Fultons called to offer prayers and support, while others like the Gideons called obviously just to glean gossip fodder. The only people I personally talked to on the phone were Benny and Nancy. It was good to hear Nancy's voice, to hear how good she felt physically in relation to the car wreck, but it wasn't good to hear her cry. Or Benny. They wanted to come over, but their parents wouldn't allow it. I told them about the Lazy Daisy cake and Nancy's card, and they were appreciative, but sadly, by the time I next saw them at Robert's funeral, the cake had hardened and been fed to the chickens, the card all but forgotten in the bottom of my chest.

Fatigue eventually got the better of me, and I fell asleep on the couch in the living room while Mom and Ruth were in the kitchen, needlessly reorganizing the pantry. When I woke, it was almost midnight, exactly twenty-four hours since Robert and Pastor Lewis had died and I'd last seen Karl. Mom was sitting in the kitchen by herself, reading her Bible. Her pistol sat on the table next to the Lazy Daisy. The radio was on again, so low it was barely audible. She looked weak and worn, like she'd been battling a migraine headache for days.

She told me Ruth had just left, which explained the absence of a tumbler on the table. If Ruth hadn't spent all day at our house consoling her, I'm sure Southern Comfort would've filled the void. She said Ace had come by and stayed for a while, too, but he didn't have any new news about the prisoner or Pastor Lewis. He'd escorted Ruth home before heading downtown to meet up with Tanis again to discuss how to proceed with the searches now that the town and immediate area had been cleared. She'd also talked to Hazel again, and they'd prayed for Pastor Lewis's safe return over the phone, asking God for another miracle like the one he'd blessed Nancy and the Garrisons with. She asked me to pray for the Lewises, too, and I hugged her, promised her I would, and headed upstairs when her eyes moved back to scripture.

In my room, I opened my window, sat on the floor in the moonlight, and stared in the direction of Regreso Creek. I prayed for Hazel and Thomas as promised, asking God to help them heal, and I did pray for a miracle, too, but I prayed for it to go to Karl. I needed for him to be okay. If he wasn't...what was it all for?

The longer I sat there alone with my thoughts, replaying what had happened in the garden, scrutinizing everything I'd done (*giving Karl the gun*), thinking about things I should've done differently (*telling Karl to run when I saw Pastor Lewis...grabbing Robert when he tried to intervene in the fight*), the more my chest tightened. Finding it harder and harder to breathe, I closed my eyes and shook my head as if reprimanding myself. I needed to calm down. I needed a distraction. I needed to hear a soothing voice.

I grabbed the letters from Dad out of my chest, lay on my bed, and read them by lamplight, over and over and over. Eventually, the ache lessened, and I turned off the lamp and lay in the dark, waiting, brainstorming new ways to help Karl to keep my mind occupied, occasionally getting up and peeking downstairs to see if Mom was still awake. She moved from the kitchen to the couch a little after sunrise and finally gave in to exhaustion.

I immediately crept downstairs and out the back door, scanning my surroundings for watchful eyes as I made my way to the chicken coop. I knew the three houses and all the other structures on our street had been thoroughly searched and cleared, but I thought there still might be a guard or two patrolling the area since we were the southernmost road in Sunray. I also expected cars of supporters to start coming and going from the Lewis's soon, eyeing our house to get a look at the site of the incident as they passed. Pretending to be scattering seed for the chickens, I took one last appraisal of the area. Confident I was alone, I ran.

I ran south toward the old windmill until I was out of sight from any cars that may have turned onto the road before cutting east toward the creek. When I reached the bend, I headed straight for the big elm with the cavity in the crook and found Dad's blanket and canteen gone. I inhaled a hopeful breath and scanned the tree shade and vegetation along the creek, focusing on the knee-high foliage where I'd found him sleeping the Sunday morning we'd fished and shared *Dad* stories. That morning, I'd called out his name as soon as I'd arrived. This time, I didn't. I searched in silence in case someone had followed me and was in earshot. I could explain coming out to the creek, to my and Dad's special spot for some emotional relief, but I couldn't explain calling out the prisoner's name.

The creek water rippled and birds chirped in the elm and oak trees as I moved up and down the bank. I searched for five minutes before I found him half a mile farther south on the water's edge. He was only visible once I got right up on him. He was lying flat on his back on Dad's blanket, hands on his chest, canteen and pistol by his side, suitcase under his head like a pillow. He was in the shade of an oak tree in knee-high foliage, wedged up against a long-ago fallen elm trunk that trailed out into the water.

I knew he was dead the second I saw his ashen face. He'd died with his eyes open.

Despair weakened my legs and brought me to my knees at his feet. I put my hand on his shin, on Dad's going-out jeans, and whispered, "I'm sorry, Karl. So sorry." Then I dipped my chin, cupped my face in my hands, and bawled. I'd never felt so broken and worthless. Not even when I had learned Dad had died. I hadn't felt responsible for his death like I did Karl's…and Robert's…and Pastor Lewis's.

Startled when a fat pigeon landed on the elm trunk right next to me, I sprung to my feet and ran home as fast as I could. I sat down on the backside of the chicken coop to wipe off my face and collect myself before heading inside and possibly facing Mom. Thankfully, she was still snoring on the couch, so I snuck up to my room and lay back down like I'd never left. Curled in a fetal position facing the wall, I silently wept on and off until my body gave out.

23

Mom sat on the foot of my bed and woke me a little before noon. She was dressed in one of her Sunday dresses, her makeup doing little to mask her despair or fatigue.

Once I'd sat up, she said, "I talked to Hazel and she would like everyone to go to the church for a few hours to pray for Pastor Lewis. She says that's what he would want, for everyone to come together in God's house and support each other. He always says there's power in numbers. I think it'll be good for her and Thomas to get out of the house, too. If you want to go, you can, but I'm not going to force you. Ruth's coming to pick me up in about thirty minutes."

"Have you heard any news from Ace about the search for the prisoner?" I asked.

She stood, straightened her dress. "They believe he must've gotten out of town somehow, but a couple of hours ago they started a second round of searches just to be sure. Ace and Putnam looked through our house and garage again while you were asleep."

Mom walked to the doorway and glanced back at me.

"I can't go," I blurted out before she had the chance to say anything.

"I understand." Her nod and slow blink as she spoke let me know she believed I thought I couldn't handle it emotionally. "There's sliced apple and a peanut butter sandwich downstairs if you get hungry."

I'm sure I would've struggled emotionally, but the real reason I refused to go was because I needed to bury Karl. I owed him that much. I didn't want him to be found and taken away by the military. God knows what they would've done with his body, the vile words and anger they would have buried him with. Selfishly, I didn't want more questions coming my way, either. I didn't know if I'd be able to keep his secret if I was pushed and pushed and pushed, and he deserved to have it kept.

I stayed in my room until Ruth arrived and Mom called me downstairs.

She was waiting at the front door with Ruth, who greeted me with a smile and hug. After Ruth asked how I was and I said I was okay, Mom said, "Don't leave the house, keep the doors locked, and call Ace or the church if you need anything." She gestured toward the kitchen with her Bible. "And I left my pistol on the kitchen table for you."

I thanked her, locked the front door behind them, and hurried to the kitchen. They'd probably be gone a couple of hours, and I didn't want to waste a second. I shoved the apple slices in my pocket and bolted out the back door. I waited on the porch until the sound of Ruth's car had faded to nothing before getting a shovel from the garage. I stopped at the coop and pretended to scatter seeds again as I surveyed the road and area for people. Seeing no one, I ran back to Karl.

I initially tried to start digging near the creek in the shade ten yards from his body, but the roots were too plentiful to make a hole any bigger than a watermelon without resistance. So I moved out into the open pasture about forty yards away, where the dirt was root-free and the sun was direct and scorching.

I scarfed down the apple slices and began furiously digging. I'd helped Dad dig and refill holes when he'd moved the outhouse every three or four years, and he'd taught me how to jump on the shovel to minimize the use of my arms. Thanks also to helping Dad bury a couple of dogs we'd had over the years, I knew I needed to have at least twelve inches of soil on top of Karl to keep the coyotes and other scavengers away. The soil was dry and brittle and easy to maneuver, but I'd never dug a hole that big on my own. Despite all the vinegar and piss I could muster, the shear amount of work began to overwhelm me. About an hour in, after a short break in the shade near Karl, but not too close (I didn't want to see his face any more than I needed to.), I took my shirt off, wrapped it around my head, and pressed on. With each scoop and toss, my arms and back ached more and more. My head throbbed, hands grew raw. As I approached the end of the second hour, I'd dug about two thirds of the shallow grave but couldn't go any more. I dropped the shovel in the hole and walked home to an empty house.

I washed up at the pump out back, ate the peanut butter sandwich on the table in the kitchen, then went upstairs and lay back down on my bed, exhausted. I don't know what time Mom got home, but she roused me around 6:00 p.m. to come downstairs and eat some potato soup with her.

As we ate, she told me a little about what happened at the church—some of the people who were there, a few of the passages they read, the way it seemed to uplift Hazel and Thomas like she'd hoped—and I told her I hadn't done anything other than eat the apples and peanut butter sandwich, wash up and rest. When she asked if Ace had called to check on me like he'd told her he would, I told her I slept through it if he had.

The phone rang while we were clearing the table, and Mom answered. The conversation was short. The only words I heard from her were yeses, okays, and fines, all in less than pleasant tones, and when she cut her eyes at me in the silences between those words, my stomach tensed with fear. I just knew someone had seen me running out to the creek with the shovel, or worse, they'd found Karl.

After she hung up, she met eyes with me.

"Who was it?" I asked.

"Greta Gideon."

"What did she want? Didn't you talk to her at the church?"

She nodded. "She wants me to come clean their house at seven tomorrow morning like I was scheduled to yesterday. She said she didn't think it was appropriate to discuss it at the church."

Relief relaxed my knotted stomach. "But she found it appropriate that you go clean her house tomorrow with all that's happened over here?"

"She said she needs it done because they're expecting company this weekend, and now that the town has been searched twice, there shouldn't be any risk in me driving over." Mom rolled her eyes in disappointment, picked a rag up off the counter, and started wiping down the table. "She said if I couldn't do it, she'd find someone who would." She shook her head as though disagreeing with a voice only she could hear. "It'll only take a couple of hours if Ruth helps me." She folded the rag and set it back on the counter. "I better call her."

"Sorry the Gideons won't let me come help you guys," I said although I was actually glad about it. Her leaving for two or three hours in the morning would give me time to finish digging Karl's grave.

Upstairs, I put on my makeshift nightgown and opened my journal, intending to document at least some of what had happened in our garden. But as I flipped for an open page, I began reading, reliving happy times I'd shared with Robert. I traveled back to the first time he'd held my hand at the roller rink to keep me from falling, the time we'd splashed around in the creek after he slipped on the bank and fell in… the time we'd kissed in the garden. The memories carried both happiness and heartache, causing me to laugh and cry on and off as I read.

Sunshine still faintly colored the horizon when Mom came upstairs, told me goodnight, and went to bed. I fell asleep shortly thereafter and slept solid as a rock until morning when I heard Mom gathering the cleaning supplies downstairs.

I threw on my fish-gut shorts and a t-shirt, rushed down and helped her load the supplies into the truck. After making the same promises I'd made about staying inside and locking the doors the day before, I waved her off, snagged an apple on my way through the kitchen, and ran to the creek.

I repeated what I'd done the day before, and although my shoulders and hips and arms were sorer than ever, I was thankful the temperature was twenty to thirty degrees cooler. Within an hour or so, I had the grave big enough—about three feet deep, near three feet wide, and close to six feet long. Then came the hard part, emotionally anyway. I hadn't allowed myself to have a good look at Karl since I'd first found him.

I removed the suitcase from under his head first. His face appeared bloated, the skin on his cheeks shiny. He smelled foul, and flies had begun to gather around his body. I put the pistol and the canteen in the suitcase and carried it to the grave, then went back for the body.

I took deep breaths as I approached him, trying to keep the tears at bay, but it didn't work. By the time I gripped the blanket beneath him and began dragging him toward the hole, I was sobbing. He wasn't really stiff anymore, and I had to stop and put his hands back on his chest a couple of times when they slipped off.

I pulled him into the hole as gingerly as possible, placed the suitcase on his shins, and buried a piece of God in the heart of the Texas Panhandle.

As I slung the shovel over my shoulder and headed home with raw palms, numb arms, and tears streaming down my face, I knew in my gut I could never leave Sunray.

PRESENT

4

In Avocado Circle, the sun had lifted higher in the sky, shifting the peach tree shade, allowing dappled sunshine to touch Alice's bare feet and Emily's entire left side. "Let's move before the sun gets us," Alice said, reaching for her socks and shoes in the mess of wildflowers at her feet as Emily blotted her bleary eyes with her t-shirt sleeve. "We have a little ways to go yet, anyway."

Unlike at previous points in the story when Emily had been marvel-eyed, exploding with comments and questions, and eager for more—when there was still hope for a happy ending—she seemed stunned and was at a loss for words. She nodded, slung her backpack over her shoulder, and carried her wooden chair back to the tree trunk as Alice slipped on her socks and shoes. When Emily returned, she silently scooped up Alice's chair and headed toward the trunk. Alice picked up the shovel and followed, using it like a cane as she moved.

At the base of the tree, Emily set down the chair and paused with her back to Alice, pulling in a deep breath before turning around. "I believe you." Her eyes briefly fell to the shovel handle in Alice's hand. "We don't have to do this."

"Do what?"

"Dig him up. That's what we came out here to do, right? You want to prove to me that you aren't lying. That Karl existed and you buried him out here."

"I didn't bring you out here to prove anything I've said or done," Alice said. "I brought you out here because I want to leave everything I own to you...the garden...the house...all of it. And it wouldn't be fair to do that without telling you everything. You deserve to know all of my secrets." A lump formed in Alice's throat. She'd thought about this conversation hundreds if not thousands of times, dreamed of having it with someone for decades, but none of that could simulate the emotion that came along with it. "You know as well as I do that I don't have much time left, and I'm okay with that. I'm at peace with it. I'm old and tired. I'm ready. But I'm not okay with taking the truth with me." She took Emily's hand in hers. "I'm not telling you this to put pressure on you or force you into anything you don't want to be a part of. What you choose to do with the garden and my truth is for you to choose, and no matter what, always know I'm okay with whatever you decide. There is no guilt or strings attached to this."

Tears poured from Emily's eyes, and she hugged Alice.

Alice dropped the shovel and wrapped her arms around her young friend, tears rippling in her eyes behind her bifocals. At Alice's self-ribbing lead, they'd always shared friendly jokes about her age and all the physical and mental loss and silliness that came along with it, but they'd never had a serious discussion about what would happen when she died. Anytime the subject of her health and a future without her veered toward serious, Emily had shut down, and Alice had never pushed. There was no need to force the anxiety of loss and instability on someone who'd already gone through all Emily had, resilient or not. That would come on its own someday without force.

They held each other longer than they ever had. When they separated, Emily blotted her eyes with her sleeve again, and Alice shoved her fingertips under her bifocals and wiped her own tears away. Before Alice could say anything else, Emily picked up the shovel and steadied her eyes with a ready-and-willing-to-press-on fortitude. "Where to, then?"

Alice gestured east, toward Regreso Creek, and they took off.

They exited Avocado Circle, passed through a mixture of chinaberry trees and Oklahoma redbuds, looped around a patch of clover-covered ground with carrots and potatoes eager to grow fat beneath, swerved through a mix-match of strawberry and blackberry bushes and the olive trees growing amongst them. They walked in silence for five minutes, staying in shade where possible, navigating thorny rose bushes waiting for the heat of summer, moving from lemon tree shade to peach tree shade, from pecan tree shade to dogwood shade, avoiding stepping on the new spring vegetable and ornamental growth in the sunlit areas.

They stopped beneath a huge weeping willow about thirty or so yards from the creek. Wisps of leafy branches that tickled the ground in places swayed in the breeze around them, enclosing them like a shield. Shoots of star gazer lilies, plants that would grow over four feet tall and produce varieties of pink, white, and golden blooms—flowers unrivaled in size or beauty—in mid to late summer, encircled the tree, expanding out twenty yards in each direction.

Facing west, Alice put her back to the willow trunk then met eyes with Emily. "You take twenty steps from here." She walked forward, counting out loud as she went, Emily matching her step for step by her side.

She stopped on twenty. The land around her looked no different than anywhere else. Star gazer shoots grew, spaced about six inches apart, blades of St. Augustine grass slithering among them, occasional weeds and mini-flowers, too. Alice pointed down. "We need to dig here."

Emily nodded, and after she unslung the backpack off her back and was about to obey, Alice placed her hand on Emily's shoulder. "Wait. There's something I need to tell you first." She inhaled a deep breath. This was it, the final act. She locked eyes with Emily, expectant, her gut telling her she'd soon see the sadness in Emily's eyes vanish and hope return. "The morning I finished digging the hole and buried Karl, I noticed something off about his hands. When I went to get his body and took a good look at them for the first time, I realized they hadn't bloated or changed color like his face had. They looked fine. Good as new. And when I'd had to put them back on his chest when they slipped off the blanket as I'd dragged him, they felt as warm and soft as when he was alive."

Emily's eyes widened and lit with wonderful disbelief.

"I know," Alice continued. "Although I'd seen it with my own eyes, I couldn't believe it either. So I went back two weeks later to prove it to myself. I dug down to them, touched them, and they were the exact same. Then I came back a month later and found them the same. I checked the first Monday of the following three months with the same result. And when spring rolled around the next year, I realized all the plants in the area around his hands sprouted a little sooner, grew a little faster, and were a little bigger and healthier than the ones farther out. Over the years, I periodically checked on them when I began to doubt myself and wonder, but they never changed. And the ring of unexplainable growth expanded. His body eventually decayed, but not the hands. The last time I checked was almost twenty years ago."

Emily scanned the growth surrounding them as though seeing it through new eyes for the first time, and Alice's heart swelled with warmth. Emily's world was changing without physically changing again, growing without growing. Deepening with knowledge and curiosity. Expanding beyond belief.

"Stargazers were his mom's favorite," Emily whispered to herself in a moment of recognition.

Alice smiled. "I put a piece of sheet metal about four or five inches above them early on so I wouldn't hit them with the shovel." She stepped back and swirled her finger over where she'd moved from. "Just dig a two-foot by two-foot area. When you hit the metal, stop, and we'll use the hand shovel from there."

Emily lifted the shovel, and after she thrust it into the ground a couple of times and set aside the dirt, she asked, "So, this is where the Garden of Sunray was born, huh?"

As Emily continued digging, Alice picked up where she'd left off with her story without provocation, reflecting on the days and months and decades after Karl's death, restating many things she'd already told Emily over the years during their dinnertime and garden conversations, filling in gaps in the timeline for the things she hadn't.

Robert was laid to rest two days after Karl's burial, and within two weeks all the guards had left town. The local watch groups remained intact for another month or so, Pastor Hughes taking over the group Pastor Lewis had led, but they eventually fizzled out, too. The prevailing belief was that Pastor Lewis had encountered the Nazi after the Nazi had fled Alice's house, been killed, and the Nazi had somehow gotten away. What had exactly happened, how he'd gotten away and why they hadn't found Pastor Lewis's body, was a matter of never-ending debate. The rumors that spawned from the debates—some implicating Alice and a few her mom as well—spread like a raging virus, and over the following decades, evolved into all the ridiculous Hollywood-driven (secret Nazi romance, illegitimate children, hidden gold, clandestine bunker, murder mystery, haunted garden, vengeful ghosts, alien, angel, demon, human experimentation, government cover-up) tales Emily heard when she was young.

By Halloween, life had returned to a confident sense of normalcy for most people in town. But for people like Alice, her mom, Ace, Hazel, Thomas, and the handful of others directly involved in and impacted by the mess, life was never the same.

Half a year after Robert's death, with no hope Pastor Lewis would be found alive, Hazel and Thomas moved back to Paola, Kansas, where she had a brother and sister-in-law. Before leaving, Hazel told Mom she had a bad feeling that if she stayed in Sunray, more pain would come her way. Alice never had an opportunity to talk to Thomas privately. The few times she went to their house with her mom, Thomas stayed close to Hazel's side, quiet and to himself for the most part. Years later, after he became a pastor like his father, he moved back to the panhandle, to a small town north of Mercy called Dumas, and headed his own Trinity Lutheran Church. Alice saw him walking out of a grocery store in Mercy once, and they'd met eyes in a moment of pleasant recognition as she'd driven past him, but that was the only other time she ever saw him.

Instigated by Alice, they did exchange a series of letters over the following years, though. In her initial letter, she apologized in general for what had happened, asked how Hazel was doing, and expressed her hope that he didn't carry any guilt about sending his father after Robert. In his, he told her Hazel had passed from a heart attack when he was twenty-two and expressed a similar hope about her carrying guilt when it came to her role in the incident. In the letters afterward, they wrote about simpler things. Alice wrote about the garden and stories about locals Thomas might remember. He wrote about his wife Loretta, two sons, Rob and Ralph, and his congregation. When she learned how he'd died in a three-car collision on I-40 in the early '80s, she attended his funeral in Dumas but sat alone in the back and didn't speak to anyone.

After everything that happened, Alice's mom wanted out of Sunray more than ever, too. Martha had been talking about starting fresh ever since Alice's dad's death, and after Alice graduated high school, nine months to the day after the incident in the backyard, she told Alice she was putting the house and land up for sale. She wanted to move to the Oklahoma Panhandle, where Ace was moving, and she wanted Alice to go with her. Ace had been offered a sheriff's job in Junction, which was about twice the size of Sunray, and was eager for a change as well.

Alice refused to move. The house had been built by her dad's family, the creek her dad's spot of Eden, the land Karl's resting place—a piece of God's resting place. She wanted to keep the house and land. She'd do whatever it took. She told her mom "Selling it would be a betrayal to Dad. You may not be connected to it, but I am." Nevertheless, Martha put the land and house up for sale in June, saying she needed the money to afford the move. The next day, Alice started a job at the same Alloy carbon black plant where her dad had been a supervisor. She also visited the bank, looking into what she needed to do to secure a loan. Before the war, not a single woman had worked inside the plant, but by the time Alice joined the crew, there were twelve. The work was hard and dirty, but it paid better than any other job in Sunray. And she needed money as fast as she could get it.

When Ace found out about Alice's plans, he pulled her aside and asked her if she was certain this was what she wanted. When she was adamant that she was staying in the house and on the land "come hell or high water," he stepped in to help. He had no idea about Karl, of course, but he understood how important the land was to Alice due to her ties to her dad, and he knew how special the land had been to her dad, his best friend. He told Martha if she insisted on selling the house, he'd help Alice buy it. But if she signed it over to Alice and let her make of it what she wanted, and if she didn't mind living with him, starting over with him as her husband, he'd buy her any house she wanted in Junction. As a lifelong bachelor with no kids, he had a huge chunk of savings set aside, not counting what he'd get from selling his own house in north Sunray. Ace's proposal and offer brought joyful tears to Martha's eyes, and she accepted without debate and pulled the house off the market.

In October, fourteen months after Karl's burial and two days after Alice's eighteenth birthday, Ace and Martha moved to Junction, and Alice officially became the owner of the Mayes house and land.

From day one, she started building the Garden of Sunray. Almost every day when she finished her shift at the carbon black plant, she drove the beat-up Chevy (her mom had given her the truck, too) straight home and worked on cultivating the land. On holidays and weekends, she often worked out there from sunup to sundown.

Initially, she had no blueprint in mind, no desire for a specific size or shape, and didn't realize the potential of her efforts. She simply planted what her gut told her to plant and where it told her to plant. She planted because it helped ease her pain and quiet the relentless *what ifs*, the *would'ves, could'ves,* and *should'ves*. She planted because when she was out on the land, she had hope.

Years passed. Camp Hutchinson was emptied and closed in the winter of '46, the buildings removed. Deputy Putnam became Sheriff Putnam. Battles with alcohol came and went. Boyfriends came and went. Her grief lessened and hope grew. All the roads in Sunray were paved, two more houses built on McGee Street, a second gas station in town. She had proper indoor plumbing installed in the house, built a barn for storage next to the garage. She quickly worked her way up to becoming the first female supervisor at Alloy—the same position her dad had held. All the while, she planted. She planted fruit trees and vegetables, lilies and roses, berry bushes and shade trees. A rose of Sharon here, snowball bush there. She decided on a field of corn, a circle of avocado trees, a huge L-shaped tangle of herbs, a clump of honeysuckle so thick you could fit a diesel trailer in the witch-broom center. She dug small canals off of Regreso Creek to help naturally water the area, repaired the broken windmill to help pump spring water up for irrigation, fenced in the entire property. She chose native varieties and non-native, spring, summer, fall, and winter crops, and everything took to the soil and flourished. There was no extreme-miracle-overnight growth, and an occasional plant here and there wouldn't take, but most things grew twice as fast and twice as thick as they should have. The fruit and vegetable and herb yields were twice as much as expected, twice as juicy and crisp and flavorful, too. Just like Karl said the food he and his mom had delivered to "the unfortunates" had been. The weeds were also twice as aggressive, some a thorny, invasive nuisance and tough to get rid of, others small and flowering and left alone.

As the output of her work grew, so did her understanding of the garden's potential and her belief in a purpose—the reason for God's hands coming to her land. For years she'd struggled with the *why* (*Is it all just luck and misfortune? What is the purpose? Why? Why? Why?*), but as her grief and guilt and questioning receded in parallel with the garden's growth, she realized the why, her purpose, her future.

She began donating food to the local food bank and churches, having giveaways in front of her house after harvests, leaving baskets on people's porches who she knew were struggling with finances, stocking the lunchroom at Alloy, decorating Sunray Cemetery tombstones with abundant flowers, making bouquets and arrangements for local weddings.

More time passed. Decades. Bars changed owners and names. Chain stores replaced mom-and-pops. Cafes came and went (Miss Carla's sadly closed in '66). Families moved away, and families moved in. The Chase Ranch was sold to Emily's friend Becca's grandparents and renamed Cattle Crossing Ranch. Two new filling stations were built, so was a second school building. All the while, Alice kept her secret. She planted cherry and apple trees, kale and chives, crepe myrtles and photinia, anything she wanted.

She bought a tractor and a small backhoe, dug two random ponds, added two more windmills. The garden's output expanded and produced enough to help neighboring food banks as well. The name the *Garden of Sunray* ("*Sunray's own little Garden of Eden.*"), emerged and stuck. People began leaving donations in a bucket Alice had inadvertently left by the gate when they came for food. Local churches began donating. People volunteered to help with harvest and deliveries. Ruth, Mr. and Mrs. Fulton, Garrett Show, Pete and Jasmine Garrison, among the first of them early on. Those who came wanting to walk the gardens and take pictures, "the knockers" Alice deemed them, offered money for their desires. She allowed walkthroughs and pictures, even the occasional proposal, but not the bigger requests for weddings. People marveled at the garden, wanted to know Alice's secret, called her "Queen Green Thumb."

Giving hope gave her hope.

The garden survived the drought of '59, the flood of '66, the tornado that tore through south Sunray in '72, and the fire in '82 that burned the Lewis's house and two others on eastern McGee Street to the ground. By the '90s, there were more people who'd been around for the whole Nazi mess resting in Sunray Cemetery than walking the streets. Ruth, Garrett, Putnam, Weber, and Mayor Wilson, were among many who had passed on. Cancer, heart issues, diabetes, dementia, suicide, accident, simple deterioration and give-out, you name it, all had taken someone Alice knew.

She lost her mom to liver failure in '84, and Ace succumbed to pneumonia in a nursing home five years later. They were buried next to each other in Junction. Alice had visited them every Christmas and two or three other times a year and was in a good place with each of them when they went. She visited their graves when she could and covered the ground with flowers from the garden.

She retired from Alloy in '95 and spent all day every day in and around the garden. PBS did a special about the Garden of Sunray just before the turn of the century. The thirty-minute segment included aerial and ground level video of the greenery to go along with the Alice Mayes interview. Inspired by the documentary, a local Mercy artist named Allen Fark painted three huge six-foot by six-foot landscapes of the garden. One was purchased by the city and hung in City Hall, one was given to Alice and hung on the largest wall in her living room, and the other was purchased by a local rancher.

In the early 2000s, the Newels moved into the house that had been built where the Lewis's once stood. They adopted Emily a few years later, and after Alice caught the little girl with grass-green eyes and a pixie chin stealing tomatoes and pears from the garden, she'd taken her under her wing, and they'd worked and given together ever since.

Emily stopped and looked at Alice when the shovel clanked metal. "I hit it,"

Alice retrieved the hand shovel from Emily's backpack and handed it to Emily. "Dig out the edges so we can peel it off."

Kneeling next to the hole, Emily obeyed. She set the small shovel on the ground after slipping her fingers under the lip of the metal and test-lifting it an inch or two, then she looked back over her shoulder at Alice.

Alice gave her a *go-ahead* nod, which also gave the sleeping butterflies in her belly the go-ahead to wake. She wanted to kneel, or squat at least, get close to the hands, but her body wouldn't allow it. Repetition was no longer her body's ally. The long walk had angered her arthritis and hip. If she lowered all the way to the ground, she may never get up.

Emily lifted the metal slowly, as though it were delicate and brittle, and set it on top of the small shovel. The ground beneath the metal looked like regular soil, the same as the dirt she'd removed. "Now what?"

Emily's eyes shone with hints of both excitement and fear, and Alice knew Emily felt the butterflies, too. "Use your hands," Alice said, keeping her gaze on the soil as the butterflies fluttered faster. "Push the soil out from the center. They're about four or five inches down."

Emily held eye contact with Alice for a moment, until Alice gave her a second *go ahead, it's okay* nod. Then she began moving the dirt. Three inches down, she paused with her fingers in the soil and shot Alice an amazed look. "It's getting a little warmer. The dirt feels warmer."

Alice smiled. "Keep going."

When the first bit of skin emerged, skin as healthy and taut as Emily's own, she looked back at Alice. "I'm there." She put her finger on the exposed skin. "It feels real."

Delighted at the sight of the hands and Emily's reaction, Alice chuckled. "It is real. Clear off the rest of the dirt so we can see the top of both hands." She removed the rag and a bottle of water from the backpack as Emily worked. When both hands were visible but still covered with dust, Alice wet the rag and handed it to Emily. "Wipe them off."

Emily gingerly cleaned the hands and fingers, smoothing down the tiny hairs between the knuckles, revealing the skin's vibrant color, the nails' glossy firmness. She rose to her feet when finished, staring down at the hands, speechless.

Also staring down into the hole, Alice sidled up next to Emily. Her fear that this day would never come—a day of confession and sharing— wilted and turned to ash like the plants Karl had drawn energy from. She felt sixteen again—as unchanged by time as the hands she looked down at. *Time*, she thought, *such an odd thing*. She'd buried them so long ago, carried the heavy secret for going on eighty years, but right then and there it might as well have been yesterday.

She took Emily's hand in her own, laced her fingers between Emily's. "You feel the butterflies in your stomach, too?"

Without looking up, Emily nodded and gave Alice's hand a firm, *holy shit* squeeze. "How do you think it works?" Emily asked. "The hands? How do they help everything grow? I mean…they let Karl move energy before…but now…what?"

"I spent years, decades, wondering about that, and I'm sure you will, too, no matter what I say next, but you want to know what I figured out after all that time?"

Emily arched her pierced brow in curiosity, still not looking away from the hands. "What?"

"Nothing. There is no understanding or knowing. There's no answer. And I don't think there was meant to be. Just belief."

Alice reached into her cargo pant pocket and pulled out a pressed, dried star gazer encased in wax paper. It was twice the size of a typical star gazer. She removed the wax paper, let it flutter to the ground, placed the flower in her palm and held it out in front of her, pulling Emily's attention away from the hands. "This is the first star gazer that ever bloomed out here," she said. "I've kept it in my Bible ever since I pulled it." She caught Emily's eyes, offered the flower to her. "I thought you might like to have it."

"Stargazers," Emily whispered, eyeing the flower, her single word seemingly carrying the meaning of an entire story. "I wonder what ever happened to his mom."

"I tried to locate her after the war ended, but information was hard to come by back then. There was no internet or anything, and many of the records that did exist, especially about traitors and the unfortunates, were destroyed by the last of the Nazis at the end."

Emily held out her palm, and Alice slid the flower to her. She marveled at it for a moment, tracing a finger along an abnormally huge petal, then scooped up the wax paper and delicately rewrapped it. As she placed it in the front pouch of her backpack, Alice reached into another one of her cargo pant pockets and removed the Toblerone.

When Emily stood, she hugged and thanked Alice before noticing the candy bar. "Toblerone. The ones Karl and his dad shared, right?"

Alice nodded. She loved how Emily remembered the details of the story. Details were important. "After that first year or two, every time I've dug up his hands, I'd bring one of these out here with me, eat half, and leave the other half in the ground. Next to the hands. You may think it sounds stupid, and maybe it is, but it's part of my secret, part of the story, and I thought you should know." She unwrapped the bar, split it in two, offered half to Emily.

Emily placed it in the hole, a few inches from the hands. Then Alice offered her the other half. "You want to do the honors? My stomach won't accept chocolate anymore."

The look in Emily's eyes as she accepted the candy assured Alice they were on the same wavelength. They had an unspoken understanding. A passing of the baton of sorts.

"I feel like the luckiest person on Earth to be here right now," Emily said, taking a bite, eyes on Alice.

"I don't believe you're lucky at all," Alice said. "I believe you are meant to be here."

Alice glanced at the hands. She wasn't lying or trying to placate Emily in order to force her into a destiny. She didn't believe in luck. She didn't believe it was luck that Emily had been adopted by the Newels when she had. Or that she lived in a house on the same lot Robert had. Or that she'd met Alice while she was stealing from the garden—the same way Alice had met Karl. Or that she'd decided to return to Sunray after moving away to Denton. No, she believed there was as much purpose in Emily's journey as there had been in hers and Karl's. They were all linked in an entwined fate. An intricate web. Destiny had brought them all there for a purpose. But she kept all that to herself. Emily didn't need tutoring or a lecture on issues with roots that ran that deep. She would think about it enough in the coming years to figure it all out on her own, come to her own conclusions, in her own time, in her own way.

Emily pulled a bottle of water out of her backpack. She washed down the chocolate bar and looked at the hands. "I wish I could've met him."

"He would've liked you," Alice said.

"Because I'm a lot like you," Emily said, agreeing. She glanced at Alice. "I wish I could've known you back then, too."

Alice gave an appreciative smile, and with the sun warming their backs and a gentle breeze caressing their hair, they quietly stared at the hands for a while.

"Do you still have your old diary?" Emily asked, breaking the silence.

Alice nodded. "Back at the house. In a trunk in my closet. With my fish-gut shorts, Dad's letters, the card I never gave Nancy, and a few other things like pictures and newspaper clippings from back then." They met eyes. "I'll show it all to you when we get home." She looked back at the hands. *We need to walk through the will, too*, she thought, *discuss where I want my ashes scattered in the garden*. But again, she kept that to herself. There would be plenty of time for that tomorrow, or the day after. "Let's go ahead and cover them back up, and you can go get one of the four wheelers so this old lady doesn't have to walk all the way back home."

Emily placed her fingers on Karl's hands one last time before gently covering them with the loose dirt, then the corrugated metal and more dirt. When she finished the job, she stood and wiped her hands on her shorts. She smiled at Alice like her world was as right as cake and pie. "Be right back."

As Emily headed toward the house, Alice walked toward the shade of the willow tree, to one of the wooden chairs they'd spaced throughout the garden, and eased herself onto it, facing Karl's grave. She felt exhausted but calm. Complete. Fulfilled. She'd tied up her last loose end. *The* loose end. Now she could move on in absolute peace. Join Robert, Karl, her mom and dad, Ace, and everyone else, wherever they were, God willing.

She closed her eyes and listened to the country. The wind. Birds. The rippling creek. Discrete insects. She opened her eyes and took in bits of beauty, the new growing greenery, a wispy willow leaf, a wildflower petal, a single blade of grass, a stargazer shoot. Soon the summer flowers would bloom and fruit would be plentiful and the air would be rich with a hundred sweet scents. She'd miss it, being witness to the majesty of seasonal change, but she looked forward to what awaited even more.

She stood when she heard the four wheeler engine approaching and met Emily at the edge of the ring of stargazer shoots.

Emily locked eyes with Alice, her expression suggesting she'd been struggling with an age-old conundrum. "Do you think there are other God parts out there somewhere? Like in the rainforest or redwood forest or something like that? In the ocean maybe?"

Alice simpered. She'd spent countless hours over the decades circling the thought, daydreaming, wondering how many others like Karl had come and gone, who they were, what they'd looked like, what their purpose had been, who knew their secret, how their God parts had worked, where the parts were buried if their time had passed, if the parts would eventually decay or if they'd exist forever. The possibilities were endless, and there were only a select few who got to journey through them, know they actually existed.

Welcome to the club, Emily.

"There have to be," she said as she climbed onto the four wheeler and put her hands on Emily's waist. "There have to be."

AUTHOR'S NOTE

If you live in the Texas Panhandle, grew up there like I did, or simply Google "Sunray, Texas," you'll know it is indeed a real town. Although I did take liberties with the exact location, dates, and business names to suit my fictional purposes, I did try to include as many of Sunray's authentic traits from the time period as possible. For instance, Sunray did experience an oil boom in the 1930s, which led to tiny homes being brought in on skids and placed all over town to house oil field workers. After the boom, the carbon black plants provided a bulk of the jobs for locals. Also, few homes had indoor plumbing at the time, the movie theater, built in 1938, was indeed the only building in town with air conditioning, bars and churches were by far the two most abundant structures in town, and other than Main Street and the roads leading to the wealthiest churches, none of the streets were paved. Everything else about the town, story, and nearby area—the people, incidents, Camp Hutchinson, and sadly, the Garden of Sunray—are my creations. As for how I came to use the town's name, well...

It's funny how some ideas stick and others don't. How some stand alone and others need a partner. Most ideas I've had for novels originated as short story ideas, and *Sunray Alice* was no different. Almost ten years ago I was brainstorming to submit a story for an open anthology that wanted dark tales about natural, physical anomalies, real or fiction. I'm not quite certain how I settled on the idea, but I decided to write about a man who arrives in a small Texas Panhandle town in the 1940s and has the ability to transfer life from one organism to another. Soon after he appears, the extremely religious town accuses him of molestation when someone sees him healing a child. He is lynched, and the spot where he is secretly buried by the children who trusted him blossoms into a garden that should never exist in the panhandle.

Back then, I knew the town of Sunray by name only, thanks to the local weather forecast, but something about it just rang true for the setting. Gardens, growth, life, sunrays, right? I liked the story (titled "Garden of Sunray"), but I felt like at only 7000 words, which was the anthology limit, something was missing. It wasn't complete. I wanted to know more about the man and the kids, dive deeper into the town dynamics. I felt there was so much more there, but I didn't feel comfortable attempting to expound on it at the time. So I set the story aside.

Two or three years later, I stumbled across a PBS documentary about a World War II internment camp in the Texas Panhandle. It was one of seventy-nine in the state during the 1940s. I'd had no idea such things existed. The camp in the documentary was the Hereford Internment Camp, which housed thousands of Italian POWs. Many of them were professional painters, sculptors, and craftsmen who had been forced to join the Italian army. They worked on nearby farms and ranches and were considered a vital part of the local economy. Five Italian POWs died and were buried on site before the war's conclusion, and to mark the graves of the deceased, a group of the artists and craftsmen constructed a small chapel in the camp.

The chapel still stands at the site today—one of the last remnants of the camp. Additionally, many of the imprisoned Italians contributed their artistic talents to St. Mary's Church in the nearby town of Umbarger, decorating the church's interior with wood carvings and frescos. St. Mary's Church continues to maintain the art works today. I highly recommend Googling the church and viewing some of the artwork. It's spectacular. Learning all of this, knowing it had happened in my neck of the woods and I'd never heard about it, blew me away. I was fascinated. My wife, son, and I took a road trip one Sunday afternoon and visited the camp chapel and St. Mary's. I did research on other camps that existed all along the south during the war, read memoirs, looked at pictures. I knew I wanted to somehow include a camp like these in one of my stories, but the time wasn't right. So again, I set the notes aside and moved on.

Fast forward to April 2020. I was in lockdown like most of the world, anxious and worried about an uncertain future, unable to focus on anything positive much less write. I felt hopeless and started falling into a depression. Realizing this and knowing me better than I know myself, my wife, Tricia, came to me one day with a stack of my old notebooks and folders and dropped them in my lap. "You need to find something in those to start writing about," she said. "Anything. That's your medicine. You need it. It'll help." I knew she was right. So I began flipping through the papers, and within minutes, the "Garden of Sunray" short story and my internment camp research notes found one another after ten years apart. I started writing *Sunray Alice* the next day. I spent the next three months traveling back to 1944 every morning, learning about Alice and Karl, falling in love with them, cherishing the time we spent together.

In the end, they did help pull me back up to the surface like Tricia knew they would. They were the medicine I needed. They did help restore my hope in the future. But I believe the best medicine I have always and will ever receive is the support, encouragement, and love of my wife and best friend. Thanks for dropping those notebooks in my lap, Tricia.

And thank you readers. I know there is a multitude of other books out there to choose from. Thank you for choosing to travel to Sunray with me. I hope you enjoyed your time with Alice and Karl as much as I did.

Jeremy Hepler
China Spring, Texas
January 27, 2022

ACKNOWLEDGMENTS

I want to thank Ken McKinley for trusting in my writing and allowing *Sunray Alice* to see the light of day. I'm forever grateful.

I want to thank Kenneth and Heather Cain for their keen insights and help honing this story into the best possible work it could be. This is the fourth time I've worked with them (two novels and two short stories), and they're top-notch.

I also want to thank Kealan Patrick Burke for creating such an amazing cover. It captures the spirit of the story perfectly! He's mind-blowingly great!

Most of all, I want to thank my two biggest allies and supporters, my wife, Tricia, and son Noah. Tricia is always my first reader and was the catalyst for this book to be born (see Author's Note). And Noah's imagination runs circles around mine (He's fifteen years old and already writing his second novel!), and his suggestions when I was stuck or stumbling with this story were more valuable than he'll ever know. Love you guys.

ABOUT THE AUTHOR

Jeremy Hepler is the Bram Stoker-nominated author of *The Boulevard Monster, Cricket Hunters, Sunray Alice*, and numerous short stories and nonfiction articles. He lives in central Texas with his wife and son and is currently working on his next novel. For more information, you can find him on Twitter, Facebook, Instagram, Goodreads, or Amazon.

ALSO AVAILABLE FROM
🍀 SILVER SHAMROCK PUBLISHING 🍀

Lee, an urban shaman, gets tasked with tracking down a vinyl copy of the Dark Light EP by the '80s hard rock band, Bad Obsession. The extremely rare record is said to be cursed. Nearly every copy of the album burned in a fire at Tower Records in Los Angeles the day of its release. With only one remaining member of the band alive and living in a home for those battling Alzheimer's, Lee must return to Maine, a place where he's battled evil forces before, and see if he can retrieve the album.

Living her life on autopilot and working in an economy motel, Rhiannon is visited by a dark force she's not felt in years. The evil is familiar but not quite what she remembered. This is something else. In over her head, she calls out for Lee, hoping her old friend can hear her.

Brought back together by a force beyond anything either has dealt with prior, Lee and Rhiannon must combat powers beyond their realm. The Master wants to come through, and should someone spin the crimson vinyl, that's just what he'll do. A portal is about to open, and the world is about to learn the true meaning of pain.

Something in the Groove is calling... Can you hear it?

ALSO AVAILABLE FROM
🍀 SILVER SHAMROCK PUBLISHING 🍀

People are stopping, bodies halting regardless of situation or location. They are still alive but completely unresponsive, vulnerable statues utterly at the mercy of their environment. Unable to run from fire, some burn. Unable to return to shore, some drown. Unable to move from the path of a truck, some are crushed. Nor are you safe at home—unable to move, you starve.

Dr Alex Griffiths heads a research department in a university hospital. As more and more succumb to this strange affliction—including his own family—it becomes a race against time for his team to find an answer before they too are affected.
Humanity has been put on pause. Will it ever restart?

ALSO AVAILABLE FROM
☘ SILVER SHAMROCK PUBLISHING ☘

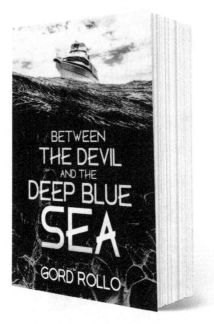

BETWEEN THE DEVIL AND THE DEEP BLUE SEA

Charter fishing boat captain, Miguel Santora, is an honest man who's in serious trouble. He's in over his head, owing money and allegiance to a slimeball mafia boss named Alberto Tonelli, who runs the shadier sections of Brooklyn with an iron fist. As payback, he's forced to let Tonelli and his goons have access to his boat, the Amada Maria, to drop some of their enemies' dead bodies into the Atlantic Ocean, chained to concrete cinder blocks.

THIS TIME THINGS ARE DIFFERENT...

Miguel's life goes from bad to worse, as Tonelli and his massive henchman, Hugo Taft, show up unannounced, with yet another body in need of disposal. Only this time, the man destined to be tossed overboard is still alive. He's been beaten and tortured, but he's still breathing. Helping these thugs in the past was morally wrong, but Miguel knows that assisting the mobsters this time means becoming an accomplice to murder. But how can Miguel refuse Tonelli's orders without becoming a casualty of these ruthless men himself?

THE HORROR HAS ONLY JUST BEGUN...

Victor Matheson, the condemned man, is someone who harbors many secrets, and he's far less helpless than anyone aboard the Amada Maria knows. Before finally being thrown overboard, chained to the heavy concrete block, he confides in Miguel that he is 'undrownable.' This revelation is only the beginning of a strange adventure that will see Miguel tested to the very limits of his sanity as he tries to uncover the truth of who this mysterious man really is. His search will take him from the docks of Brooklyn's East River to the small coastal New England town of Newburyport, where a secret race of horrific creatures and a century's old curse foretold in the fantastical stories of H. P. Lovecraft are preparing to unleash Hell on Earth.

Made in the USA
Coppell, TX
03 April 2022

75924076R00152